NO TITLED LADY

JUDITH LYNNE

JUDITH LYNNE

BOOKS BY JUDITH LYNNE

Lords and Undefeated Ladies

Not Like a Lady

The Countess Invention

What a Duchess Does

Crown of Hearts

He Stole the Lady

No Titled Lady—Series prequel

The Lord Trap (Forthcoming)

Cloaks and Countesses

The Caped Countess

The Clandestine Countess (Forthcoming)

Ladies' Own Bakery

The Regency romance comedy serial

DISCLAIMER AND GENTLE WARNINGS

This is a work of fiction and as such, its characters, events, words, and places are the product of the author's imagination.

This is a generally sunny book but does have occasional references to domestic abuse, character death, and slaughter of animals. If this isn't your cup of tea today, I mention it so you may peacefully pass this by.

PREFACE

Love stories are stories about families, good and bad, and the love story of Sir Michael and Letty in *Not Like a Lady* always felt to me a bit incomplete.

A child's view of their parents' love is notably limited; and our Regency London is so full of characters now that my readers might wish to go back in time with me to almost thirty years before, and see how some of these love stories started.

Enjoy our visit to Georgian England. Especially Roseford, one of my favorite places to be.

Your obedient servant,

Judith Lynne

CHAPTER 1

A man's shaggy shape slid toward the garden door like a beggar, or a thief.

The housekeeper, Mrs. Peterborough, met him there, gave him the bread she'd been carrying for two hours in her pocket just hoping the mansion's new lord would come home.

The baronet, for such he was, grunted his thanks. The deep rough noise was all of a piece with the faint sounds of horses neighing in the stables, the whispering parched herbs in the garden, and the owl asking *who?* on the roof.

The time since they had buried his father could still be measured in hours. He might now be baronet of Roseford, but he'd also been a child here, a youth, a strapping young man. All his life he'd shared with his father the driving need to see that all was well in his lands.

Still was, though he now walked alone.

So alone that he spoke little. Death did that, Mrs. Peterborough knew. It took away the words.

So his words were a shock many times over. "We must go to London."

"Sir John—"

"—is my father. Not me, Mrs. Peterborough." His voice was as ragged and torn as the rest of him.

"Sir," she murmured, and cut herself off before she said a name. "Don't think about that now. You've buried your father. Give yourself time."

"I've wasted *too much* time! This house should have been full of children by now. My God, I'm nearly an old man myself."

"You're not forty yet. Many gentlemen marry late. You have time—"

"We'll go to London tomorrow."

Warning bells pealed in the back of her mind. "To London? To get married, just like that?" Did she have to remind that grief clearly had the better of him? It wasn't the time to tell him that his clothes were as ragged as his hair, and his manners were... exactly what one could expect of a man who'd had only his father for company.

The father who'd thrown him bread across the table.

Not as a child. Last week.

"You're not ready."

He bent over to scrape the dry earth with one scarred-knuckle hand. The dust painted his fingertips. His eyes slid towards her, bright between gnarled locks of hair. "If I'm not ready now, I never will be. In the morning, Mrs. Peterborough. We'll have to take advantage of a friend of my father to do it, but in two days I will be where the ladies are. It's overdue. Roseford should have had heirs long ago."

He stalked past her and down the echoing, lightless hall. Mrs Peterborough followed him with the candlestick; the other servants were long since in bed.

Did Roseford look different to him now? The candle's glow showed carpets and chairs, but the carved ancestral wood wasn't soft. It looked like a place where two like men had barely slept for a lifetime. A place abandoned in favor of the village, the farms, and the woods.

Empty. And lonely.

"The Duke of Gravenshire still remembers my father fondly. He'll know a house I can let."

She paused at the foot of the stairs, but the new baronet did not stop. His voice floated down the dark hall as he climbed. "Two days, Mrs. Peterborough. We must leave tomorrow."

* * *

IT WAS THREE DAYS, and Jesper had met no ladies. But the hard London cobblestones under his feet felt like progress.

He needed an heir, but he *wanted* company. His father had been a good friend, the kind who laughed when the mud sucked off Jesper's boot. Surely London held at least one woman who could laugh.

If he did this right, he'd pay time's bill and get himself the family he should have had long ago.

The city was taller than Jesper remembered. Gray and disapproving. So were the people who frowned and muttered their way across his path.

There was little sympathy among these high-hatted, bewigged, tight-coated people, it seemed, for a country baronet.

At least the Duke of Gravenshire had greeted him kindly.

"I will provide your house." As if leasing a townhouse was a birthday gift for a little boy, as Jesper had been on his last visit.

Time must flow differently for older men. "There's no need, sir."

"Hmph. You don't gainsay a duke, boy. Well, please yourself. But you'll use my tailor, and you'll like it. Of course you want a wife; of course you do. There's no lack of choices, but you have to meet them first. When you do, be a credit to your title."

Jesper didn't comment on the *boy*. Dukes could do as they liked. Even to dictating his clothes.

Jesper's father had made few comments in the last years of his life that weren't about the day's work. *Don't wear mourning*, he'd said on a birthday that must have reminded him he was mortal.

Well, the Duke seemed to think the same. Perhaps he'd known his father's wishes that well. Or Mrs. Peterborough had slipped him a note.

She followed Jesper all over the townhouse, staring at him with

3

worried eyes, opening her mouth, and then closing it again.

Why? Jesper was fine. His father was gone, yes, but he'd had a long, full life. At Jesper's age he could surely go on without him.

He told himself that a hundred times a day.

Jesper liked his clothes fine. They were washed enough to be comfortable, withstood all weather, and kept him warm even at night under the trees. He'd followed in his father's footsteps, always charging in and out of doors in the same suit.

Now suddenly his clothes were wrong, his hair was wrong (this he deduced from Mrs. Peterborough's new habit of scattering combs everywhere), and his boots and teeth and fingernails no doubt failed to measure up as well.

His father would say...

The howling emptiness inside him since he'd held his father in his arms, watching him go, threatened to swallow him down.

Jesper could keep it at bay if he kept moving.

There, that was the wool importer's shop. The Duke had suggested he see finer fabrics, he would just—

An awkward wrench brought his attention back. He'd collided with someone, and Jesper had size and speed.

The man stumble-crashed into a woman.

She went flying toward the street.

Seeing it all in an instant, Jesper lunged for her and seized her waist, tight. Rather than fight her fall he whirled with it, so hard her arms flailed like ribbons in river water.

So fast that a swaying tower of feathers flew off her vast hat, into the street.

Where they landed in a pile of horse manure.

All of them, Jesper, the woman dangling from his arm, the staggering young man who'd almost fallen himself—even passers-by—all came to a halt, staring for a moment at the sad spectacle of a majestic tuft of white feathers billowing, flag-like, atop a stinky heap of dung.

Her hat was askew but somehow still attached. Her elbows knocked into him as she righted everything atop her head.

"Sir!"

It was the most affronted, the most belittling, the most off-putting "Sir!" Jesper had ever heard in his life.

He put her down on her feet. Her waist was tiny, and she seemed small, but everyone was small to Jesper, who strode around the village like a hairy church steeple.

Her wide skirts swayed with the speed of her desire to be away from him. She had a trick of looking down at him from below.

He gestured vaguely toward the street. "Should I fetch that for you?"

"*No.*"

"I thought you should have the option."

"I want none of your *options.*" She said it like *assaults.*

The battle-ship rig she wore, from wide beribboned hat to frill-plumped hips, lied about the slender curves he'd just felt against his arm. He couldn't even tell the color of her hair under all that stuff. All he could see was disdain, and lips the color of deep June roses.

"How *dare* you," those lips said. "I do not speak to men in the street." Then she went on speaking to him in the street. Though it was more like clubbing him with words. "I don't wish to be flung about, I don't wish to be bruised, and I don't wish to lose my new hat to—"

Even she couldn't bring herself to say *horse dung.*

Shoving her great mass of powdered hair upward to get the curls back around her face, she backed away, and a crowd of people went with her. The man he'd jostled, a boy to carry things, an older woman who might be her governess—or her housekeeper, thought Jesper, since she was full old enough to marry.

The little crowd all looked at Jesper as if he were more objectionable than the horse dung. Then they bustled away, protectively surrounding the fine lady at the center.

This was what he was up against. Women who wore huge hats and buttressed skirts and hated him on sight. Women who hid their tiny waists and rose-colored lips and traveled with coteries of servants.

Clearly tough enough, but not good company.

Grim, Jesper lengthened his stride.

And he did pay more attention to what was in front of him.

CHAPTER 2

"*I*t's right in front of you. Mr. Taggart is not going to ask for your hand."

"Mrs. Willowby, I've asked you not to say that."

Mrs. Willowby had run out of exclamations about Eleanor's accident and the loss of her hat feathers. Eleanor could withstand the loss of feathers. She could not withstand the loss of hope.

And she didn't wish to fuss with her beloved Mrs. Willowby. Eleanor had fought tooth and nail to keep her old governess as her lady's maid. It was the only fight with her father Eleanor had ever won.

Lord Fenlock dictated when she danced, to whom she spoke, and what she wore. That cursed cockade of feathers had been his dictate too. In other circumstances, she might have been glad to lose them. But the jostling and being whirled around *off her feet* had shaken her, in every sense.

She still had a quiver in her stomach, thinking how brusque she'd been to that big farmer. To say things she shouldn't say had a thrill to it, and nauseated her all at once.

At least her father hadn't heard. He corrected her temper more than anything else—which was to say, all the time.

And he was waiting. Eleanor turned to let Mrs. Willowby tie her overskirt. "I'm not yet dressed for dinner."

Mrs. Willowby pinned a sheet snugly round Eleanor's neck and reached across the toilette table for the powder bellows. "I'm not trying to fret you, pet. I just want you to be happy. Would it be so bad to marry the marquess your father wants?"

Eleanor shuddered. Yes, it would be. On the surface he was all bluster and self-admiration, but below that Eleanor sensed something darker. She had no intention of marrying Lord Burden or any other titled lord. She intended to marry Mr. Taggart.

She would have already, but he hadn't asked her.

"I will be more help to my father once I am wed. He doesn't see that London swoons before titles, but admits money." If her father thought she could help direct London society—and he did—he must see the wisdom of her being a merchant's wife. She could make her father happy and still have Mr. Taggart look at her with those kind eyes.

She *wanted* that.

His kind eyes had been at every social affair this season, even when the gentleman lacked a title, and that ought to say all there was to say.

Eleanor preceded Mrs. Willowby into the powder closet and plopped the powder shield against her forehead.

"Close your eyes," warned Mrs. Willowby as she closed the door, and blew a torrent of fine white powder over Eleanor's hair.

The sweet pomade in her hair caught the powder and held it; Eleanor could feel her hair getting heavier.

It took some time, but eventually Mrs. Willowby pronounced the job done.

Eleanor maneuvered her wide skirts out of the closet. They were complexity and brilliance, her skirts, fortified by panniers and bum pads and turrets and battlements, and Eleanor loved them.

Still swathed in the protective sheet, hair shedding a slight rain of powder, she sat at her toilette table. Mrs. Willowby began the detailed business of hair arrangement.

"Perhaps," mused Eleanor, "Mr. Taggart will dance with me at the Gravenshire ball tomorrow night."

In her head, she'd already worked out a whole evening of delights.

He would see her and, unable to resist, follow her into the garden, where he would admit he loved her. Forced to return to the crowd lest they be missed, he would lead her onto the floor for a dance, then another, then another, until everyone realized his clear intention.

Then he would walk her back to her father and offer for her hand. Right there in front of everyone.

The way she imagined it, she didn't have to say a thing.

She was too old for this fantasy. She clenched her hands in her skirts. She'd seen too many London seasons.

But surely Mr. Taggart understood. Eleanor had made her dreams very plain to the city's most discreet wigmaker, a woman who liked to walk out with the valet of the prelate who ran a charity with Mr. Taggart's mother.

That was a deeply reliable chain of communication, and Eleanor had faith that he had received the message.

"There's always more than one path forward," Mrs. Willowby said, pinning crystal drops in Eleanor's hair.

The drops recalled raindrops, which were Parliament's current obsession. If Britain's dry spring continued, corn crops could fail.

Even Eleanor's hair was forced to talk about corn crops.

That was her day, every day. Bills and budgets, Parliament and prelates.

Mr. Taggart would talk about something different, she just knew it. She'd known it from the moment she saw him. All of Ranelagh's pleasure gardens, every London ballroom, had a new sparkle because of him. He was so pleasant, so kind.

This would be her year.

Tomorrow night, Mr. Taggart and the Gravenshire ball.

Tonight, turtle soup, toast, and tweaking from her father. She'd survive. She always did. And no matter what, she would not snap.

* * *

His Grace liked entertainment, and at this point in the season everyone was known to everyone else. Young people exchanged giggles like calling-cards, and the questionable ladies had painted on extra beauty spots.

Eleanor would have a busy evening mining the social crush for useful details.

Her father liked to mix flattery in his thanks. "Your Grace. Your invitation was kind."

Beside him, Eleanor was more conscious of his eyes than the Duke's. She could feel him measure the depth of her curtsey, the height of her powdered curls, and the exact angle at which she held her fan.

His Grace tossed out a response of perfunctory politeness. "Good of you to come, Lord Fenlock. Miss Henry."

Then the Duke turned away, more quickly than Eleanor's father would like. Eleanor would, she knew, be blamed.

And she was. "You ought to have curtsied lower, Eleanor. Why do you think your neckline is cut like that?"

Eleanor reminded herself for the millionth time that she was lucky. Her much-older brothers had to sit in the Lords and try to maneuver their way into the government. She only had to survive her father's idea of social affairs.

Which was always humiliating, but never more so than at the ball of someone with a title of greater precedence than his own.

"I wouldn't want to curtsey so low that I discredited the family, Lord Fenlock." She gripped her fan so tightly the wood ridged her palms.

Only a little longer. If she could just keep her temper a little longer, gentle Mr. Taggart would offer for her hand.

There he was now, seeing everything from behind the punchbowl. He didn't need high-heeled slippers to be taller than Eleanor.

Truth be told, she'd worn this neckline for him.

So why didn't he come peer down it?

Her finger tapped out her irritation against her closed fan. *Because he was a gentleman*, she reminded herself. *And because her father glared at him.*

If he didn't at least approach, her father would never consider the benefits of money rather than title.

Ugh. Now he was locked in conversation with that potato-shaped Miss Bligh. Why must she stand in the way of true love? Miss Bligh was already betrothed!

"Perdition and pox."

"What?" Lady Hortense turned to see what had set off Eleanor this time.

"Oh, Miss Blight." Eleanor's eyes dipped away.

Hortense's wig slid an inch across her head, she peered around so fast.

All there was to see was short, plumpish Miss Bligh holding Mr. Taggart's attention. And making him laugh. What had she said to make him laugh that way?

Eleanor's fan creaked in her grip.

Hortense had no sympathy. "You're too old to get so hot if your cold-blooded suitor lets himself be detained by Miss Bligh!"

"I'm too old to wait! You know what my father will do if I reach my twenty-fifth birthday still unwed."

"He can't really send you to a nunnery, El." Hortense's fondness for wigs might be extreme, but in some ways she was practical. "There aren't any more in Britain. And you're not Catholic."

"You've known my father all your life. What makes you think he won't dispatch me to France as he threatens? A nunnery, you can count on it. With cold baths. And spiders."

No other threat came closer to breaking Eleanor's resolve. Her father said it so often just the thought pushed her close to crying. Eleanor wasn't proud of her temper, but she preferred temper to tears.

"Oh, he… he couldn't be so cruel." Hortense's reassurance trailed away limply. Lord Fenlock certainly could.

He'd aimed his sons like arrows at Parliament, and Eleanor at a peerage. And even if his arrows fell short, he would never admit the fault had been his.

"Never mind. I'm sure Mr. Taggart will ask me to dance in a moment."

Miss Bligh showed no signs of moving. Her teased, powdered hair was unfortunately wider than tall, and did her shape no favors.

Eleanor worriedly touched her own curls, and the fashionable knot of ribbons. Would Mr. Taggart be by her side if she wore more powder? Any more and it would rain upon her dress. Perhaps she should have worn the blue powder. Or the pink.

And then, because the man could smell hesitation across the room, Lord Burden started toward her. At this distance, all the way across the Gravenshire ballroom, he stood out like a moving shadow slithering through all the laughing merrymakers.

"Hortense," she said grimly as her least favorite lord circled towards her, no doubt to grip her in sweaty hands and very obviously stare down the front of her dress, "we need to get married and get out of here."

CHAPTER 3

*J*esper usually danced in wide swings on the village green. In the glittering Gravenshire ballroom, apparently, smaller movements were required.

He'd have to replace that vase.

His fresh new coat swung wide at the bottom, and his waistcoat was embroidered, appropriately, with roses. He'd discovered white at his temples when he brushed his hair back. He considered it Mrs. Peterborough's fault for making him do it.

Jesper was as pretty as he was going to get.

He'd squashed his inner emptiness and pasted on a smile. Surely a smile worn like a disguise would soon be real. And at least among all these potential wives, he needn't feel alone.

Some girlish giggles here and there were prompted, he suspected, by his plain, low boots, the scars on his hands, or something else that fell short of fashion's requirements. But he was too old to squawk at children. If a woman were moved to laugh at him, well then, she wasn't one to marry.

The right wife would laugh *with* him. At least most of the time.

Any type of laughter would be better than silence.

Even with this sensible approach, he found these young ladies, with flashing slippers under dresses that swayed like ships, a terrifying crew. Lace wreathed every snow-powdered bosom, attached to necklines so low he suspected the lace was to keep him from a very entertaining show of pink tips.

Jesper had never before thought of terror as an effective distraction. He'd never before thought gold-embroidered people in gold-plated rooms to be terrifying, either, but then he'd never spent time with them.

A few ladies cast wandering glances his way, making him think his chances might be good. If a woman's head could be turned by height or broad shoulders, he had those.

And this dancing was manageable. Jesper had seen a room spin around him before—he was no longer young—but here he'd do the spinning, as many ladies as allowed. The last one curtsied and staggered off looking dizzy herself.

Before he could pick another lady, the Duke of Gravenshire approached; the crowd parted for him. He was all elegant fashion and dignity, in his wine-red waistcoat and deep blue suit; and his hair didn't need powder to be white. He said nothing of Jesper's father, but his eyes had edges of grief. Sir John had been an old, dear friend.

"Your Grace," said Jesper, who faintly recalled the rules of good society, enough to avoid being too familiar in public. "I will replace that vase."

His Grace waved off the small loss, clearly still thinking of the large one.

"I'm glad you waited to come till my son was married." He surveyed Jesper's gold-trimmed coat. "Though perhaps I shouldn't have worried you'd steal away any options. You still hardly look fit for a ballroom."

All right. Half set-down, but also half-cheering, for a duke to consider him competition.

"He's married already?" The Duke of Gravenshire's heir, in the thick of the dancing, looked stretched, like very young men did. Was he even twenty?

"He's promised, which is just as good," said his father shortly. "So let's turn our attention to you."

"I'm not a green boy who needs to be arranged, Your Grace."

"No," his host said with the bluntness of a family friend. "You're old and worn and we have no time to waste."

Jesper made a face. He didn't need the reminder. And it was a bit rich, given that the Duke hadn't married till well into his 30s.

His Grace saw the silent sarcasm and shrugged. "You've sown all the oats you can sow. Get yourself a wife."

"I haven't been sowing oats. I've been busy."

"Yes, you and your father made Roseford bloom. But a wife would have helped."

"She still can. Let's find a woman with a practical hand and a head on her shoulders that I wouldn't mind looking at."

"You've set your sights high. Come, my Duchess may have some good advice for you."

* * *

TWENTY MINUTES with the Duchess of Gravenshire, and Jesper wisely followed her advice. He settled into a dance with a young Lady Hortense. She had a big smile, a lack of reverence for her own vast wig, and a very promising *décolleté*.

Jesper was already congratulating himself on finding a wife.

"You're remarkably patient, Lady Hortense," he said as he trod on her toes a second time. It wasn't only dancing in the cramped space. He did insist on turning left when he should go right.

Lady Hortense just laughed. She had a laugh like a box of diamonds rolling down the stairs. She let it all go and it sparkled. "Perhaps I like to have my toes trod upon," she said.

"Do you?" She was so forward, Jesper had to smile.

"No," she said quite honestly, eyes sparkling with fun, "but I'd rather dance than sit aside and watch, wouldn't you?"

She would admirably suit a house where holidays had long featured two men throwing bread across the table.

Jesper's good mood fizzled. Why hadn't his father remarried? Finding a wife clearly wasn't hard.

His father had only shared stories of his mother that would interest a child, like of picking berries, or singing through the house. Now Jesper wished he'd asked more.

"Do you drink ratafia?" Lady Hortense asked, offering him a glass.

"I seldom drink," he demurred. She might take it for flirtation. It wasn't. The slow swirling feeling he sometimes got reminded him of too much wine, so he avoided spirits.

"But I thank you for a delicious experience," he said with a half smile that made his double meaning clear, and Lady Hortense blushed attractively. Whew. He'd managed a pretty speech at least.

He wasn't ready to ask her for a second dance. But she was definitely the top of his list.

Jesper had rushed to London vaguely picturing someone practical. Someone to manage the manor and help keep order in the village. Someone who *didn't* throw buns across the Easter table.

That idea was sliding away. After all, the first requirement of his lady—the only real requirement—was that she provide him with an heir. Surely that should be fun. The emptiness inside him subsided a little at the idea of someone *fun*.

Someone sparkling and gay. Like Lady Hortense.

Would it be crass for him to ask how many siblings she had? Large families tended to produce large families. It felt a bit like bringing up cattle breeding. But ladies' skirts, with billowing sides and covered with bows, made it impossible to tell how wide Lady Hortense's hips were. She could have been built like a door under there for all he could see.

"Have you any brothers and sisters?" he asked her, hoping she wouldn't understand why.

"A few," she grinned, "would you like some?" Yes she was incredibly forward. Pretty and pert.

"Have you many suitors this season?" He was terrible at flirting. Doing his best. With any luck, he was already nearly done.

"I don't think that's a question that you can properly ask me," she said with a nicety of distinction that made him wonder if her father had studied law.

"It's *not* a question that he can ask you, Lady Hortense."

The young woman who appeared at Lady Hortense's side had eyes like slammed doors. She was much taller, and graceful where her friend was lush. In every way the opposite of Lady Hortense.

And he'd already met her. "Your hair is on straight." Perhaps not the most polite thing to say, but it was the first thing that struck him.

He recalled those lips very well. They curled to one side with disdain. "How do you come to be so brash, sir?"

"Living a long time," he told her, with half a bow.

He ought to thank her. Meeting her had revised his goals. From that moment, he'd wanted someone entirely different.

He hoped his brusqueness would make her leave.

It didn't. "You may be old, but you do not understand how to treat a lady. Lady Hortense, I do believe that Lord Overburg would love to have the next dance with you."

"Would he?" Did Lady Hortense look torn? She knew, just as her friend did, as Jesper did, that their conversation had already passed the bounds of propriety and ought to be cut short. She fluttered her fan, and her eyelashes, for Jesper's benefit. "Unless you were planning to drive to Gretna Green…"

Her friend gasped, but Lady Hortense looked half hopeful. He suspected that, had he proposed they leap into a carriage and start for Scotland, she would have come with him.

He wasn't *that* ready to be done with his search for a wife.

When Jesper hesitated just a second too long, "Of course," Lady Hortense said to her friend, "I would be delighted to dance with Lord Overburg."

Jesper expected them both to leave, but instead the sober young woman merely nodded and let Lady Hortense trail away, sparkling laugh and sparkling slippers disappearing with her.

Then the lady's friend turned on Jesper. Unlike Hortense, she had her head-toppings perfectly under control, and the delicate lace edging her sleeves never shivered as she sliced her fan down through the air like a government minister's gavel.

"Lady Hortense is very sweet," she pronounced her judgment. "She does not deserve trifling."

"I was not trifling with her, I assure you." Nor was being scolded the least bit amusing. "I have a very legitimate wish to marry. And Lady Hortense, I suspect, doesn't hate the idea."

"Lady Hortense likes everyone she meets. If you have any regard for her, you will pay her proper court and get to know her before making any improper suggestions. Or better yet, don't make any improper suggestions at all."

"I hate to disillusion an innocent young woman," Jesper said, watching how she gripped her fan like a club, "but I didn't begin the improper suggestions."

Her jaw snapped shut, and the ice in her eyes snapped with sparks.

"Be a man," she finally exclaimed, skirt swaying away from him in a way that recalled how he'd swung her around in his arms in the street. "Pox and perdition! How hard can it be to ask a thing politely? It's not as though her father is intimidating. He's quite pleasant. Things between you and Lady Hortense could be perfectly delightful if you'd only get over your self-infatuation, pull your head out of your armpit, and speak as if you had a brain between your ears instead of wet moldy straw from the countryside!"

"Whoa. Madam." She looked like smoke might shoot from her nose at any moment. This steaming young miss couldn't be Lady Hortense's chaperone, not with a neckline cut like that. "*Are* you her chaperone?"

"You can consider me her chaperone until you learn how to behave," the young lady said, with a snap of her fan that could have broken a small animal's neck, finally following her friend into the crowd. It wasn't until her slender figure disappeared that Jesper realized he still didn't know her name.

CHAPTER 4

*E*leanor's anger stayed at a simmer. Not only did she have a stomach-ache from giving that oaf a piece of her mind. She'd begun to suspect that Miss Bligh had captured Mr. Taggart's attention just to spite her. "Mr. Taggart hasn't come near me all night."

She'd even made Hortense cross. "I'm not speaking to you! Why did you chase off that enormous baronet? I think he was just remembering how to dance!"

Eleanor didn't even look his way. She knew where he was; he was tall, and it was easy to see his silver-templed head and broad shoulders over the crowd.

What was he *doing* here? On the street yesterday looking like a farmer, and then today at a *duke's* ball, with his hair actually brushed and wearing a decent coat.

The coat did not repair the rest of his shaggy appearance. But it was at least decent.

"He's old, Hortense! Surely too old for you. I swear. What possessed you, flirting with him like that?"

Hortense straightened her wig so she could give her friend a long, long look right in the eye. "Eleanor, your father will go to his grave

18

never having had one minute of fun. He wants the same for all your brothers *and* you. Don't oblige him."

"Oh, Hortense."

Out of the corner of Eleanor's eye—as she didn't dare to look straight at him—she caught sight of Mr. Taggart. Miss Bligh had finally let him go, but he hadn't moved one step closer.

He was looking her way with those fine, soft eyes, but his feet hadn't moved.

That wasn't how she'd imagined this night at all.

And here came her father's choice. A man likely to soon be an under-secretary in the treasury. Perfectly coiffed, with jeweled slippers, and hands like a lust-addled lizard.

"Lord Burden." Eleanor tried to curtsey low enough to be appropriate to an earl but not so low that he could see everything he'd come to see.

It never bothered him that Eleanor was taller. "I was engaged with His Grace on matters of state," he sniffed, no doubt turning a random remark into a personal relationship with the Duke.

She loathed his clawing, possessive hands and his eyes that never lifted higher than her neck. But most of all she loathed how he addressed her, as though they were, horrifically, already married.

"My lord," was all she said, as otherwise she might rip off his wig and beat him to death with it.

A quarter century of patience. She'd come this far. All she needed was for Mr. Taggart to offer for her. She could convince her father to accept the role that would give her in London. If he would only offer.

She cast one more glance back over her shoulder. Hortense, the sweet girl, was talking to Mr. Taggart now. Perhaps even pleading Eleanor's case.

But Mr. Taggart didn't meet her eyes.

Lord Burden led her to the dance floor like a sheep to be slaughtered.

She couldn't. She simply couldn't do it. Not one more night of being treated like Lord Burden's wristwatch, not when Mr. Taggart was *here* and could do something about it.

Trying to keep inches between herself and Lord Burden, desperately searching the faces of the crush packed into the Duke's ballroom, Eleanor only managed to spot that huge sore thumb of a farmer.

He stood to one side, his arms folded over his chest making his shoulders look even wider. His big foolish face now wore a half-scowl.

Eleanor didn't know what *her* face said, but no one was more astonished than she when the man stalked over.

"Your pardon, sir," he said as though someone had once taught him how to speak to his betters. "This dance is promised to me."

"Of course not," Lord Burden said, not moving an inch. Around them, other couples took their places for the dance.

The music would begin in a moment, and people were whispering behind fans at the effrontery of the interloper.

But he went on interloping, saying "I'm afraid it's true." Eleanor thought his grimness was genuine. "You must excuse us."

No one ever told Lord Burden what he must do. Out of sheer astonishment, he stepped aside.

The farmer—had Hortense claimed he was a baronet?—took his place at Eleanor's side, one arm behind his back, the other very correctly holding up her hand for all to see.

"What are you doing?" The question bouncing around Eleanor's mind finally burst out.

"About to dance." He said it with the same grimness that he had used to Lord Burden, as if he were about to put his hand in some completely necessary fire.

"Do you know how?"

"We danced yesterday." With a meaningful side-glance.

"Is that how you dance? Flinging women about?"

"If there's room." He looked around, easily seeing into the corners from his height. "Not in here."

"I don't wish to dance with you!"

"You don't wish to dance with that old lizard."

Eleanor was so taken aback by the accuracy of his description of

Lord Burden that some of the words she held back shook loose. "My father wants me to marry him."

"Good God."

The flutes started playing, and he had to step forward, Eleanor at his side.

Over the music, he said, "He has a face like something you'd find under a rock."

"He is an earl, and well placed in government."

The man's eyes slid over to survey Eleanor again. "You want to sleep with the government?"

Had she forgotten for a second how crude he was? "New clothes haven't made you a gentleman."

"I'm a grown man. Clothes don't change me much."

He'd clearly mistaken grown for *over*grown. Eleanor had to look up to see the cut of his profile.

He did have a strong chin. Not that it mattered. It was only that Lord Burden had so little chin of his own.

Eleanor cast her eyes about for Mr. Taggart. She wanted to reassure herself that his chin was sufficiently manly.

"Who do you keep looking for?"

"For whom am I searching, you mean?" She didn't bother to hide her disdain. "A friend of mine."

"Not that wet rag with the puppy eyes."

"Yes—No!" He'd noticed looks between her and Mr. Taggart? "He does not have puppy eyes!"

"He doesn't have balls, either. Clearly thinks you good enough to gawk at, but hasn't spoken to you once."

"*Sir.* Speaking of rocks and crawling. One doesn't speak to a lady that way."

"True." His big shoulders shrugged in that coat, and the rich brocade looked fake on him. Every movement of his body spoke of strength, moving mountains, not tracing the steps of the *quadrille.* "Maybe I'm not looking for a lady. Just a woman who wants to be wed."

21

"Thank goodness for that." Eleanor ignored the pull under her ribs at the way he said *woman*. He was like a bull charging through a room full of dolls: heavy-footed, wild, and dangerous to all concerned. "No titled lady would wed a man like you."

"No? Lady Hortense seemed keen." He looked straight ahead, but she thought she saw humor sparkling in his eyes. "It might just be you who isn't, Lady...?"

It was too much. He wanted her to introduce herself? He had no manners at all. "Gentlemen are introduced to ladies. Ladies do not introduce themselves."

"No?"

And just like that, he broke out of the dance to lead her, hand still in his, across the room to where the Duke of Gravenshire stood.

The crowd parted, with some titters of amusement, and Eleanor felt her face grow so hot no amount of face powder would hide it.

"Your Grace," said the big lumbering ass, with the slightest of necessary bows, "my partner has reminded me that we have not been properly introduced."

"Introduced enough to dance, surely," said the Duke, his bushy eyebrows pulling down into a fake frown. "Miss Henry, may I introduce Sir John Grantley? He's currently captured your hand."

"*Miss* Henry?" Yes, the big ox's eyes were dancing with fun as he bent over her hand. When his lips brushed her knuckles, the rest of Eleanor's skin felt as hot as her face.

"Yes, my father is the Viscount Fenlock," said Eleanor with a kind of desperation that he understand what that meant. He didn't expect her to lecture him on titles and precedence, surely. Everyone was listening.

"Ah. And the daughter of a viscount is only Miss Henry? Well." He dropped her hand finally. It left her fingers feeling cold. "Then you would be in a position to know, Miss Henry."

"Know what?" Why did he have to be so tall she had to keep looking up at him? It almost unbalanced the way her hair was tied on her head.

"What no titled lady wants. Miss Henry. Your Grace." And with that the big ox left her standing there, unpartnered, in front of a duke, with the entire assembly watching.

CHAPTER 5

"*I* can't do this."

Jesper slumped over the planks of a kitchen table that wasn't even his. He'd begun the evening in high enough spirits, buoyed by hope and an apparently violently needed new coat, but it had been a hash of poor dancing, no dancing, and barbs from Miss Henry. Yes, he'd met Lady Hortense, but hadn't dared dance with her again.

He was right back where he started, still haunted by loneliness, his father's absence, and Mrs. Peterborough.

She was pressing little cakelets onto a dish to be baked, and now that he'd brushed his hair, she didn't seem perturbed at all.

No doubt she was pleased that at least he wasn't roaming out of doors, stewing in his own failures as a son. That was partly because London didn't really have an out of doors.

Regardless, she seemed to regard his seeing people and saying things as progress. "You need to give yourself more time, Sir John. Bread doesn't rise in a minute."

"Bread makes sense. Women don't."

"Hey now." Reaching over, she slapped his wrist lightly, like she had when he'd been just a boy, eating everything in the kitchen before

24

it was done. She didn't seem to mind at all that the wrist was thick and hairy now. "I'm a woman and I won't be slandered."

"This girl at the ball. Has her eye on a cow-eyed sack of straw that couldn't lift a hand to help her. She clearly didn't want attention from Lord Burden. Why didn't that puddle-man do something? For that matter, why didn't her father?"

"Sounds like her father *wants* her paired with this Lord Burden." The smell of the cinnamon should have lifted his spirits; it didn't.

"And she stopped me dancing with Lady Hortense, who was fun. Lots of fun. Why didn't I just let her suffer?"

"Indeed, why didn't you?" Mrs. Peterborough pressed an almond into each cake.

"She just looked so miserable. Kind of a tall girl, but thin. Too thin, really. Perhaps she needs cake."

Absently he reached for an almond; Mrs. Peterborough slapped his wrist again.

He ignored it but left the cakelets alone. "I just... she looked help-less. That was what it was, surely? Helpless. Like a... heifer. Or a colt."

"When you see her again, don't refer to her as a heifer. If she's still a girl, and one looking to marry a lord in government, you have no reason to cross your path with hers."

Jesper thought of those lips. They looked as soft as rose petals, too. Whatever made them so appealing, it wasn't just the color. With all that powder and brocade, it was as if she had erased every part of her that was real except those lips.

"She's a woman at that," he muttered, "but no, no reason to cross her path again. Unless she comes between me and Lady Hortense."

"That one sounds no better than she should be. Why don't you try finding a woman who *wants* to marry a country baronet and come to Roseford?"

"Do you want to come to the next ball and choose for me, Mrs. Peterborough?"

His housekeeper didn't blink. "If only you were that lucky."

The hired footman stumbled down the kitchen stairs so quickly his head thumped on the ceiling beam.

Jesper winced. "No rush, boy."

"Yes, sir. Of course, sir. It's just that a Lord Faircombe is calling, to see you, sir."

Jesper's eyes widened; he looked at Mrs. Peterborough. Their closest titled neighbor? In London?

"Go on, you must receive him. Go on." Her waving motions were accompanied by one last hiss as he went up the stairs. *"Button your coat."*

In the drawing room paced a thick-chested man, lace spilling from his rumpled neckcloth and his sleeves. He smelled like stale burnt cotton, and brandy.

"My boy!" he called as he caught sight of Jesper, opening his arms wide.

Jesper felt his lip curl almost into a snarl. He rubbed his chin to hide it. Damn it, already bristled. How often did these London men shave?

He preferred coarse hair to Lord Faircombe's looks, behavior, or attitude. He had never regarded the neighboring Marquess as a father figure, and he surely didn't now.

"My lord," Jesper said as politely as he could.

Lord Faircombe didn't seem stubbled by Jesper's reception. He dropped his arms but not his toothy smile. "You should have told me you intended to come to London and find a wife! I never expected it."

"No?" Jesper decided to keep scratching his chin. It was better than leaving his fists free, if this insult were going where he thought it was going.

The Marquess treated every deviation from his own path as a failure of manhood.

And so with this one. "Didn't think you the right sort of man," he shrugged, and Jesper resolutely refused to imagine what he meant. "If you need a wife, you should have come to me! I know all the tastiest girls in London."

Jesper also refrained from saying that he didn't want one to eat, he wanted one to marry.

He ought to offer his lordship a chair and some refreshment. He didn't.

"Now that tempery bit you looked at tonight." The Marquess helped himself to a chair, shaking a warning finger. "She's not for you and she's trouble. The kind who will constantly fight tooth and nail. You don't want that kind of girl."

"I don't?" The words made Jesper's teeth itch, halfway to claiming that he very much wanted that kind of girl, just to spite the man.

"Lord Burden is a bit of a collector and he has his sights on that one. No, you want someone pretty and biddable who won't cause trouble. Met the girl I found for my son?"

The Marquess of Faircombe's only son was younger than Jesper, and no more appealing than his father. He kept his mouth shut and did what his father wanted, and Jesper mostly felt sorry for him. "I haven't had the pleasure. She is in London?"

"Of course! You had it right to come to London, I'll give you that. Whatever you want, it's here. You want a girl deep in the pockets? Fertile? Both?"

He'd only ever maintained civility with the Marquess of Faircombe, Jesper realized, because he'd spent little time with the man. Every second that ticked past revealed more and more of his oily, repulsive personality, and Jesper just wanted him gone. "Thank you, Lord Faircombe. I believe I've found myself an option."

He was thinking of Lady Hortense, but as he said it, the fake smile dropped from Lord Faircombe's wattled face, and he leaned forward.

"See here, son, you've got to be serious about this. That girl belongs to Lord Burden; he has plans for her."

By nature Jesper didn't rush, and even the pounding of his own blood didn't drive him into hasty action. His father had raised him to hunt successfully; a slow attack meant a clean kill.

He never, by nature or training, felt the kind of pressing urge to leap at someone's throat that he felt right now.

Jesper possessed not only Roseford's manor, but its village and all its lands, from the strips of farm all the way north where his wild woods connected to the farther edges of Faircombe. And he never once thought of anything or anyone as *belonging* to him the way Lord Faircombe seemed to mean. His tone implied control, not responsibility. Or care.

"How does she *belong* to Lord Burden? What right does he have to make that claim? Is he betrothed to her?"

Faircombe waved a dismissive hand, flopping his lacy sleeve. "It's understood. Not settled yet. Pushing her father for a better dowry, or simply making him sweat. But it's understood."

"And what the lady wants?"

At that Faircombe looked genuinely surprised. "Who cares what the lady wants? If Burden wants her, she should be honored. As I said, he's a bit of a collector. Never married one of his pieces yet."

The word *collector* used this way sounded chillingly sinister.

"Lord Faircombe, I am a simple country man and these late London hours tax me. You'll forgive me if I bid you good night."

Surprised at Jesper's resistance to being sensibly directed, Lord Faircombe looked agog even as Jesper strode to the door. And opened it himself.

Even he couldn't mistake the pointed sign that it was time for him to leave.

"I'm in no hurry!" sputtered the Marquess.

"But I am. Not to find a wife; as I said, I have that in hand. Only to get to sleep."

Faircombe came heavily to his feet, both hands pushing up from the chair arms in a way that made Jesper wonder how much brandy he'd had.

He approached Jesper at the door slowly, and there was something menacing about his fake smile, which had returned.

"No need to take offense, boy. Merely offering the help of a neighbor. You and I live so close by. It would be unfortunate to clash unless we have to."

"Would it?" and Jesper merely looked down at the man, holding his place as unyieldingly as an oak tree.

Once Lord Faircombe went out, Jesper followed to make sure he left the house by the nearest door.

The Faircombe carriage drove away and a drizzling rain began to fall, wiping away the smells of London's streets and the ashy feeling of this encounter.

Jesper thought to himself that Lady Hortense would still be his best bet for a jolly, comfortable wife, and he'd like to see her again.

But he had better keep an eye on Eleanor Henry.

* * *

"YOU'VE MADE a grave mistake tonight, Eleanor. In fact, you've made *several.*"

Eleanor fought to suppress a shiver.

This was her father. She had known him all her life. He had always been like this, tightly bound in gold buttons up to his chin and looking down on her like a game piece. He was still her father.

"I know, Lord Fenlock. I should never have danced with him." They both knew what *him* she meant: the big country oaf, Sir John Grantley. Eleanor had never heard his name before tonight, which was damning enough; it meant he had no important place in government.

"Danced with him? Of course not. Yet you did, and you *spoke* to him, and you let him force the Duke himself to introduce you. You didn't just insult Lord Burden. You showed him you cannot control your situation. Something a lady of his wife's station must know how to do."

"I do apologize, sir." She had lost control of the situation the moment that ox had entered it. Why had he even bothered?

Because she had shown her distaste for Lord Burden's pawing, that's why.

She simply had to keep herself in check. She loathed Lord Burden, but if she showed it, she could be on a ship to France before Mr. Taggart stepped in.

Why didn't he step in?

She had no intention of marrying Lord Burden. But if she'd simply agreed to dance, it would only have been one dance. Afterward, perhaps Mr. Taggart would have said something. Perhaps *he* would have asked her to dance.

Instead, that ox left her standing in front of His Grace, who looked amused but did nothing to rescue her, and she was left to fan herself on the sidelines while the dance continued. And the next, and the next. No one was quite sure what to make of her abandonment of Lord Burden, or of the country baronet's abandonment of *her*, and the Duke did nothing to resolve the situation. She was simply... left.

She needed to see Mr. Taggart.

That was it. She would find some way to pass him in the street. She could imagine it now. He just needed to be free of crowds. He would speak to her, and smile, and before she knew it, he would be speaking to her father.

Perhaps even asking *her* for her hand in marriage.

Perhaps if she went for a horse ride in the park—or visited the Pine Apple tea shop? It had been some time since Eleanor had been among those who flocked to the famous confectionary, but Hortense would accompany her, surely.

Eleanor had been leaving too much to chance.

CHAPTER 6

*L*ord Fenlock did not allow Eleanor to visit St. James' park.
His suspicion dated to the riots, when soldiers camped in
the park had harassed many women. He accepted Lord
Burden's ogling of his daughter, but wouldn't allow her to be
subjected the ghostly memories of common soldiers from five years
before.

Well, the marks of tents and horses were long gone, and Eleanor
would face a great deal more than soldiers' ghosts to speak alone with
Mr. Taggart.

Alone except for Hortense. "Lord Overburg is past thirty if he's a
day, but I never saw such a man for dancing. Of course I didn't let him
dance more than once with *me*, but I never guessed he would dance
every dance. I don't think he cared *who* he—Eleanor, are you
listening?"

Eleanor craned her head. It was difficult to seem nonchalant while
also peering around Hortense's vast bonnet. "Do you see him yet?"

Hortense *tsked*. "I see you, and Mrs. Willowby trailing behind us,
and too many trees. Honestly, Eleanor, this is taking your obsession
too far."

A leaf floated down to land on Hortense's wide panniered skirt; she whacked it away.

Eleanor, buoyed by determination, was in a much better mood. "Mr. Taggart's housekeeper told her laundry woman that he takes the air in St. James' park on Tuesdays. Her laundry woman mentioned it to a fellow who drinks with Mrs. Willowby's son. That's reliable information, Hortense."

"Where *do* you get all this?"

Hortense knew perfectly well that Eleanor's habit of listening, planting spies, and drawing inferences had been learned from her father at a young age. As a motherless girl in a London house full of servants silent enough to please her father, Eleanor had always needed to ask questions to find out what was happening. Surely the same methods applied to Mr. Taggart.

"He is always here on a Tuesday morning, always. If we keep our eyes open, surely we can see him."

"It's a lot of trees, Eleanor. A *lot*."

Eleanor just pressed on. Her own hat never swayed, but her eyes searched in every direction.

"The French king's spies could learn something from you," muttered Hortense, but Eleanor didn't hear her.

There, *there* was the lovely Mr. Taggart. His suit shone in the sun, its green silk of a piece with the sunlight through the trees.

It was the work of moments to cause their paths to cross. Moments, and a hike across the grass. Eleanor would do a great deal more than stray from a path for this.

She would even speak to the man in public. "Why, Mr. Taggart! What a pleasant surprise."

"What nonse—"

Eleanor stomped sideways onto Hortense's foot.

"Ow!"

Eleanor ignored her. "What brings you into St. James' park on such a fine day?"

The man looked stupefied. Was it *so* astonishing, to see a woman in a park?

"Oh, ah—I often enjoy the air here, Miss Henry."

"Do you? Now isn't that odd, Lady Hortense? I don't recall ever seeing Mr. Taggart here before."

"Nor do I," Hortense said drily. Eleanor shot her a look. She would tread on her friend's foot again if she must.

"Lady Hortense," said Mr. Taggart belatedly, lifting his hat, then bobbing it awkwardly in Eleanor's direction as well.

"Perhaps one of these days we will see you in a more familiar location, Mr. Taggart. Perhaps at the Pine Apple, for the ices?" Eleanor was treading perilously close to shocking behavior, and then she trod closer. "Perhaps tomorrow?"

Hortense swallowed a gasp—Eleanor heard her choke—and even Mrs. Willowby, upon whose complete discretion Eleanor relied, made a disapproving sound far behind them, and rustled her skirts.

Mr. Taggart, his fine profile ruined for the moment by a slightly gaping mouth, seemed transfixed by Eleanor's gaze like an insect upon a pin. "Oh, ah—you honor me, Miss Henry, but I—ah—it was my belief that you, ah, ...elsewhere."

All her attention focused on the small space between them, between her hands and his. "Your belief? *What* elsewhere?"

"That is, it is plain that Lord Burden—"

The lump in Eleanor's stomach turned to ice. "What about Lord Burden?"

The slicing sharpness of her tone seemed to force Mr. Taggart to take a step back; Eleanor stepped forward to stay just as close. "*What* is plain, sir?"

"That you were, that is, that L— That another gentleman intended to offer for you."

Yes, that was ice in her stomach. "And yet no gentleman has."

"Ah. Truly? Well. I am no one to cross your understanding with anyone."

"*What* understanding?" Behind her Eleanor heard another warning noise from Mrs. Willowby. She ignored it. She couldn't imagine what he meant. She had never had an *understanding* with anyone. Her first season had not been till she was twenty-one, her father judging her too childish until then to attract the right attention. In the four years since there had been no *understanding*.

Till this season, she had never even wished for one. This season, when Mr. Taggart had arrived with his fine suits and the look in his eyes that said he would never, ever tell a woman that she should behave better.

"Mr. Taggart. Have you not, in the past, found me attractive?"

"Really, Eleanor!" gasped Hortense, but Eleanor just threw up a hand, stopping her friend's bluster.

She'd rather be consumed with fire than succumb to the ice.

Her gaze pinned Mr. Taggart again. Had she never seen him fidget? She had imagined him the sum of his fine clothes and manners, but compared to even the oafish Sir John—surely the bottom of London's barrel—Mr. Taggart fell short.

The way he squirmed, as if he only wished himself elsewhere, told Eleanor that her own imagination was a traitor. Her golden girlish dreams had been phantoms. He had never been her knight in shining armor. He never would be.

Still, she wanted the truth.

He couldn't meet her eyes for more than an instant. He looked away, then again, but her eyes remained fixed; and, trapped, he finally answered.

"You are very attractive, Miss Henry. Of course I have *looked* at you, but any man would in your company."

Any man would look at her the way he had.

Eleanor had thought only her father could make her feel this demeaned.

It was the humiliation, not of his rejection, but of that *any man*.

"Mr. Taggart."

Her tone made Hortense mutter next to her, "Now it comes."

Indeed, Mr. Taggart himself looked rather pop-eyed with worry.

How could she have ever thought those eyes soft and kind? They were placid, true, but there was no fire to them either.

They simply weren't as disapproving as her father's.

"I just want you to admit one thing," she said, so quietly that

Hortense, braced for a blast, stumbled while standing still. "You *didn't* look at me the way you looked at every other woman, did you?"

Trapped in open air between whatever repercussions he feared from Lord Burden and Eleanor's inescapability, Mr. Taggart opened his mouth once, closed it. Finally he said, "You *are* very attractive, Miss Henry."

Attractive. Like something sticky for a bee.

She had spent *hours* imagining the talks they would have, over breakfast, at night by the fire. Hours imagining he cared what she thought.

There was no reason to subject him to her temper. *She* had been the fool.

"I see. I am sorry to trouble you, Mr. Taggart." And, heart beating like a drum, Eleanor charged off again over the grass, not looking to see if Hortense or Mrs. Willowby followed.

*   *   *

"Why aren't you eating? William, serve Miss Henry the butter."

Eleanor looked at her plate. The colors and shapes meant nothing to her; she wasn't sure where she was supposed to put butter.

It was the same meal with her father that she had every afternoon. Her brothers, so distant from her that she thought of them more as her father's heirs, had rooms elsewhere in the city, closer to the King and the riverfront bureaus of government. It was her duty to entertain her father at dinner.

An endless chain of such dinners lay before her, snapping closed like a trap she would have to drag through day after day. Without hope of Mr. Taggart, she had no hope left.

Her father was clearly displeased when she took none of the butter. The footman, at a loss, simply replaced the dish on the table.

"You haven't decided to reduce, have you? You're too thin now."

That brought Eleanor out of the fog of hopelessness. She peered sharply at her father. His powdered wig sat perfectly balanced on his head as he carried each forkful of food the same distance to his mouth and then chewed each one, equally repetitively.

Lord Fenlock was the soul of repetition. And he'd called her thin and childish for years. But not since her first season. So who had reintroduced the thought?

"Am I?"

Her father regarded her measuringly, the same way he looked at his plate. "What matters is that Lord Burden thinks so."

Her sudden sharp attention cut like ice now; she felt it in her fingertips. "And why should Lord Burden's opinion matter to either of us?"

Lord Fenlock rolled his eyes. "Come, Eleanor. You have never been stupid. Lord Burden's opinion matters to everyone in London."

And that was it. It wasn't an endless line of dinners; she would be traded to Lord Burden in exchange for good opinion. She had always known that, but imagined Mr. Taggart would somehow thwart her father's plan.

Mr. Taggart couldn't thwart a fly, and Eleanor had always been lost.

Foolish to hope, really, and yet now she saw how that hope had kept her heart beating all these years.

"Why hasn't he offered already?" Eleanor managed to ask carelessly. She wanted some water, but thought the glass would shake too much in her fingers.

CHAPTER 7

The question intensified her father's constant frown. "These are delicate matters of negotiation, far too delicate to summarize."

Meaning that her father hadn't yet been offered what he wanted. That was the only reason she was twenty-five and not yet under Lord Burden's odious roof.

She stood so suddenly she overturned her gilt chair.

Its crash to the floor drew a disapproving tap of his fork on his plate. "Really, Eleanor. You have become a lumbering elephant. I ought to have paid closer attention to your marriage in your first season. You are on the verge of becoming so unappealing that only a French convent will *have* you."

That would be best, Eleanor's frenzied thoughts chased each other round and round. She'd rather spend the rest of her life scrubbing floors among spiders than with Lord Burden *or* her father.

The thought of food sickened her. "I must dress," she provided the first excuse that came to mind. "Lady Hortense will be at Ranelagh this evening, wearing blue; I have promised her my ribbons will be yellow."

"Lady Hortense is no example for a young lady of your quality," her father said, and Eleanor so wanted *not* to hear more that she simply sailed out.

"Eleanor. *Eleanor!*"

For once, Eleanor didn't heed her father at all.

* * *

"Ah! Sir John! Come meet two men who've already won the marriage game."

Jesper had been planning to slide past the Duke of Gravenshire. Ranelagh's laughing crowd of peers, darting about its garden in laces and silks, was equal parts appealing and daunting. Jesper thought the easiest approach might be to simply get lost among them and see what would happen.

But one couldn't slide past a duke.

"Your Grace." His eyes measured the Duke's companions as he made his bow.

"The Marquess of Ashbury. The Earl of Rawleigh. Meet Sir John Grantley, my lords."

His Grace made the titles sound easy. Neither gentleman looked easy. Rawleigh was a good-looking enough fellow, severe, with powdered hair pulled back from a careworn brow; Ashbury had a head like a hawk, busy looking about, giving Jesper the impression he'd rather be talking with someone more important.

But Jesper would stop out of courtesy for his father's old friend if nothing else. "Honored for the advice, Your Grace."

Lord Ashbury just shrugged, still looking elsewhere. "You look old enough to know what a wife should be. Choose one."

"What should a wife be?"

"Compliant."

Lord Rawleigh's expression did not change, but his chest puffed out a bit with pardonable pride as he said, "That quality doesn't determine whether she provides an heir. Lady Rawleigh, I'm glad to say, has provided two."

"And Lady Ashbury three," said that gentleman with a sniff, "yet that does also require compliance."

Jesper suppressed a shudder at the man's tone.

Just then, a gentleman passed by, wearing as much embroidery and lace as the Duke himself. A knot of footmen followed, surrounding a boy swathed in similar finery, who could only be the gentleman's son.

"The Duke of Talbourne," muttered His Grace, and the fact that he did not greet his peer was evidence enough what he thought of Talbourne.

The boy at Talbourne's heels looked all around with big gray eyes that missed nothing. But he did not speak, or run after the peacocks, or point. He said nothing.

Suddenly Jesper realized why his father had never married again.

Had his father wished to marry a lady of his station, he would have had to come back here. He would have had to come to London, and he would have had to leave Jesper at Roseford alone, or bring him, too, to London, where these stiff, sad people would have infected him with their stiff, sad lives.

A crashing din from the music pavilion meant it was easier to bow his goodbyes than say anything else, so Jesper did. He didn't want advice from these men on finding a wife; his feelings about marrying, given London and his father's example, were decidedly mixed.

* * *

"It's cold baths and spiders for me for certain," Eleanor moaned quietly to Hortense as they walked side by side down the path at Ranelagh.

Despite the drought, gardeners had coaxed the footpath borders into life, and forced some early flowers to bloom. The shrubs were stunted, and no water ran in the little brooks under the footbridges; but the gardens still smelled fresh and green.

In the Music Pavilion, the musicians struck up a lively air.

"Your father has never actually sent you anywhere." Hortense loved believing the best of people. "Perhaps he will relent."

"My father has never relented," Eleanor pointed out.

She did not want to be here, in her silk jacket tied with yellow bows. The *pouf* of her hair was subdued, suitable for garden walking, and her feather-trimmed flat straw hat would have been the envy of any French courtier.

On another night, Eleanor might have enjoyed it all. Tonight, Eleanor wished to be somewhere else, anywhere else.

It all seemed like a flowered, straw-hatted cage.

Everyone in London had watched her moon over Mr. Taggart for nearly the entire season. They were watching on all sides tonight, and they were laughing. They *knew*.

They didn't know about the cold spiders. But she had the feeling that if they *did* know, they'd be glad.

She hadn't just stopped visiting the Pine Apple tea shop where Mr. Negri and Mr. Gunter dispensed candy and ices. She had fallen out with too many women her age. She'd snapped that Lady Lawson was a terrible flirt, and the lady's daughter had stopped speaking with her. She'd told gloomy Lady Ashford to pull together the heart to leave her horrible husband, and the lady had avoided her since. One by one her circle had fallen away, shot down by bursts of intolerable truth. Had they ever been really her friends?

Were they glad she would soon be as miserable as they were?

Wasn't she already?

"Lady Hortense." Before them, a gentleman's powdered hair framed a majestic nose capped with round golden spectacles. "We have met before, do you recall? Lord Dunsby? Perhaps you would care to walk to the Chinese pavilion?"

"Shall we, Miss Henry?" Hortense seemed to genuinely want Eleanor's opinion.

Had Eleanor done as she wished, she'd have grabbed Hortense and run the other way. Surely she deserved to have one good friend all to herself?

But she didn't wish to spoil Hortense's evening.

Lord Dunsby was pleasant enough, aside from his peculiar enthusiasms. He wore a lightning rod on one side, pocket microscope on the other, and if past experience was any predictor, had pockets full of dull-looking rocks.

Eleanor just nodded weakly, fell into step behind the two, and made noncommittal noises whenever Lord Dunsby stopped to show Hortense a flower or a twig through his microscope.

He seemed genuinely interested in pleasing Hortense with these mild entertainments, and Eleanor felt a little tug inside as she watched. He was not so young as Mr. Taggart, and his eyes were not that particular shade of brown. But he was earnest, and kind, and that was what Hortense needed. Perhaps what every woman needed.

Why could she not have seen that earlier this season? Or last? Not that she wanted Lord Dunsby's attention for herself. She only regretted months, *years* of seeing what wasn't there, and realizing she should have been looking for something else.

* * *

THE HUGE ROTUNDA space at Ranelagh made it seem as if half the earth were enclosed in one stunning honeycombed dome.

There was far more space for dancing than in any London ballroom, and Jesper should have tried swinging a lady or two.

Instead, he found himself surveying each lady present and, when they were not Eleanor Henry, looking for Eleanor Henry.

There were taller women, and shorter ones, thinner, fatter, and several whose fluttering eyelashes (somehow darkened) promised him a much sweeter conversation. Still, he kept looking for the young lady with the sharp tongue.

It could have been only to keep clear of her, as one paid attention to where one found stinging nettles.

The nettles hinted that unlike the rest of London, her artifice was all paint and paper. There was something in her trying to get out, and Jesper, who had seen every animal born from butterflies to oxen, was interested in what would be set free.

He paused when he spotted Lady Hortense.

That lady's companion tonight was a gentleman only a few years younger than himself, draped in all the trappings of ocular science.

He adjusted the lenses on his nose as he took in Jesper from top to bottom, no doubt measuring him as a rival.

Jesper took it upon himself to do the duty. "Sir John Grantley. It appears we have a mutual acquaintance in Lady Hortense. Delighted to make your acquaintance as well, sir."

"The Earl of Dunsby. Your service, sir."

Well. If Lady Hortense had caught an earl—no, if she *wanted* this earl—Jesper wouldn't stand in her way.

Indeed, as he watched her laugh, that sparkling-diamond laugh rolling out for Lord Dunsby, Jesper thought to himself that he needed more in a woman than a beautiful laugh.

"Have either of you seen Miss Henry?"

"Yes, just there." Lady Hortense was too well-mannered to point, but nodded toward where Eleanor stood unhappily between her father and, of all people, Jesper's neighbor, Lord Faircombe. "We, ah, have delayed a dance until we might assure ourselves that she will be well."

Hortense looked gratefully up at Lord Dunsby.

Jesper admired the man. He might be truly gallant, or he might be only wishing to ingratiate himself with Hortense; either way, it was a decent thing to do.

"I believe I will stroll in that direction, so why don't you two take a turn?" Jesper nodded toward the *quadrille* whose sets were just forming.

And he felt good about letting Lady Hortense have her fun, but soon forgot her as his steps drew closer to the lady with no title at all.

CHAPTER 8

"*Y*ou'll dance, Miss Henry." From Lord Faircombe, it was not a request.

Eleanor wondered if he would go so far as to order her to perform, like an opera dancer. "Not at the moment, sir," she said as if Lord Faircombe had been polite.

Instead of letting it be, her father chose to chime in. "If Lord Faircombe wishes to dance, Miss Henry, you should oblige him."

Finger tapping on her fan, Eleanor wondered how many times a day the word *should* passed her father's lips. "Perhaps later," she said.

Lord Faircombe narrowed his eyes. "Lord Burden has the ear of many ministers." Thwarted of the chance to harangue her during the dance, he went ahead and harangued. "He may climb very high in his position. Very high indeed."

Vibrating with irritation, Eleanor gripped her fan tight. "Has he done anything clever? Solved any knotty problem?" *Helped anyone besides himself?* she resisted the urge to say aloud.

Lord Faircombe only looked more disapproving. The powder on his dark head made his hair the color of hard steel. "It is not a matter of what he has done. It is a matter of the sort of man he is."

"And what sort of man is he?" Out of the fountains and flowers came Sir John Grantley, the country baronet.

Eleanor closed her eyes. He could only make things worse.

Though she did find herself drifting a little closer to his side as he faced Lord Faircombe, his hands folded behind his back emphasizing the breadth of his shoulders.

The oaf was appalling, she told herself; but she felt safer standing by him than Lord Faircombe.

Who only answered Sir John's question after an insultingly long look. "Explanation isn't needed in the right sort of circles."

"I can only imagine. Miss Henry, your friend Lady Hortense has decided to try the *quadrille.*"

Why was he telling *her*? Eleanor felt her heart pounding harder. At close range, Sir John's silvered temples looked nearly white. Somehow he didn't look old; he looked seasoned, calm, and very aware that he couldn't trust either of the gentlemen before him.

In fact, the wariness in his eyes made her realize, for the first conscious time, that her father *couldn't* be trusted.

"Sir John!" Lord Faircombe's false good cheer grated on the ear. "You ought to attend some young lady for this dance. Let me introduce you to a few."

Just then, a wing of the dancers spun nearer, one lady tossed so high by her partner that Eleanor could see her ankles.

"I *would* care to meet some spirited dancers. Like that young lady." Sir John's admiration was obvious.

Well, at least he wasn't the kind of man whose opinion took an entire season to discern. For one thing, he made his feelings plain; for another, the ladies who interested him had far more obvious charms than Eleanor.

"Lady Lawson has a grown daughter," Lord Fenlock muttered under his breath and rolled his eyes. "It is a splendid idea, Lord Faircombe, for you to introduce the gentleman to some of our finer young ladies." Which category clearly did not include Lady Lawson *or* her daughter.

From his height, the baronet looked down on both the men. "I doubt we would have the same opinions about what constituted a fine young lady."

Eleanor had no control over this interaction; like her father and Lord Faircombe, Sir John paid her no attention at all. Yet Eleanor couldn't shake the feeling that he was standing near her. Just her.

Between his overbearing presence, her father's watchful eye, and Lord Faircombe's grating false cheer, Eleanor's nerves were stretched to the snapping point.

Which was of course when Lord Burden decided to show himself.

Before he could speak, Sir John re-introduced his mild topic of conversation. "Lady Hortense is dancing this *quadrille*. I wondered if Miss Henry wished to walk the outside of the figure to see."

Without a moment's pause between his arrival and his words, Lord Burden answered, "Lady Hortense is a coarse slattern who should be grateful anyone offers to do anything but tup her."

Inside her corset, Eleanor felt her ribs swelling, taking in air for a shout. How dare he speak so of Hortense? He didn't even know her!

Sir John spoke quickly. He wasn't looking at her, but she knew somehow he was gauging her response, and running ahead of it. "I find Lady Hortense lovely in conversation and in dance. I doubt there are many here who would agree with you."

"Few dare to disagree," and the man lifted his chin, attempting to intimidate Sir John from many inches below. "Miss Henry, you ought to sever that connection now."

The swelling anger was still inside her. She didn't trust herself to speak, only stared at the man's effrontery.

He took her silent stare for a question. "I would prefer my name not be associated with hers."

That was it. Eleanor felt herself pop.

"Trust me, it won't be."

He might still have escaped had he let it go. But no, he had to continue opening his mouth and letting his stupidity out. "I meant through our connection."

"I know *exactly* what you meant. So let me be equally clear, Lord Burden. I would rather be *dipped in spiders* than connected to you."

45

She saw his face redden but once started, she couldn't stop. Her hands balled into fists in her skirts.

"Your importance resides entirely in your own mind. I have no doubt that your work consists of dictating foolish letters to secretaries who are all much cleverer than you. The only thing more foolish than you are the people who flatter you thinking that it will somehow line their pockets. I want no connection to you at all, Lord Burden, much less any as intimate as marriage."

She wasn't shouting, but her voice carried like a bell, and concentric circles of people paused their conversation to listen to her diatribe, more with each passing word, until their entire portion of the Ranelagh rotunda was quiet.

Except for Eleanor's voice, ringing like a bell carved of ice.

Lord Burden's face was now purple, its soft parts stabbed on both sides by his stiff gold-threaded collar. If he felt half the rage she felt, Eleanor welcomed it. She had a quarter century of fights tamped down inside and was more than ready to let one out.

It was Lord Faircombe who spoke. "Well. I have misjudged your readiness for marriage, Miss Henry." As if he made Burden's, and her father's, decisions for them.

"I am entirely ready for marriage," Eleanor shot back, "but not to Lord Burden."

"Clear enough," said Sir John. "Miss Henry, perhaps you would care to walk the ballroom, if not to see the dancers, then to find more congenial company." Sir John offered it again with exactly the same tone as before.

This time, he crooked his arm.

For some reason, Eleanor took it.

"Miss Henry," hissed her father, clearly hoping his voice wouldn't carry yet rigid with anger himself, "if you walk away, you need never return."

For once she let her father see in her face everything she held back.

The rage must have been like a blow; he recoiled.

But his hissing voice persisted. "Careless, thoughtless, stupid—"

"Intelligent, compassionate, loyal, lovely." The deep lines worn around Sir John's eyes showed his devotion to sun and laughter. He wasn't laughing now. "We could stand here and compliment your daughter all day, but I fear Miss Henry needs some respite from all your fatherly love." He nearly spat those last words. "Miss Henry, if you would not consider it a fate worse than death, I will accompany you around the Rotunda—or anywhere you care to be that is not here."

His speech stunned the words out of Eleanor. She had already taken his arm, this rough country farmer, and the only possible course of action was to walk away from the men who wanted real harm for her, away *with* the man who wanted—what?

* * *

HER HEART WAS POUNDING. Jesper could see it in her delicate throat. Well, his was pounding too.

The thought that she had been subjected to that sort of treatment all her life made him want to break something over his knee. Possibly her father.

"It's astonishing you manage to be even as pleasant as you are," he said as he walked with her around the edge of the dancers.

Her slipper caught on a floorboard; he held her arm tight to keep her from flying.

"Is that more of your compliments?" She sounded choked.

"My apologies. Just—your mother must have been far sweeter than your father. He seems to have no fine feeling at all."

Miss Henry ignored this. Jesper could have kicked himself. Why speak of her mother who was gone? If nothing else, it gave away that most of his conversation tonight with new London acquaintances had been about her.

Her hand trembled. Jesper felt it against his sleeve. Ought he take more liberties and press it? Hadn't he just taken the greatest liberty, removing her from her father?

"Everyone is watching," she murmured, barely moving her lips, which had gone pale.

Without turning his head, Jesper glanced around them. Yes, many were watching, but many were not. "Some. Can it be scandalous, for us to simply walk together? What else should we do?"

It seemed to brace her a little that he wanted her opinion. A fresh wave of rage against her father washed over him, but there was no time to go back and punch her father in the head.

"We must find Hortense. I must see if her parents will shelter me."

"That's a good idea. By tomorrow this will have all blown over." Though the idea of returning her to her father's house held no appeal for him at all.

She glanced up at him. Her eyes were dark in Ranelagh's dim candlelight. "I can never go back to my father's house."

"Are you serious?" She looked serious.

"My father means what he says. He said not to go back. I can't go back. He won't *take* me back. And even if I did—" He felt her shudder.

"What?"

"He has long promised to send me to a nunnery in France if I displease him further, and I have now surely gone as far toward displeasing him as it is possible to go." Her fingers on his arm spasmed. "I should not mind it, I suppose. Perhaps it would be peaceful. If only there weren't the cold baths. And the spiders."

The young woman was in shock, and her words sent Jesper into something of a shock himself.

He was far more entangled now with Miss Henry's fate than he had planned. This would do nothing for his goal of finding a wife, and having an heir, for Roseford as quickly as possible.

Unless...

He closed his eyes. No, it wasn't possible. Miss Henry was a creature of London from the top of her powdered hair right down to her high-heeled slippers. She would never go so far as Roseford.

CHAPTER 9

hough Eleanor Henry was clearly resigned to going much farther, if she expected to land in a French nunnery.

No. He'd begun his search with the idea of a practical woman, but along the way he'd remembered that lives were short, and he wanted to be happy. He needed a wife who would be good company as well as sufficiently interested in bedding him to produce at least one heir, preferably more.

The young woman beside him was as brittle as glass and looked as easy to break.

Though, he reminded himself, she wasn't. Pushed to her breaking point she had snapped, but towards her odious father and the men who wanted to trap her into a marriage that would be not just loveless, but demeaning.

They were halfway round the huge rotunda before he thought of asking her what to do next.

"Have you no other family?" he said as pleasantly as he could with eyes on both sides watching them promenade across the floorboards. To himself he admitted he was glad now for his newer coat. His usual clothes might be comfortable and warm, but London eyes needed a different sort of protection.

"Three brothers," and his heart swooped at this information, first with hope, then a more nebulous feeling. She added, "They are all grown and have taken rooms closer to the King, and Parliament. My father required them to take important positions."

What a crew. "And they do what your father requires, I suppose."

She kept walking, looking straight ahead. "Invariably."

Did anyone in Miss Henry's family stand by her? Far from worrying about her temper, Jesper now felt that any good humor from her would be astonishing. Were he in her position, he'd be waspish.

"Look, there's Lady Hortense, and Lord Dunsby dancing." Had it only been the course of one dance? The last few minutes had felt like hours. "Let us consult with your friend. Surely there is a calm solution."

"Nunneries are very calm," said Miss Henry under her breath, but she smiled a fake little smile for anyone who was watching, and applauded as the dance drew to a close.

Lord Dunsby had eyes only for Lady Hortense, and Jesper took close note of the way she too smiled back up at him. No improper flirtations, just a smile so wide none could miss it.

Ah well. Jesper was several inches taller than Lord Dunsby, but perhaps the gentleman had something Lady Hortense found more appealing than height.

As she curtsied to Lord Dunsby, preparing to part, she caught sight of Miss Henry, and rushed toward her, leaving Lord Dunsby behind. "What is it? What's happened?"

"A falling out with my father, I'm afraid," and Miss Henry's fake little smile held tight. "Hortense, please may I visit with you for a few days? Please?"

Lady Hortense glanced up at Jesper. "Did you make things worse?"

He bowed slightly. "I didn't make them better."

"Oh dear."

Jesper thought she might be twitter-headed in a crisis, but Lady Hortense firmed up like a cake turned to concrete. "I must speak to my mother. She will be happy to have you. My father, though, he won't really cross yours, not really. For a day or two, but—"

"Just a little while," whispered Miss Henry. "It will only be as long as it takes my father to arrange my travel."

"Oh no! He won't really—"

"He is quite finished. With me."

The way she said it incensed Jesper again. What kind of father treated a daughter this way? His only daughter?

He had spent his life at his father's side, building, hunting, breeding the animals, plowing if need be. How would his father have treated him had he been a girl?

Not like this, Jesper thought to himself grimly.

Jesper was far more acquainted with daughters in Roseford's village than London ladies. Village women worked hard, all of them. They cooked and cleaned on top of working with the men, planting in season and reaping when due.

Eleanor Henry's only work was to marry at her father's command, and that seemed the hardest work he'd ever seen.

Even with no first-hand knowledge of it, Jesper couldn't imagine that marrying was the same sort of work as baking a pie or raising sheep.

"What sort of work can you do?" The words were out before he could stop them.

Miss Henry only glanced his way with confusion. "What do you mean, what sort of work?"

Lady Hortense patted her friend's hands and scowled a sweet little scowl at Jesper. "She isn't going to a nunnery."

"I didn't say she was, only asked—"

"I suppose that's why they have you sweep the spiders," Miss Henry said in a hollow voice. "I suppose one must begin learning somewhere."

"All right. That's enough of the spiders." These young ladies were *very* young, and this evening had borne all the excitement it could bear. Even he felt worn. "Lady Hortense, please do speak with your mother. We should settle Miss Henry somewhere quiet for the evening. And Ranelagh will be loud into the small hours."

"Yes. Let's walk."

As Lady Hortense led a subdued Miss Henry away, Lord Dunsby stepped closer, his lightning rod swinging and hitting him in his knee. Distantly Jesper wondered at his determination to conduct an experiment at any time. Or ward off sudden lightning. Must get quite a bruise.

"Excuse me," his lordship said, looking over his spectacles, and Jesper realized he had watched the entire exchange at a distance. "Lady Hortense isn't upset, is she?"

"No no. Only Miss Henry."

"So I hear."

Gossip must be traveling around the room like electricity even Dunsby's lightning rod could not deflect.

Jesper was getting a sense of how London worked for young ladies, and it was appalling.

"I only wondered if Lady Hortense was quite all right." The gentleman looked slighter than Jesper in his brocade and gold braid, but everyone was slighter than Jesper. He squared his shoulders. "I don't wish any harm to come to the lady."

Nor did Jesper. But he was thinking of a different lady.

"See here." Surely this fellow was some sort of ally. "Miss Henry believes her father is going to send her away if she won't marry as he says."

"Shouldn't be surprised." Reassured that Jesper didn't seem that interested in Hortense, Dunsby just shrugged. "Happens all the time. And he's a cold fish."

"Yes." Jesper couldn't see him now, all the way on the other side of the crowd. "Yes, he is definitely a cold fish."

* * *

"Let me speak to my mother. I can calm her pretty quickly."

Eleanor let Hortense go, even though she did not want to stand alone before the curious onlookers crowding Ranelagh's walls. She well knew that Hortense's mother was quick to flap, but also to calm. Though she'd never had a flap because of Eleanor.

Not only were Eleanor's dreams dead, her nightmares were coming true. She had held herself in so tightly all these years, and now she was unraveling. In public.

In fact, here came Miss Bligh.

"Perfection," she muttered to herself, not caring if the other young lady heard.

"It is," nodded potato-shaped Miss Bligh, with a haughty nod that did not match her diminutive stature.

"Are you too having a perfect evening, Miss Bligh?" Eleanor would not let her shattering show.

"I am." A few years younger than Eleanor, she had never traveled in Eleanor's social circles; but now she nodded with complete familiarity, as if they dined together often.

"Do you enjoy the dancing? The gardens?"

"Watching you brought low."

Eleanor could only gape.

Miss Bligh nodded again, as if at a particularly pleasing hand of cards. "You would have known what a limp rag Mr. Taggart was, had I let you speak to him more often. He has a certain taste, he was always going to stare at you from afar, but he has no interest in crossing your father or any of his allies. It was work, I don't mind telling you, to keep you from discovering that for so long."

Eleanor's knees were shaking now, whether from fury or fright she could not tell.

Miss Bligh? Miss Bligh had purposefully trailed along Eleanor's hopes? And surely knew how those hopes were now dashed, if only because for once, Eleanor had *not* gone looking through the crowds for Mr. Taggart all night like a ghost.

She had been watching *Eleanor* all this time?

When Eleanor hadn't paid the least attention to her, not since her presentation at court, except to note her knack for appearing where she wasn't wanted.

"Why?" Eleanor asked in a voice like paper.

CHAPTER 10

$\mathcal{T}$he shorter woman's face took on a hard, white look. It matched the powder on her hair; she looked much older. "Why indeed? Why call me *Miss Blight* at my first ball, before we had even really met? I despise your type and your judgments." She smiled, but not a smile; only a grim thinning of the lips and some self-satisfaction. "You might join Lady Villeneuve's coterie of spinsters—but no, you'll be leaving England, won't you? Too bad."

Oh no. Had she really called Miss Blight—Miss Blight even at her first ball?

"I'm sorry," croaked Eleanor.

"Yes, most people are when they've had their just desserts. No thanks to you, I've made my match. And since I'll soon be Lady Winpole, I will not give you a second thought. I doubt you'll say the same."

And with that, the little woman sailed away.

Eleanor longed for Hortense to return. Hortense would reassure her she was not so bad as all that. But Eleanor couldn't move her feet. And instead of her friend, here came the lumbering baronet.

"I suppose Lady Hortense's family has a carriage?"

Eleanor only nodded. She couldn't say anything at all.

* * *

ONCE HE SETTLED the young ladies in Lady Hortense's carriage, with a fluttering mother unsure of what to say to her husband and a paper-white, silent Miss Henry, Jesper set out to catch the cold fish who was her father.

But he was gone.

With some quiet swearing, Jesper realized he would have to track the man down to his home. He couldn't just walk away from something this broken.

It meant leaving Ranelagh, where dozens of pretty young maidens still kicked up their heels and laughed behind their fans, but Jesper hadn't found the crush an appealing prospect before, and it definitely palled now.

Lord Dunsby also looked a bit forlorn since Lady Hortense's departure. He was all too happy to provide Lord Fenlock's direction.

At the door of that house, a prim footman tried to block the way. "His Lordship isn't receiving."

Jesper pushed past him. The footman sputtered along like a puppy at his heels as Jesper searched room after room till he found Lord Fenlock in his study.

The man came to his feet as stiffly as a marionette. "Leave."

"Even in London, a gentleman cannot toss a daughter out of his home like rubbish."

"My family affairs are no business of yours."

Even as Jesper silently agreed, he found himself arguing. "It's an injustice to punish your daughter for not wishing to marry Lord Burden. The man's appalling."

"He is crass and selfish," Lord Fenlock said with the same lack of passion one would use to count spoons. "You also are crass, and lack polish. You cannot see his more important qualities. He has the ear of the King."

"Likely only a desk in a government office the King has never visited."

"He has visited the King's court. The King will value his counsel."

Jesper folded his arms over his chest. There was calculating, and then there was stupid. "The King values *family feeling*. And his wife. Do you think he and the Queen had fifteen children for politics?"

"One necessarily involves the other," said Lord Fenlock, still stiff as a board.

"Well, I have never met the King. Perhaps you know better than I what he likes in a courtier. But I have met your daughter. And she loathes Lord Burden. It is a particular cruelty, I would say, to force her to marry a man she loathes."

"Cruelty implies intention. I don't intend for her to loathe him; it is her affair if she does."

This twist of words nearly made Jesper's head spin. "I beg your pardon?"

"The alliance with Lord Burden is necessary. For myself, my sons, and what we intend to accomplish for England. My daughter does not look for ways to make the necessary palatable; she has stubbornly decided to stay hateful. I don't know why Lord Burden has put up with that stubbornness for this long. But clearly, that is over. And if she cannot help my cause, she must not hurt it."

Here was a type of stupidity Jesper had never encountered before. Roseford had no people this foolish.

He couldn't resist the attempt to repair the man's understanding. Perhaps he was simply so priggish that he could not imagine the depravity of a man like Lord Burden.

"If I were to guess, I would guess that Lord Burden enjoys the prospect of making a proud woman cry. I have little knowledge of him, but everything I have seen tells that story."

"I could barely have imagined that anyone who would marry my daughter would not have the same goal. An excess of feeling is an excess of feeling, whether toward sunniness or tears, and that is her main fault."

Again Jesper faced his own lack of experience in the ways of the world. Lord Fenlock was not stupid; he simply did not care.

"I have never felt as sorry for anyone as I do, after this conversation, for Miss Henry."

Lord Fenlock swept his coat back to resume his seat. "Your feelings are obvious as well. Take her if you want; I have no more use for her. I will give no dowry. Though I will send her clothes."

Unbelievable. Miss Henry had once more been correct. One serious mis-step, and her father had cut her out of his life.

She erased herself with powder and padding under her dress to force herself into his mold, Jesper saw now.

"You are revolting." He could not restrain the words.

"Your opinion is unwelcome." Lord Fenlock only waved one arm languidly toward the door.

He didn't bid Jesper goodbye.

The man threw away a daughter like a piece of paper. The very coldness recalled the moment his own father had died in his arms. Looking at Jesper as if he were the whole world.

Well, Miss Henry still lived, and surely her life would be better off if she had no further contact with this man, who was in no way a father.

* * *

ELEANOR COULD BARELY BE SEEN in the bed. She had wrapped the featherbed around her, and bolstered both sides with fat pillows.

"Please, just throw a quilt on top and let me never be seen again," she whispered. The stomach-aches had tried to warn her. It might feel good for a moment to say what she thought, but it always ended in horror.

Hortense, released from her finery and now in a dressing gown herself, put her hands on her hips and huffed. "Fine, mope for a moment, but then I expect a smile."

Eleanor flopped the quilt back to glare out of the pillows. "*Smile?*"

"Yes!" Hortense wiggled onto the bare edge of the bed that was left. "The tie that bound you has snapped, don't you see? I'm only surprised it didn't happen years before. You can do anything now, anything at all!"

"Do *what?*" Hortense was speaking madness. A woman who didn't marry was...

She sat up in bed. Was what?

Hortense shook her finger with a sly smile. "Ah, now I see you're getting it. You are *clever*, Eleanor. What might you do if you aren't spending every waking moment trying to please a father who won't be pleased?"

"I don't know! I could... oh..." The burst of excitement that had filled her—travel! Independence! New society! New chances!—trickled away. Deflated, she sank back, disappearing again into the pile.

What *could* she do? She hadn't any money. She couldn't travel, she couldn't even get to Bath. She hadn't a penny.

Hadn't she just been worrying over learning to sweep? She knew nothing about how to keep alive, much less find a place anywhere.

She had a vague idea that this was how women wound up becoming mistresses, or worse. Though she had only vague ideas of *that* work, it didn't seem to require previous knowledge.

"I can't do anything," she moaned into the pillows. "I don't appeal to men's passions. And where can an unwed woman go without falling entirely into disrepute?"

"Then marry," shrugged Hortense, "but cleverly."

Eleanor peeped out again.

"There's something in what you say." The words came slowly because the thoughts were piling up fast. She had wanted to help her father rule London because that was what *he* wanted. She had wanted to help Mr. Taggart, too. But what did *she* want?

"I could have helped rule London," she said, word after word arriving very slowly, "but London's not the world. What if I... *leave* London?"

"You could do it." Hortense conveyed the perfect confidence of an excellent friend. "You have always managed whatever you decided on, Eleanor. You must now decide on something for yourself. This is an *excellent* development."

Eleanor had no home, no money, and no husband. She relied on a friend for this very bed, as otherwise she'd be sleeping on a stoop. Or outside Ranelagh, in a ditch, a cautionary tale for young ladies. Laughed at by all of London.

But she wasn't in a ditch. And she needn't stay in London to be laughed at either.

She had no family who would stand against her father, and her father was now against her. Eleanor simply had to be for herself.

CHAPTER 11

"You've picked up the stray kitten now. You might as well just marry her."

Jesper had found the Duke of Gravenshire at home.

His Grace had not changed his clothes, and the lace at his wrist showed white in the dim light of the library fire. He waved his hand; a footman leapt forward and poured Jesper a crystal tumbler of brandy.

Jesper didn't want it, but he needed Gravenshire's help. He took the tumbler, even as he refused the Duke's wave toward a chair.

"I don't want to marry a stray kitten," he said, absently sipping. The liquid had fire.

The Duke scoffed. "It isn't a kitten, it's Eleanor Henry. She's got backbone, and that's what your country wilderness needs. If stubbornness gets sons, you'll have ten. If she won't bed you, you can divorce her."

"Is every man in London so crude about a lady's prospects?" Jesper slammed down his glass. "She's human! She's not a cow!"

"Ah." The Duke's eyes twinkled. "So you like her."

"Does a man have to like a woman to treat her as a human being? I wish every lord in London had to do a year's farming. You'd soon know what life was like without a wife to turn your sour apples into pie."

The Duke's half-grin faded. "Miss Henry is no farmer's wife. I don't see her baking pies. You're right, you'd best leave her alone."

"Except then she would be entirely alone. Are you willing to help her?"

The Duke of Gravenshire watched the son of his old friend pace his library, too agitated to sit. He had a number of thoughts about this which he had no intention of revealing.

"Why should I?" was all he said.

"Her father's heartless. Burden's a pig. She made none of this situation. You ought to help a helpless woman."

The Duke snorted. "Miss Henry is far from helpless. She is known for a cutting tongue when she is not getting her way, and that's often. In fact, I take it back. A farm might suit her. I think she could slaughter animals without qualm." He shrugged one shoulder. "She's made her enemies in London, and I can't fix what she herself has broken."

"I thought dukes were supposed to be of some use," muttered Jesper, still pacing.

"Did you? What a romantic idea for such a practical man." The Duke's dry tone made it impossible to tell if he meant to be funny or not.

"This is absurd. A perfectly good woman perfectly suited to London life—court, even—and no one wishes to marry her? London's askew."

"Hm." The Duke watched Jesper pacing back and forth a few more times across his library. His guest had barely touched his brandy, and the Duke began to wonder if he should insist on it as something medicinal.

"Very well," the Duke finally said. "As you say, there are any number of unmarried men in London. One is bound to want a wife. I'll find one."

"There! That is the sort of heroism Britain needs. Good man." Jesper actually stopped in his tracks and heaved a sigh of relief.

His Grace's eyes widened. "Good you think so! I had thought there for a moment you might have a *tendresse* for the girl. No, it's just as you say, she's pretty enough. She won't have a life at court, but she'll have a roof over her head and she'll be grateful for it. She'll give someone an heir or two."

Jesper's relief faded, and a frown pulled his forehead down again. "She ought to have a husband who wants more than an heir."

"Why?" The Duke had every intention of enjoying his fine brandy, even if his guest did not. "Isn't that just what you came here to offer a woman? The chance to have your son?"

Confusion, denial, irritation, all chased each other over the big man's features till the Duke wanted to laugh.

Oh, his old friend's son had grown up and was growing old, but he still didn't know himself well at all. Perhaps Sir John should not have kept the boy beside him; he was a man now, and yet had never wrestled with the complexities of other people.

Or at least, thought the Duke, remembering Sir John's reports of his son's skill at resolving village arguments about sheep and fences, he'd never wrestled with a complexity that had to do with himself.

Jesper—the Duke had trouble thinking of him as Sir John, having called him the other name since birth—slowly lowered himself down into one of the low club chairs.

"I did come to London to find a woman who would give me sons," he admitted. "And here is a woman in want of a husband. Yet the fit is poor."

"I just said, I don't see her baking pies." Oh, the Duke was enjoying himself now.

"I have a cook, you know. *And* a housekeeper."

"Still. She's not the sort to sweep up after pigs and all that."

"I don't have pigs in the house! What do you *take* me for?"

"There are pigs out of doors, I know that." The Duke savored the vanilla and fruit flavors of the brandy, and licked his lips. It was delicious, the chance to help an old friend who was gone. "You want someone who will get in among the pigs, and the sheep, and probably horses too. I know you. Your father never stopped traipsing around his lands, and neither do you."

The younger man let his head fall against the leather back of his chair. He rocked it back and forth for a moment, then fixed the Duke with one tired eye. "I know what you're doing."

"Do you?"

"No, I don't need a wife who bakes pies. Nor one to muck out stables. Roseford could perfectly shelter a gentlewoman who did nothing at all. As long as she bore me an heir."

"Really?" The Duke drew out his enjoyment. "And her mother bore three sons in a row. Huh."

"Your Grace..." Jesper sounded beaten down. "I have lived a life of quiet. I do not know how to live with a person who is sharp-tongued."

"You can still learn." The Duke refrained from rubbing his hands together.

"You think I should spend my remaining years listening to lectures about my looks, my manners, my clothes, and my house?"

"I think you have lived in a dream world till now, Sir John." Time to put some spine in the boy. "To whom will Roseford go if you die without an heir? Your mother was orphaned, your father an only child. You think there's a distant cousin out there who will treat Roseford as you wish to see it treated? The manor, the village into which you've put every waking moment of your life?" This was no act. It was easy for the Duke to shake his white head. "The King would take your lands and keep them. Or give them to someone he favors. Faircombe, perhaps."

"Ugh." Jesper's hands dangled over the arms of the chair to the floor. "I don't even have puppies. What would I do with a small, fragile creature?" One hand waved. "Besides the obvious."

"You owe the girl nothing." The Duke sounded utterly serious now, as he was. "She'll land somewhere, probably better off than you think. She's a clever one, Miss Henry. Don't worry about her."

"I *do* worry about her. Her spine is like oak, but she's so thin."

With this nonsensical remark, Jesper launched himself from the low chair. "Regardless. Miss Henry is one thing, my marriage another. I've wasted enough of your time. Your service, Your Grace."

And before the Duke could answer, he'd barrelled out the door.

Well. Young men.

The Duke heard him practically racing down the stairs—he definitely had his father's habit of diving into whatever must be done.

Then the Duke heard a heavy sliding *crash*.

In short moments, he'd swooped down his staircase to follow.

There was Sir John—Jesper—the only son of one of his oldest friends, lying like a felled tree on the carpet of his hallway.

He wasn't moving.

"You." The Duke of Gravenshire never put his hands on anyone, but he grabbed a footman by the collar. He shook the boy to drag his attention away from the prostrate body on the floor. "Fetch my physician." The boy nodded and raced off. "Mrs. Wilcox. Did he trip? Fall?"

"No, sir!" His housekeeper was straightening Jesper with her own strong, knobbled hands. Her fingertips probed his neck. "He reached the bottom on his own two feet, I saw him myself! Then he paused just a little—he still had his hand on the rail—and just pitched forward. Landed like a felled ox." She looked up. "His heart still beats."

The Duke's blood ran cold.

The Duke's first wife had died slowly, from an illness of the heart no one could cure. He well knew how secretive the heart really was, and how it could bring a strong person low.

His hand closed on Mrs. Wilcox's arm like cold iron. "Get Dr. Baillie. His uncle too. Whatever they want. They must be here in minutes. Go yourself."

That placid woman flew as if pursued by flocks of crows.

The Duke of Gravenshire himself felt Jesper's neck for signs of life. For the first time, the white at his temples seemed a terrible omen.

"You're not done yet, boy," the Duke whispered.

CHAPTER 12

"*I* feel fine."

The grim crew of physicians staring down at Jesper from the bedside made him feel he'd already died.

He wanted out of this bed, out of the Duke's house, out of London.

And he would be, too, as soon as he settled his mind about Miss Henry.

"*Do* you feel fine?" The physician peered through his spectacles, looking oddly bald without a wig. His thin hair was scraped back from his face, so Jesper could see he wasn't watching Jesper's expression. He was minutely examining the back of Jesper's hand.

"Fine people don't collapse," the younger one said with a brutal directness Jesper found unnecessary, given that they were discussing him.

Beside him a third fellow, who had apparently grabbed his wig on his way out the door and clapped it on nearly straight, pressed his fingers into the hollow of Jesper's throat in a way that was distinctly uncomfortable. "His pulse is fast."

Jesper thought about trying to explain this evening and gave up.

The young one tossed back the sheet and poked at Jesper's bare foot. "*Oedema*," he said.

This was about enough.

"I don't know what you're about," he pointed a sun-browned finger at the man at his feet, "but poke me again and I'll kick you. If my heart beats fast, at least it's still beating. Your Grace. This is too much hospitality. I must go."

The Duke looked just as serious as the physicians. "Sir John, you did collapse."

Jesper didn't wish to admit to fainting, but fainting was clearly all it had been. "It's been a trying evening."

The bespectacled physician pursed his lips. "The gentleman takes natural exercise, obviously, in congenial air. Heavy musculature, such as one sees in farm animals. You've experienced no other symptoms? Have you ever found it difficult to breathe?"

"Never in my life. Well, a fever years ago, but that was years past."

The physicians exchanged meaningful glances over his body till Jesper wanted to shake them. "Years to onset of symptoms. Just what you say, Dr. Pitcairn."

"I'm not ready to present."

"Cautious fellow," agreed the one by Jesper's head, "but here it is all the same."

"Here *what* is? Gentlemen, I have business to attend."

Throwing off the sheet, Jesper stood. His chest and feet were bare, breeches hanging unbuttoned at his knees, but surely he could find at least his boots?

The one with spectacles spoke again. "Your joints swelled when you had that fever. It hurt to move. You were disinclined to rise from the bed, even as strong as you are."

Jesper's head whipped around. "Yes." This felt like walking among lions, now. "How did you know?"

"Sir John, you have clearly suffered a bout of rheumatic fever. You survived. Congratulations. However, it has been our observation that once survived, the fever may not leave you."

"Or rather the fever is gone, but its damage remains." The youngest one didn't poke his foot again, but he bent low, clearly trying to continue to examine Jesper's foot even as he stood. "I would like permission to examine your organs once you have deceased, Sir John."

"Dr. Baillie!"

"One doesn't get without asking," the youngest one said imperturbably, "and he's not a sentimental fellow. Look at him. About to rush off anyway."

Jesper did indeed feel weak in the knees *now*. He sat heavily on the bed.

His voice rasped in his throat. "You're saying I'm dying?"

The bewigged one gave Jesper a look Jesper couldn't read. "Death is the inheritance of all mortal men," he said gently, "and as you say, you have not yet died."

"Then what are *you* saying?"

The others fell silent and let the bewigged man speak.

"Sir John," the man said in the same direct but gentle way. "We have observed that the fever damages the heart. The sac around it. Perhaps its very material. It is connected with the fever, though that mechanism we do not yet understand."

"My heart... is *damaged*?"

"Yes." Still serious, still gentle, the physician nonetheless nodded his head. "You clearly work hard. You move about. Perhaps some of the injury has healed. But not all, as you found this evening."

"I just had too much to drink." But he hadn't, he knew he hadn't. He'd barely touched the Duke's brandy.

And when he met the man's eyes across the little candlelit room, he saw the Duke knew it too.

"You may feel some similar sensations," the younger one said, now standing straight and keeping his hands behind his back, perhaps to avoid continuing to probe. "Light-headed. Fatigue. You are very lucky not to experience any pain."

The fever *had* hurt; Jesper remembered it very well. Every joint from his knees to his knuckles seemed to swell and had hurt even to touch.

Afterwards his father had suggested he keep walking, riding, carting stones and lifting sheep.

He *had* felt pain in his chest, Jesper realized now, but had thought it only the bellwether of healing. He'd ignored it. It had largely gone away.

One brown hand came up to rub the hair on his chest.

"When will I die?" His voice was still rough.

"No one knows when." The older physician looked kindly now. "Perhaps you have the span of a normal life before you. Thirty years? More? Perhaps tomorrow." He shook his head. "It is a failing of our profession that we cannot look inside you as a telescope pierces the ether to show what is on the other side. We may not be correct. We've studied this for years, but find only so many cases. That also obstructs our view."

"But you have seen patients—" How could that word pertain to him? "—like me. Of those, how many survive? For years?"

The doctor's kind eyes didn't waver. "A few."

A few. He was in the few already, perhaps. That fever had been six or seven years past. He had come through it. He had *survived*.

Half of his mind noted his shirt, ripped open down the front and lying on the bed. The shirt the Duke insisted he have to find a wife. Mrs. Peterborough had said the same thing.

To find a wife.

Sliding it over one arm then the other, he shrugged the torn shirt up over his shoulders and turned to face the physicians.

"This wound is invisible, but there. Scarred, perhaps. Do I have that correct?"

"Just so, sir," the bewigged man agreed, startled.

"Thank you, gentlemen. I will see to your financial thanks—"

"Never mind it, son, the physicians will be paid." The Duke pressed forward, and all three gentlemen bowed.

"Our thanks, Your Grace."

"And mine," Jesper said, sliding his open waistcoat over his shirt. The buttons were intact. It hung open over the snowy linen as he said, "I have much to do and little time. You'll excuse me, Your Grace."

"But Sir John!" The youngest physician reached out a quelling hand. "Powerful muscles you may have, but not a powerful heart. You must be gentler with yourself henceforth."

"Gentlemen," sighed Jesper, "a word with His Grace."

They all clearly wanted to say more, but, throwing glances back and forth, they withdrew.

"You advised better than you knew," Jesper told his father's friend once they were alone. "I was right in the beginning. Roseford needs a practical lady, and a strong one. She must not only give me an heir; she must rule my lands."

"An interesting conclusion, but this is no moment to make rash decisions." The Duke looked sadder than Jesper himself, whose face was stony.

"I do not gamble, Your Grace. I assume, like any sensible man, that I may always lose the next toss of the dice. Apparently I've won my every hour for the last few years, thanks to the power of a fate that may at any moment change its mind." His shoulders relaxed minutely. "I'm glad my father did not have to bury me."

"The most horrible fate," agreed the Duke. "Yet perhaps having few days means they should be merry. Be sure of what you are doing."

"I have been gambling for years, unknowing! How much time is left?" Jesper thrust the coat in his hand angrily toward the door.

The Duke said nothing. His wife, Jesper remembered, had been attended by just these physicians; and she had still died.

Every passing moment brought more sobering thoughts, and he must escape this room.

"I have played like a child too long," Jesper said, sliding on his coat. Without a collar, his powerful chest showed through the snowy linen, belying any unseen wound. "No more time for games."

Before the Duke could stop him, for the second time that evening, Sir John Grantley charged out of the room.

The golden light of the rising sun shone through London's omnipresent haze to peek past the velvet drapes.

The Duke of Gravenshire, looking out his window, took it as a good omen.

"What woman could resist a proposal like that?" he murmured to the empty room.

CHAPTER 13

*T*he sun slowly crept up, and Eleanor's only evidence was that the room changed from pitch dark to murky light.

It had been impossible to sleep. Her mind kept tracing and retracing every thorny path through the people she knew, cycling again and again through all the men she had ever met.

Freed from the glamor of the mythical Mr. Taggart, Eleanor could see she'd set her sights on him partly because no other men seemed the least bit appealing. She had been in society for years, collecting news for her father and waiting for a suitable marriage. She had *met* the London men.

Her mind kept circling back to a man who *wasn't* from London, and Eleanor kept stubbornly shoving the thought away.

Her husband needn't be perfect, but of all the things she disliked, *that* man was most of them. Uncouth. Badly dressed. Barely washed. Blunt. Simple in his outlook. Insensitive to when he wasn't wanted.

No, there must be something she could *do*. Some chain of events to put in motion that would reveal a more suitable choice.

Lord Overburg wasn't ugly. Could not Eleanor find out if he was indiscreet with his affections the way he was with his dancing? His valet would know, but how to find out what acquaintances in common they had?

Or even the Ayles son. He was young—perhaps younger than her —but he seemed... pleasant.

Her unhelpful mind supplied the image of the Ayles son whose name she couldn't even remember, looking as slender and young as he was, next to a fully detailed portrait of Sir John: powerful, weathered, like a castle turret who had seen many years and would see many more.

I don't wish to be locked in a tower, Eleanor thought, legs twisting in her nest of pillows. *I am free of my father. What life do I want?*

No daydream formed. She'd easily been able to imagine a whirlwind courtship to Mr. Taggart; now she couldn't imagine any future at all.

Sir John's arms came to mind, but that was no imagining. They were hard and real, just as real as his blunt words to her father. *Intelligent, compassionate, loyal, lovely.* The only compliments from a man she'd ever received, and all the more believable because he uttered them offhandedly, and had not mentioned them again.

That wasn't a *future.*

As she lay in the quiet dawn, staring at the blue ruffled canopy overhead and preparing to go over the list of eligible London men again, Eleanor noticed the sound of voices outside her room. Distant, but growing louder. The servants couldn't be making all that clamor arranging breakfast, could they?

The commotion drew closer. Eleanor could hear shouting. In fact it was an alarming amount of noise, someone crying out "Sir! Sir!" over and over again, and a collection of voices calling out to one another to grab an arm, or a leg.

The noise was like a human hurricane... and it was growing closer.

When the door crashed open, Eleanor squeaked, and sank back into her protective barricades of pillows.

It wasn't a hurricane. It was Sir John Grantley, standing in her *bedroom.* His clothes disarrayed, shaggy hair flying loose, and his collar gone. She could see his throat right down to—

How *dare* he approach a lady looking like that?

Fury launched her from the bed, coverlet wrapped around her night dress and tucked under arms. She would behave just as if armored in panniers and corsets. The *nerve* of the man.

"If speaking to a lady in the street is bad manners, accosting her in her chambers is far worse!"

He shook a servant off his shoulder. "I hate waiting to be announced."

Seeing her stand up to him, wearing a quilt like a breastplate, seemed to take the momentum out of his advance.

He might have nice arms and nice words—four—but how could she seriously consider a life of *this*? He didn't converse; he randomly charged in and out like a buffalo.

She couldn't even raise both hands, because one was holding the edge of the quilt.

She was raising the other to point—*get out*—when Sir John forestalled it.

"You're going to marry me." Clipped and curt.

Time slowed. Eleanor saw each shocking word being formed by his lips.

And he continued to shock. "No titled lady would want the life I offer; so take it. You'll have to be fair. With Roseford's money and lands. Will you do that?"

A road to the future opened.

Marry? She could. Leave London? Yes. Take a chance on one man she doubted, rather than the hundreds whose failings she knew?

"All right, I will," she said, matching his brusque, business-like tone.

They stared at each other a moment. Clearly, he hadn't planned what to do next.

But he formed some idea. "Leave us," Sir John said without taking his eyes from hers.

Murmurings of discontent broke out among the servants massed behind him, dark mutters and one outright "Oh, we mustn't!"

Sir John turned. They fell silent.

"You have all witnessed the lady agree to marry me. What other assurances do you want? She is of age. She can make her own decisions. Leave."

She shouldn't let him. But the very idea was deliciously shocking, as if the buffalo occasionally showed people the door.

Slowly, one by one, they backed out, some tugging on one another's sleeves. Eleanor thought some of them were looking to her for guidance, but she kept her eyes fixed on the man. What he did now would determine whether she'd keep the agreement she'd just made, or break it.

She wasn't afraid of him, and wondered why.

In moments Eleanor found herself alone with the man, the tension between them ratcheting tighter and tighter till Eleanor could not breathe.

The door had barely shut when he said, "You know I need an heir."

"Yes." She didn't have breath to say more.

"You are agreeing to provide one."

"Yes."

"I'm not unreasonable, Miss Henry. I know you may not be able to. I don't wish to pressure—"

"Why wouldn't I be able to provide you an heir?" Why had *that* come out of her mouth?

A tiny shrug of one massive shoulder. "You're just so thin."

Against her will, she looked down at the wad of quilt around her.

He said, "You forget I've had an arm around you. I know what's under all that stuffing."

The easy way he said it made Eleanor so angry that her insides felt like pooling fire. It must be anger. She still couldn't breathe. "I am perfectly healthy."

A shadow crossed his face. "Good," was all he said.

Still, they stared at one another in an empty room. Distantly Eleanor thought she heard various servants complaining about one thing or another, but the space between them was quiet. And small.

"The Duke will obtain us a special license," he said.

"I see." Married by special license. There would be even more scandal. She needn't worry; she wouldn't be in London to hear it.

"I saw your father. He won't object."

"Ah." That was lowering. Her father must have spent two whole minutes deciding he had no daughter.

"Say it."

"What?"

"Say what you're thinking. I see you thinking something. Say it."

No one ever told Eleanor to *speak*.

She waited for the flip-flop her stomach made when she spoke and it wasn't wanted. Her insides were quivering—still shock, still anger, surely—but her stomach was fine as she said, "I thought that my father has nothing to do with my marriage. Not any more."

"Good." He liked that answer, she could tell. "I am sorry for you, Miss Henry, for all the years you must have truly suffered under his roof."

His words melted some sort of weight, like a cage Eleanor hadn't known she was wearing.

She felt lighter.

"Very well," she said. "I understand. You wish me to help your estate; I'm sure I can. You'll have to teach me; I've had no practical instruction. And you wish me to bear an heir. I have no—"

She wanted to say she had no practical instruction there, either, but despite her newfound freedom to say what she liked, those words wouldn't come.

He saw it, the hesitation, the melting away of her confidence. "Don't be frightened."

"I'm not frightened! Don't order me not to be. If I were, that wouldn't help."

His frown made his whole weather-browned forehead wrinkle, like it took his whole mind to be concerned. About *her*.

"You *are* frightened. And ordering me not to order you is precisely the sort of circle that will make this marriage hell if we let it. Let us be cordial. You should kiss me."

"What?" Cordial? Hell? Kiss him?

"Kiss me. You'll feel better if you are the one to do it."

"I don't know how!" Inside the quilt she was trembling now, and it felt like fury.

Opening his arms and eyes, Sir John was the picture of exaggerated surprise. "Miss Henry. My God. Your whole life has been about making things difficult."

When she still didn't move, he did.

With a step his whole massive, hard body had pressed against her, and one arm caught her up at the waist.

Just like that there was *no* space between them, like when he had flung her about in the street. But this time they were behind a closed door.

His mouth swooped down to capture hers.

His lips were warm, surprisingly soft, but just as strong as the rest of him.

After her first instant of rigid surprise, Eleanor's mind with all its finicky details simply stopped. He was hard and hot; the heat of him went through everything he wore, the quilt, her skin, right down to her bones, which melted.

She forgot to think.

When his other arm surrounded her, hers floated up of their own volition to lie around his neck. He pulled her closer, tighter, till she floated off her feet. Pinned against him, she felt as though she were flying.

Slowly his lips parted from hers, and she realized he knew now how she tasted. As she knew him.

She slid back down to earth.

Still, her lips felt new. They lay open; she hadn't the thought to close them.

But Sir John laid a finger against them as if in a gentle *shush*. "No critique."

"I wasn't about to."

"Good." He looked stunned, too, as if something about that kiss hadn't been what he expected. Her knees started to shake at the thought of what he expected. "Will Lady Hortense be your hostess until we can be married?"

"Yes." She wasn't sure at all. But it might soothe Hortense's parents to know that Lord Fenlock's difficult daughter would soon be out of their house and out of London. She'd hide in the pillows for days if she had to. "I won't show myself."

"That," and his lips murmured it against her forehead, giving her another shock, one that sent inexplicable prickling sensations to weaken her knees, "would be a shame."

And with that he set her away.

"All right then," he said, as if not wanting to leave but unable to think of anything else to say.

"All right then," she said back.

So he strode out.

"Lady Hortense," she heard him greet her just beyond the door.

As Hortense rushed in, Eleanor found herself staggering backward to let the bed catch her before she fell down.

"Not really!" Hortense was all aflutter. "Not really!"

"Yes, really." She really was going to marry Sir John Grantley.

And she'd soon find out if kisses like that were more dangerous than cold baths and spiders.

CHAPTER 14

*H*ortense was good enough to attend to everything about the wedding that Eleanor couldn't. The few preparations were all over so fast, and Eleanor stood in the great stone church with cold air echoing all around.

The huge arched buttresses sheltered only her and Sir John, Hortense, and the Duke of Gravenshire himself. Eleanor's youngest brother was there, slipping in sheepishly moments before the ceremony. He sat far off to the side as if avoiding contamination. The Duke's son hung back; Eleanor barely saw him.

A few words, a posy of flowers, her traveling shoes, and she was married. She hadn't even managed to catch her brother's eyes before he'd disappeared. Hortense had walked her in; Sir John waited to walk her out.

She sank into the last bench on the aisle, looking around at the bare choirs.

"Anything wrong?" Sir John stood in the aisle, tugging on his gloves.

She had to go with him. Right now. In a carriage he'd hired, to a country manor farther from London than she had ever been.

Where she wouldn't know a soul, because her beloved Mrs. Willowby refused to come with her.

"You'll be married now," she'd said, dabbing at her eyes. "You don't need a governess, or a nursery maid. You must engage a proper lady's maid; you'll need it."

"I haven't time! Mrs. Willowby, surely you won't—"

Then she realized. Mrs. Willowby *had* a family. Her son and her daughters were all here in London. She even had grandchildren.

She didn't deserve to be stripped of all that for Eleanor's comfort.

No, Eleanor must now be hardy. Resolute. The kind of person who presided over country manors. She imagined that there would be muddy holes in the grounds, and some sort of animal slaughter. Perhaps dead ducks. She wasn't clear on the details, but she'd seen paintings.

"Never fear, Mrs. Willowby," she'd said, holding back the sobs she'd wanted to indulge, "I will be fine. And I shall write to you often! Who knows, perhaps we shall see each other again!"

They both knew perfectly well Sir John had spent little time in London and probably never would.

So Eleanor had already felt bereft before taking the vows in this vast church that meant so many slamming doors. She hadn't wanted to marry any London men; but she never would now.

She'd married the man who stood in the aisle asking if anything was the *matter*.

"No," Eleanor managed to say faintly. "It was all just so much... smaller than I had expected."

No other friends had come.

Sir John, standing next to her, cleared his throat.

"You should warm your blood before sitting for hours in the carriage. Climb up with me."

Unlistening, she gave him her hand.

She only paid attention when they reached the ironbound door that led to the stairs upward. "Not really?"

"Why not?"

Why not indeed? She'd just married a man she didn't know, just to escape London's bitter whispers. Why not?

It was impossible that Sir John had ever done the journey before, yet he directed her up tiny winding stairs, across creaking platforms, and out the last door without a moment's hesitation.

"Well, I know you don't hesitate to go places you've no idea how to escape," Eleanor said crisply as he handed her out of the door. Her shoes teetered on the grooved stone.

But when he led her to the roof's edge, she fell silent.

All of London lay before her, tall and squat buildings of every color, the Bridge, and the silver ribbon of the Thames. The river, studded with ships and small boats, seemed to tie together the whole city. Cold, damp air in her face made the view clearer and cleaner. Up here, all sounds blended together to just a soft whisper.

She had not been happy in London. She'd had every luxury, but few friends.

Perhaps she'd be different in her new home. She must keep an even tighter hold on her temper than she ever had before, and she must learn how to listen, and not just for gossip.

Sir John's boots sighed against the stone. "This isn't small."

What? Oh, her comment about the wedding being small. "No, it isn't." He was kind, in his rough way.

And Eleanor had better learn to appreciate that. He was the only man in London who would have her. What would happen if she disappointed him as she had disappointed her father?

Wondering how many ways there were to disappoint a husband, and how many she would stumble into before the night was over, Eleanor felt knots tighten in her stomach and listened to the quiet.

She was resolved to live differently.

* * *

SMALL? She'd thought the wedding small? In a thousand-year-old church that could have married kings?

He'd been mad. Why had he settled on a woman who could never be happy at Roseford? He'd had some wild thought, once the doctors delivered their doom-laden verdict, that Miss Henry would be the person to see to Roseford if he couldn't.

Blinking in the daylight on the roof, behind his new bride looking out over the panorama of a London she was clearly loath to leave, Jesper pulled the little velvet pouch from his pocket and shook its contents into his hand. The brooch, an ear of corn made of rubies and diamonds in shining silver, winked red in the light. Even more red than Miss Henry's lips.

But if she thought marrying in a cathedral too small, she wouldn't care for this as a wedding gift, either.

Sighing, Jesper slipped it back into its pouch.

The young lady clearly had no interest in his person. Whatever had motivated her acceptance of his proposal, it hadn't been his charms.

Damn it. Perhaps he should get some.

It would be a long ride back to Roseford in the back of the carriage. He'd arranged to ride with her, thinking it would give them time to become acquainted before they were home.

Now it seemed like a daylong ride to hell, and he questioned every decision he'd ever made.

She was thin, and pale, the breeze from the river ruffling the hair ribbons on her enormous hat as she surveyed her London kingdom. She jumped when he approached behind her.

"Did you bid Lady Hortense farewell?"

"Yes." He couldn't see her eyes under the wide brim of her hat, which balanced on a huge arrangement of powdered curls and sported a carved ship in full sail.

Well, they might as well get this disaster under way.

* * *

AFTER THE SECOND hour of watching Miss Henry—Lady Grantley now, of course—silently brace herself against the walls of the carriage and try not to fall on the floor, Jesper realized he'd have to try some conversation or the silence might kill them both.

Mrs. Peterborough and the few servants who'd come to London, he'd sent ahead. He'd engaged drivers and changes of horses to get him and his new bride home by the next morning. It was a hell of a way to spend a wedding night, but it had seemed easier than awkward questions about beds, and he wanted it over with.

Perhaps he shouldn't have married someone with whom a journey was something to survive. But he had, so there it was.

He scratched his chin; the rough masculine sound made her jump. "Miss Henry."

She looked at him warily.

Damn it, she was young and barely knew him.

"We're not starting on the heir right now."

Her eyes narrowed into sharp slits. "I didn't think we would."

"Then stop looking like a chicken riding with a fox."

"I've never seen a live chicken," Miss Henry said with a sniff. "I doubt they wear hats like this. And whatever you call me, please do not call me Miss Henry."

Damn it again. He wasn't this ham-handed.

Yes he was. That was why he'd been unmarried this long.

"Lady Grantley. My apologies."

She nodded and opened her mouth, but he interrupted. "And I'd prefer not to be called Sir John. I was always Jesper."

Mouth agape, she simply blinked. "Sir, I barely know you."

"We're married. We're acquainted."

"A nursery name?" It seemed impossible, but her long neck grew even longer. "Simple etiquette forbids me from using such an intimacy in public. Most wives never use it at all."

He wanted to know how she knew what *most wives* did, but he didn't ask. "We're not in public."

"We certainly are. This is a public carriage on a public road."

And just when he thought an early grave might soon be welcome, she tipped a finger to the brim of her ridiculous hat.

"This is a public hat," she said. Could that be a glimmer of a smile?

A smiling Miss Henry—Lady Grantley—*his wife* was worth a

moment's pause. Her lips were truly lovely, and so eloquent; they told him things about her mood that she wasn't willing to share.

She was nervous, but also on the biggest adventure of her life.

Well, so was he.

"Why do you wear such a ridiculous thing?" He didn't care, but wanted to see if she would rise to the bait.

She did. "Sir!" She puffed like an angry summer bird. "I pursue the latest fashions from Paris. The Queen of France herself set this fashion."

Jesper folded his arms over his chest, letting the carriage rock him back into the cushions. He eyed the scaffolding of the thing. "Is her ship bigger than yours?"

CHAPTER 15

*E*leanor felt her lips twitch. Was laughing an acceptable response? It never had been for her father. "Quite," she said, trying to squash her smile. "Her entire head was one vast ship. It was extremely famous."

She had resolutely refused to imagine this coach ride; she could never have imagined what he said next.

His eyes softened, and even in the dim light of the carriage Eleanor thought she saw something in them—approval, or amusement, perhaps. She could tell he was primarily keeping the conversation alive when he said, "She isn't popular with her people. Likely because of that hat."

Until Eleanor understood why he was teasing her, best to stay as serious as she could. "A queen need not be popular. She rules because that is her right. It is what she was born to do."

Sir John's hidden smile faded, and Eleanor felt half-sad, half-comfortable thinking that now he would begin the river of correction she expected. It was disappointing, that he was so like her father; but it would be comfortable from familiarity, at least.

But he didn't say what she thought he would say.

"Birth bestows responsibilities, not privileges," he said. "You will be the lady of Roseford. Remember that."

Shocked, Eleanor braced her arms against both sides of her seat so she could study him more closely than the violent rocking allowed. "What are you saying? The King's privileges come to him by right of birth, just as the Duke's do. Just like yours."

"I don't see it that way." He was frowning now, a forbidding frown that made Eleanor uncomfortable to be alone with him in the carriage. "I think privileges come to few, and those earned."

That truly was shocking. "What year is this? Am I riding with a Parliamentarian? This is England, sir, and the King rules here."

"You will be at Roseford, Lady Grantley, and I rule there. If you wish to be the help you promised to be, remember that. They'll show you deference—but you should deserve it."

The pounding of her heart calmed. He was correcting the *King*, not her. It was a relief, Eleanor realized, not to be braced for the next correction.

Such a relief that she took him at his word.

"I should expect nothing different from a man I first mistook for a farmer. You said I should learn to manage the affairs of the estate. Well, instruct me."

He spread his scarred, sun-browned hands. "Here?"

"What else is there to do for the rest of the day and night?" Eleanor's words drilled past his disbelief.

She *had* been braced for him to—well, attack her, she supposed, in the carriage. But he wasn't. And what else had they in common to talk about?

"Very well." And he began to list his rents, from memory, and each of his tenants, and Eleanor found it easy to be swept away by the sound of his voice distracting her from the rocking carriage and their solitude in it.

* * *

SHE MIGHT NOT HAVE WISHED to marry him, thought Jesper, but she paid attention.

Over the course of several hours she drew out of him all the details of his tenancies, his financial support of craftsmen in the village, how he got on with his local magistrate, his too-obvious disdain of Lord Faircombe as a neighbor, and as much detail on work that lay ahead as he cared to give.

In the middle of a long dissertation on how there was no more river stone, yet they must still build new walls, he realized he'd just outlined his whole plan to convince one tenant to give up a wall so it could be moved to the land of another.

She sat watching him with those serious dark eyes and said so little, Jesper hadn't realized how much he was talking.

He interrupted himself. "You aren't truly interested, are you?"

"We had a bargain," was all she said, and waited for him to resume. It gave him a most peculiar feeling. Her attention was so intense, focused on him and only him.

Suddenly he remembered their promise kiss. She had kissed the same way, giving herself up to his arms and focusing on him and only him. He was no expert on women but he knew when one had forgotten the rest of the world.

Though how did he know that? Thinking back, he couldn't remember any woman being that way in his arms before.

"If you are letting me talk of walls so you forget that we're married, you don't have to be wary." Her widened eyes told him that speech was too blunt, but he didn't know how else to be.

"I'm not wary."

"Don't look suspicious, then."

"I don't!" One carriage wheel bounced in a rut, shaking them both; she braced one arm against the carriage side again, the other gripping her hat. "But if I did, it would only be sensible. You burst into a *private chamber* to demand I marry you."

That was what she chose to remember? "This private-public business matters to you."

"It matters to *everyone*. Why do you consider yourself an exception?"

"One, because it is news to me. And two—" He stretched, hands pushing against the roof and his feet on the floorboards. The carriage barely held him. "It's easier to be the same person wherever you go."

If that wasn't a wary look from her dark eyes, he didn't know one.

His brittle bride had a lot of lines not to cross, and Jesper didn't have time for that. Relaxing with her, talking with her gave him something to think about besides her mouth. Sharp or giving, he was on his way to an obsession with it.

He wanted to know the real version of the rest of her.

But it wouldn't do for him to push her too fast, despite his urgency for an heir—and the way her mouth reminded him that marriage was supposed to be ready access to the type of comfort it was otherwise hard to get.

"I don't wish to rush you." He had no other way to be but himself, and maybe Miss Henry could do with some bluntness that wasn't cruel. "Things happen in their own time. We don't need to begin tonight. Or the next."

He could see her puzzle through what he meant by *begin*, and her eyes widened more.

But she said, "We had a bargain, and I will do whatever I must."

The way she thrust out her chin spoke of battle campaigns, or possibly torture.

A wonderful way to approach marriage.

He ought to leave it, but the way she'd said it pricked what was left of his pride. "You make it sound like someone will be shot. It is supposed to be *fun*, Miss Henry."

"If I hadn't just been married to you by a bishop, I would suspect you of fraud, Sir John. You cannot seem to remember my name. Regardless, I have heard marriage mentioned thousands of times. I have never heard it described as *fun*."

Jesper stretched again in his stiff clothes. Lot of good it had done, wanting to *look nice* for his wedding. She drew her knees aside, from distaste or to make room for him, he didn't know. But she clearly thought him as polished as mud.

He smelled the scent of her powder; even that brought to mind the taste of her lips.

He snorted. "What I saw of London would lead me to think there's not ten people in it having fun in their marriage," he admitted, "and yet fun it can be."

She cocked her head. The prow of the little ship on her hat-brim turned up. "How do you know?"

She sounded so genuinely curious that Jesper started to wonder. How *did* he know? He had never seen his parents' marriage, nor been married himself. Though he had benefited from knowing a widow or two over the years, they'd seldom spoken of their dead husbands.

After a moment's thought all he could say was, "It only makes sense. If two people are to spend a lifetime together, would they rather enjoy it? Or suffer through?"

"You have odd ideas. You should have mentioned some of them before we were married."

She meant it, and her tone was sharp. But the way she said it, so quickly, as if her words were only something she couldn't hold back, made Jesper keep silent. Whatever she made of life at Roseford, she didn't have to hold back the way her father had wanted. Not ever again.

Even if he bore the odd barb or two in service to the change.

"I suppose I should have," was all he said.

CHAPTER 16

"*M*rs. Peterborough. Have you secured a maid for Lady Grantley?" Finally free of the carriage, Sir John sounded hale and hearty, while next to him, Eleanor could barely stand.

The ride had been a day and a night of sheer hell.

Eleanor had assured Sir John it would be no bother; but she had never made such a journey before. By the tenth hour her bruises had bruises, and time had ceased to flow. It had been endless, with no possibility of sleep.

And now, standing in a dewy morning Eleanor did not have the power to appreciate, Mrs. Peterborough looked doubtful about something of which Eleanor was sure. She *needed* a lady's maid.

She wanted to snap that Sir John should just *do* something about it. But what could he do?

And what sort of opinion would he form of the wife he'd just gained if she couldn't even ride in a carriage?

She must be free of this hat.

"There hasn't been time." The housekeeper addressed Sir John but glanced apologetically toward Eleanor.

Eleanor just nodded as though this news hadn't sent her innards plummeting. "Perhaps you will show me to my room, Mrs. Peterborough. We needn't bother Sir John with every detail. I am sure he too wishes to rest."

She hadn't been able to imagine her new life, but she'd expected something like this. Discomforts she must simply endure. She could do this.

Her new husband nodded, but said, "I'll look over the grounds, just to assure myself all is well." Eleanor must look surprised, for he added, "A night without sleep is no great matter to me."

Well, it was a great matter to Eleanor, and she felt grubby and battered besides. "I will be grateful to rest."

She knew she sounded weak, and he already thought she was too thin to bear an heir. But she simply could not sound more robust after a night like that.

Fortunately, Mrs. Peterborough seemed to be made of very strong stuff indeed. "Sir John, you ought to rest too. And eat. Lady Grantley, I have a tray in your room. Please come with me."

Eleanor barely noticed how Roseford's timbers created graceful space rather than sitting cramped like a London townhouse. The entry was oak and carpets, with Greek touches carved into the pillars; but Eleanor grasped only the sweeping staircase and that she must climb it.

There'd been no mention of a bath, but when it came, it would likely be cold.

At least, she thought as she climbed each stair, muscles screaming, *I can't see any signs of spiders.*

The room Mrs. Peterborough opened for her had tall, airy windows, with cream-colored draperies embroidered with deep pink roses. Round the bed, matching drapes were fringed with tassels in the same rose pink. The wallpaper's stripes showed a few marks of age, but every piece of furniture from the dressing table to the lounging chair had been polished to shine.

This hadn't all been prepared by Mrs. Peterborough. Not just since yesterday. There must be maids, and they must have started work when Sir John had left.

On his clear errand to obtain a wife.

This wasn't for Eleanor. It would have been for whatever woman he'd decided upon.

Eleanor didn't care. She untied the hat ribbon below her chin and sank gratefully onto the bench of the dressing table. "Please." She was nearly hoarse from exhaustion. "Please take off this hat."

Mrs. Peterborough approached the thing with some hesitancy. Eleanor felt her fingers prod at it. "How?"

"Never mind." She put aside her sinking sensation. Eleanor could find the pin, she was fairly sure. "Let us just remove the dress."

Mrs. Peterborough didn't even poke this time, just stood staring intently. "How?" she said again.

Eleanor would not weep. She *would* not. She was in the middle of nowhere, without a maid and only a housekeeper staring at her as if a *robe à la polonaise* were something peculiar.

She couldn't just collapse and let someone remove all this for her. She'd have to do it herself.

"Well," she said, proud she could keep the tremor out of her voice. "I barely know myself. We can discern the fastenings together, I'm sure."

And they did. The steel pins holding the frill-trimmed front, the tapes of the petticoat, the ties of the bum cushion, the laces of the stays—they found and unfastened them all, piece by piece, until Eleanor felt she'd been shredded.

Gingerly she felt for her hat-pin.

Mrs. Peterborough regarded the discarded pile. "It's a lot to wear at one time."

"Barely more than you wear yourself." For Mrs. Peterborough wore a version of the gown too, albeit in one piece of plain linen and wool with no rear padding, no frills, and no lace.

The housekeeper just shook her head. "Seems like way more."

Eleanor nearly wept again, from relief, as the hat finally came off. Why had she worn such a foolish thing on a day like this?

Because she'd wanted to look nice for her wedding. She told herself sternly to forget it.

Her hair would also need to be prepared for rest. Mrs. Peterborough poked her *pouf*. "Powder?"

Had no one at Roseford ever been to court? Ladies in London had powdered their hair for decades. "It lets me stack the hair and keeps it clean."

"*Clean?*"

"Quite. One brushes out the pomade and powder, and reapplies; it removes any oil."

Mrs. Peterborough had a longish nose and chin, and they squashed toward one another as she surveyed Eleanor's hair. "This is a new type of clean."

Though her arms felt like wet noodles, Eleanor herself reached up to untie the ribbon that pulled back her side curls, and steadied the bulk of her hair brushed backward and over the *pouf*. The tulle knot in the center of it all, which gave her hair height, came loose.

Every hair on her head prickled with pain, finally set free from its moorings.

The luggage held large supplies of both powder and pomade. But Eleanor simply could not dress her hair by herself.

"I am quite resigned to the difficulties of country life, but I do need a lady's maid."

"I see that." Mrs. Peterborough set about folding the ribbon. With combs not yet unpacked, there was little else to do. "I will find one, my lady. There simply wasn't time."

"Of course. I suppose there is some way to wash?" Time to start the cold baths.

"Just there." Mrs. Peterborough pointed to a copper basin by the hearth fire.

"It's warm?" Eleanor's surprise couldn't be suppressed.

"Sir John said your bath was never to be cold."

He'd heard her? He'd said that?

Something melted inside. She'd been threatened with cold baths in nunneries for so long that they had taken on a huge, looming presence inside her. Just like that, Sir John had banished that shadow.

Heartened, Eleanor felt buoyed. She'd be able to bathe alone.

The thought gave her strength to address the rough bread slathered with butter, alongside a tumbler of water. While a lady never took large bites, Eleanor devoured it all in many small quick ones, trying not to think how a nunnery might serve similar bread and water.

"If you can find a clean chemise among the luggage, I must bathe. And sleep."

He'd said her baths mustn't be cold. Perhaps five more kind words, even if she hadn't heard them. Sir John was so rough to look at, but he must have some smoother edges.

* * *

JESPER HADN'T EVEN BOTHERED to enter the house proper, striding for the stables before he remembered two things.

His new clothes, and the physicians' orders.

They'd counseled rest. More than he usually took.

He hated to shirk work. And he felt fine. But until Roseford had an heir, he should take no chances.

Reluctantly, his steps turned back to the house.

I'll at least round it, he bargained with himself, *before I go in and lay myself on my bed in the daytime like an infant.*

Roseford Manor was older than London's fashionable town-houses; his great-grandfather had added the main hall, high and airy, with public rooms on the ground floor and sleeping chambers above like an old medieval castle.

He saw a flutter at the window. The drapes in the lady's chamber. He hadn't seen them move since he was little.

Hopefully Miss Henry—his *wife*—found the room adequate.

Now that she was here, he'd no idea what to do with her. He knew what they *ought* to do, but he hardly knew her. And she definitely didn't know him.

He could see that he'd overlooked some problems with the idea of immediately producing an heir. He wasn't a fussy lover, but this was damnably complicated. She wasn't a widow who wanted pleasuring

and then to be left alone. She would *be* here, day after day, doing...
lady things.

Whatever those were.

The grounds were the same. Had it been only a week? He circled
the kitchen garden and the wing behind before going inside.

Nothing was truly different. Just a wife alone in the lady's room.

At the top of the stairs, he laid a hand on her door. She was
sleeping in there. Strange thoughts. Stranger still was his urge, almost
a need, to go in there and lay himself down next to her. To curl
himself around her in the same bed, luxuriously. He wanted that more
than sleep.

His eyes drifted closed. She had handled the journey like a soldier.
Never one complaint, even when she was tired to the point of
slumping in her seat. And Jesper hadn't thought once about Hortense
during the drive. Hortense was many delightful things, but he didn't
think she had the fortitude of the new Lady Grantley.

Thank God she had that.

He was glad she didn't know how urgent was the need for an heir.
That burden was his. Centuries of family history came down to him.
He couldn't bear the thought of dying before the work was done.

But something in him rebelled at bringing the task to her like
work. He wouldn't rush her.

It felt even worse to picture her in the marriage bed with the same
determined, workmanlike attitude she'd brought to learning of his
accounts. Jesper wanted *her* in his bed, not a soldier. The last few
hours of the ride in the coach had been hell, watching her dig in and
endure, knowing she wouldn't lean against him, even as he became
more and more consumed with simply gathering her up in his arms...
which would naturally lead to kissing her again. He hadn't expected
that promise kiss. He wanted to know what it would be like to share
her marriage bed.

Burden was a pig for wishing to break her. But would she take
more kindly to Jesper's wish to break her *free*? He wanted the cat
under the barricades, ice, claws, and all.

He doubted she had any such curiosity about him.

95

Perhaps because he didn't *have* hidden depths, Jesper thought as tossed his coat over the room's one chair. The bare, spartan room looked different to him after London, where he'd slept among draperies, fine paintings, silver snuff boxes. This room, which he'd occupied since he'd left the nursery, had a bed and a chair.

Well, he thought as he tugged off his boots. At least the lady's chamber was fairly fine. As he recalled. He'd rarely been in it.

That would have to change, he thought as he lay down atop his coverlet. If Roseford were to have an heir.

He fell asleep, dreaming about her lips, before his eyes even closed.

CHAPTER 17

*J*esper's afternoon had started askew. It annoyed him that he'd woken only briefly, swallowed the bread and butter left by his bed, and fallen back asleep. It made him feel old *and* ill, and before he'd gone to London, he hadn't felt either.

Finally roused, he'd visited the stables, then decided he would walk around the lands. It had felt familiar, stumping along in his usual clothes without the overhanging threat of tall buildings, but also as though something were missing.

Then he'd stumbled over a cow in a bad calving, and while he'd managed to save both cow and calf, now he was covered in muck and mud and badly needed to bathe.

It was his own fault that he'd sent the steward to the village and lacked footmen, so there was no one to go to the house for clean clothes but himself.

Of course, instead of successfully sneaking in and out unseen, he encountered his new wife, smelling of flowery London powder and wrapped in more ruffles than he'd ever seen in his life.

She was pointing to a spot on the rose-patterned carpet and lecturing Mrs. Peterborough. "Surely you can better direct the maids than this."

Seeing her focused all his attention. The moment before he'd been distracted, his mind on his animals. Now he felt too tall, bumbling, and filthy. Well, he *was* filthy.

And he suspected he knew why there was a stain on the carpet. Even as he stood there, a nameless blob dropped from the side of his boot.

Now there were two stains.

"A cow calved," he said by way of explanation. No need to describe the heavy struggle.

The new Lady Grantley's dark eyes ran over every inch of him. She visibly resolved to make no comment.

Then the smell hit her and tested her resolve.

"Never mind, Mrs. Peterborough, I see the problem." She folded her hands tight and said to Jesper, "I was about to dine." He could see her re-think this plan.

"I'll join you."

"Please don't." Her chin tilted up. "The most minimal courtesy requires that you dress, and wash, to reflect your station before appearing in public."

Did she really think he would sit down to eat like this? Jesper twirled a finger around in a circle, pointing to his hall. "This is not in public."

"Quite in public, sir. The servants are at their tasks, and anyone may call."

If she waited for someone to call, she'd wait a long time. The nearest gentry were at Faircombe Hall, hours away. And he suspected neither of them wished to entertain that family.

Trying to distract her, he pointed his waving finger at her head. "Is that a public hat?"

Yes, there was the quirk of a smile, though she tried to hide it. "By definition, a public hat."

The thing was a cap, but easily a foot wide and sporting three rows of ruffles. The way its fluttering ribbons slid across the smooth skin of her shoulder, just slightly showing under her neck kerchief, made him want to tear the thing off her with his teeth.

He'd never thought anything like *that* before.

He stepped toward her, and she drew back. He wondered if she was truly frightened of him; then he remembered he was covered in muck.

"I must ride past the village, to the mouth of the woods." He'd been longer than a week without seeing to the land. He didn't know what to do other than what he always did.

Though for once in his life, he'd rather stay inside.

Jesper shook himself. By the time he'd bathed and shaved where the stablemen did, at the trough out back, he'd be halfway to mounting his horse and on his way; no point in changing his path. "You'll be well?"

"Of course," she said so quickly he suspected she was lying, "but when will you dine?"

"I'll dine in a minute." He wasn't about to explain to someone in so much silk that he did not *dine*, he *ate*, and that when it was necessary.

"Good day, then," and he spared his hat by not touching it before he went on his way.

* * *

ELEANOR KNEW how to seat enemies at table, how to flatter ladies according to rank, and how to laugh at jokes that were not funny.

Nothing prepared her for the boredom of a morning where there were no upcoming parties, no need to choose more than one dress she could put on herself, and no morning chocolate.

She was going to miss that chocolate.

Roseford was clearly more home than house. All the bones of life showed: the stables, the kitchens, the ash bins by the fires. But it wasn't *her* life.

It belonged to the man who charged in and out like a wandering buffalo.

Eleanor had been flattered, she realized now, at the way he'd stormed her room to demand she marry him. It was less flattering now that she realized that was simply the way he came and went.

Sir John was clearly not about to help her accustom herself to the place. He'd barely been inside since she'd come, and she suspected that was normal. Still, she'd spent hours in that carriage growing used to his company, and he'd disappeared once they'd arrived.

It felt like she'd driven him away.

"Is he always so abrupt?"

"Likely just came to fetch clothes." Which errand Mrs. Peterborough took up without further prompting.

Eleanor could entertain herself trying to find fault with the housekeeping, but Mrs. Peterborough obviously knew what she was about. There was nothing to ask of her if Sir John habitually tracked in filth.

"Bathing at the stables?" She raised an eyebrow as she turned back to Mrs. Peterborough.

Mrs. Peterborough nodded, foot already on the first stair. "There's a trough behind the stable the men use when it's not too cold."

Eleanor was glad there was at least a trough. She reminded herself she couldn't possibly miss the company of a man in that condition. "Do they use soap?"

Mrs. Peterborough drew herself as tall as she could, which was several inches shorter than Eleanor and yet still disapprovingly lengthy. "Yes, a soap I mix myself. With lavender buds and coriander seeds to scrub. When they're done with that they smell just fine."

"Of course." Now she'd offended the housekeeper. If Eleanor weren't careful, she would wind up just as friendless here as she had in London.

It was up to her to learn if that had been caused by being her father's instrument, or her own personality. She squared her shoulders and asked a question she'd never asked in her life.

"Should I clean the carpet?"

Softened by the mere suggestion, Mrs. Peterborough waved it away. "Of course not, Lady Grantley. Please. The parlor is just there, shall I show you?"

"No, it's fine." It was oddly disappointing not to have something to do. Eleanor was going to have to take up needlework to avoid death by boredom.

And here she'd thought all she had to worry about was bearing an heir for a strapping oaf she barely knew.

Marriage was a cascade of surprises.

She remembered. "Oh! I had planned to dine. Ought we wait for Sir John? Can you?"

Mrs. Peterborough put her foot back down on the floor and looked at Eleanor with something like pity. "I'm used to making his food wait for him, Lady Grantley. You'll often be waiting too, or you've got some work ahead."

* * *

ELEANOR SOON GRASPED what Mrs. Peterborough meant.

By the time Sir John arrived at the dining table, in clothes Eleanor wouldn't have considered for rags in London, another hour and a half had passed.

She'd given up waiting in the parlor, hoping by sitting at the dining table they could begin eating faster.

As Sir John entered, she rose.

And her stomach rumbled.

The noise was shockingly loud in the quiet room, and Eleanor felt her face turn red.

Sir John was now clean *and* astonished. "I never thought your stomach would do that."

Today was the day to see how red her face could turn. "Why? I'm not made of stone."

"All that stuff you wear seems the next thing to it." He waved vaguely toward her dress.

"It is nearly three, sir. I am famished."

"Why didn't you eat?"

"I waited for you!"

"What for?"

"Mrs. Peterborough, the cook, and the kitchen maid have plenty to do without serving lunch twice."

He looked at the table as if he supposed the plates just grew there. "My father always ate when he chose, and so did I."

"I know." Eleanor pointedly looked down at her chair. There were no footmen in attendance.

Belatedly, he came to hold it for her.

Yes, he did smell of lavender and coriander. That and some warmth that Eleanor didn't think came from soap. It was so distracting that she nearly leaned back against him just to smell it more closely.

But they *were* at the dining table.

She seated herself, and Sir John, after a moment, went back to his chair and did the same.

"I am now aware of many things," Eleanor said as if her thoughts weren't still following the elusive trail of herbal scent back to his chair.

CHAPTER 18

*H*e was clean, but still ragged; she could see his shirt cuffs, and they were deeply frayed. There was nothing attractive about that.

The shabbiness of his shirt steadied her and reminded her to hold her tongue. He hadn't let loose with a flood of corrections; that didn't mean he wouldn't, but Eleanor couldn't brace for that all the time. He could use a lady's advice; she'd give it. And she wouldn't be distracted by the arm muscles bulging the soft old sleeves.

Or by wondering if he'd been cold when he'd stripped to wash.

What had they been discussing? Ah, dining. Eleanor refrained from patting her cheeks; they felt hot.

"The cook keeps a pot of soup by the fire at all times, and the bread flour is mixed with peas and rye. Nourishing, heavy, and soft for days. That way she can feed anyone in the house at any time." The cook, clearly from somewhere farther north, had called the bread *bannock*; the kitchen maid called it horse bread.

"Right." He ladled her soup himself. It gave Eleanor a little flutter of pleasure, that he would do it with his own hands, which she tried to squash; he was only doing it because there was no one else to do it.

"Then you know."

"I didn't know it burdened the kitchen to serve meals twice. I'll remember that." He had a direct way with words that Eleanor liked, too. She believed he *would* remember it. "But my servants eat this; so shall I."

He *was* a secret Parliamentarian. There was equality, and then there was laziness. "If you simply came to dine at a set time, the cook is quite capable of making much nicer food for *everyone* here."

Sir John paused in the act of buttering his coarse bread. His eyes met hers. "You don't say."

"I do say. A properly managed house has meals at specific times for a reason."

"Hmm." He looked down at his bread. She thought the big oaf was actually embarrassed.

And he didn't deserve that. His clothes were shabby and his mealtimes haphazard, but he clearly cared for everyone and everything at Roseford. She'd bet the cow whose life he'd saved today was glad dinner was late.

He'd tasked her with looking after Roseford. There was a great deal more to take into consideration than she'd expected.

"How did your mother organize things?" Eleanor asked, buttering her own bread. She was starving.

"I don't know." His big shoulders shrugged. "She died when I was small; I don't recall her."

"I'm sorry." Eleanor's appetite vanished. Of course there had been no mistress of the house for some time. Clearly Mrs. Peterborough did everything she could, but in a bachelor house, she could only do so much.

His eyes softened a little. "It's fine. Eat. If your stomach has anything to say about it, you should."

Why must he be so rude as to mention it? Pricked, Eleanor picked up her bread. "Your stomach would serve you better if it reminded you occasionally too. Or is your whole constitution so used to disorder that it can function no matter what?"

He paused, spoon arrested mid-air, and Eleanor could just hear all her father's speeches about what she should have said instead. Sir

John looked around the room, the table, and his plate as if seeing it all for the first time.

"I'm sorry," she hurried to add. "I should speak less."

That made him frown, and at her. "No one told you to speak less."

"Everyone *constantly* tells me to speak less."

"Not at Roseford." He applied himself to the soup, which was likely nourishing, but also bland and mushy, its vegetables and barley one indistinguishable mass. "You clearly know more than I about kitchens. Arrange the meals as you like. I'll do as you say."

Whatever Eleanor had expected to follow her outburst, it wasn't that. "You'll what?"

"You know more about it; you direct it. I'll follow your direction." Clearly thinking. "I'll have to tell someone where I've gone so they can fetch me. Or wear a watch. I've never had a watch."

Eleanor shuddered to think what would happen to a watch in an adventure such as Sir John had had that afternoon. "Perhaps we can arrange a dinner bell. Though it would be prudent to have someone go with you wherever you go."

"Who has time to do that?"

The day had given Eleanor the obvious answer. "I do."

"What?" Now he looked as though her face were purple.

"I do. I doubt you have many callers? Nor do you hold social affairs? The function of London's society is largely for young ladies to marry. I have." Calling attention to it seemed forward; Eleanor rushed on. "You said I needed to learn how to manage Roseford's affairs. I should come with you."

"Lady Grantley, I don't wish to offend, but I can't imagine... all that..." He waved his spoon vaguely towards her person. "...trotting through the woods with me. Even the garden would seem heavy work."

That stung. Eleanor had chosen the dress because it was among her sturdiest, a tight linen that would last forever, with ruffles but no lace. "If you have suggestions about how I ought to adjust a *robe à la polonaise*, Sir John, please share them."

"No idea," he said, going back to shoveling down the soup.

* * *

TRUE TO HIS WORD, that evening Jesper arrived at the supper hour requested by the new mistress of the house.

This was going to be a lot of trouble, he could see that. He'd left the village with the argument between the miller and his neighbor unsettled, and if the miller didn't forbear invasions by his neighbor's geese one more day, there could be blood shed. Likely of a goose.

Villagers adored occasions for excitement, and this had drawn all onlookers. Even Mrs. Wright, massive and round with her baby about to arrive, had waddled out to see his tenants Beardsley and Hatch scream dire threats at each other.

But Miss Henry's—Lady Grantley's words had rung a bell Jesper couldn't ignore. Those London physicians would likely want him to eat regularly too, as well as sleep. And perhaps better fare. Though perhaps Jesper had only lived this long because of the plain food.

Damn, how was he to tell? How could he guess? He had no idea why he had been so lucky to date, and how to prolong his luck.

He only knew he wasn't ready to leave the new Lady Grantley alone with the responsibility for his lands.

And no heir.

It stung when he arrived at the supper table nearly on time, with clean hands and face, and his new wife, upright as a board in all those ruffles, still winced at the sight of him.

If the sight of him made her wince, this heir business would be going nowhere. "What?"

"Your hair looks like you caught it in a hedge."

"Ah... I did." He'd forgotten that. He'd thought he'd seen an adder's nest under a hedge; while the poisonous snakes had free rein in the woods, he preferred they stay away from the house. Backing out, his hair had snarled on a branch; it was quickest to cut it free.

Yes, a loose hank of hair hung over his right ear.

"I see," was all the lady said.

Embarrassed, his mood darkened. "I am never the picture of perfection, Lady Grantley."

"Obviously not."

"What does it matter?"

"I thought you ruled Roseford's lands and village."

"So I do." That had been a stupid, medieval thing to say. But in its way, it was true. The village and its environs followed his edicts. "Despite what you think of my hair."

"Then you want your people here to be proud of their village, and the manor." She raised one of those delicate eyebrows. "And its baronet?"

That stung, too. "They seem to think I'm all right. And how do you know what they think of me? You haven't met them all."

"I know some reasons people look up to their lord."

"Hmph. And now against your plans, you are a titled lady after all. And no titled lady, I suppose, would sit down to supper with a man whose hair was so ragged."

He'd meant to distract her with the mention of a title. He still wondered a little if she truly had some reason to prefer Mr. Taggart to him.

Instead, her focus remained on his hair.

"Ragged doesn't begin to describe it." Her eyes wandered over his head, and Jesper felt conscious of it in a way that was entirely new.

"Then you fix it." The words were out before he knew he would say them. What was he on about? He didn't want himself fixed!

But her eyes lit up as if he'd given her a present, and, stomach sinking, he knew he'd just given a promise he'd have to keep.

CHAPTER 19

*H*alf-grumpily, he pulled out her chair for her so she wouldn't see his face. Then, still standing, handed her the nearest dish.

He expected another barb for waiting on her as would a footman; instead, she simply said, "Thank you," and ladled out the contents, filling his bowl, then her own.

When the smell hit him, Jesper forgot his hair and hurried to his chair.

"Why does it smell so good?" It was a purer green than the usual fare, speckled with leaves that smelled like mint.

"The cook is really very clever. There are only a few early peas, so she mixed them with dried, and some mint."

Jesper was too busy spooning it into his face to comment, but the lady went on. "It's one thing to listen to men's dry arguments about a drought. It's quite another to see the state of the garden and realize that the villagers must be suffering too. No one will have the peas they need this year unless the rains come."

The platter she handed him was piled high with... "Are those cakes? Bread?"

"Muffins. The cook was quite excited to make something that would go dry by tomorrow."

It was another revelation as Jesper buttered the stuff and put it in his mouth. Soft, delicious, full of little dips that held the butter; a man would walk across England to eat this. "And everyone gets this?"

She nodded. "Everyone right down to the kitchen maid and smallest stableboy. They're easily made. I thought you'd be pleased."

She could connect the gossip of Parliament to a villager's farm. She could make the food better, not just for him, but the whole house. And she wanted to please him.

She'd have made a fine wife for anyone.

And he'd nabbed her for his own because of one burst of temper.

Unsure whether to feel dishonest or clever, Jesper just said, "I am."

Again her face lit up, and it was as if the clouds of gray that hung over her in the form of powder and panniers lifted, and he could see the ripe luscious woman underneath. "You are?"

"I just said I was."

"I'm sorry, I— Well. I rarely hear that someone is pleased."

"I believe that." Jesper felt a very reasonable urge again to pound her father right into the ground. "And you must tell the cook, too."

"I did. I just—" She shrugged.

"What?"

"I never expected you to say it." Then she looked at him with the first open smile he had ever seen her wear. "If you insist on complimenting me, and I spread compliments around too, this will only spiral into a whirlwind of compliments that will make this marriage hell for both of us."

"Oh yes. Hell." He waved his muffin.

She laughed, and that was even better than the food.

* * *

Sir John had been pleased at dinner. Eleanor knew it; he'd *said* so. It made a bubble of happiness inside her that felt new and a little bizarre as she retired to the front parlor.

She'd managed to hold her tongue and not correct the way he chewed (with his mouth open), wore his napkin (tucked into his collar), or ate his meat (with his knife). And he'd promised to let her dress his hair!

The hair was daunting, as it was neither long nor short, quite bushy, and now lopsided. But Eleanor felt that something would be better than nothing. After all, it had appeared nearly decent in London.

The thought of touching it herself had her preoccupied.

"Lady Grantley." Someone was trying to pull her from her reverie. Eleanor still wasn't used to answering to the name.

It was Mrs. Peterborough, with a woman beside her. A portly, pleasant-looking woman with apple cheeks.

It was nice to see the woman wore her hair neatly tied. Eleanor was willing to practice being gentler, but not every moment had to be a provocation.

"Rebby Coombes, Lady Grantley. Her children are grown, and she would like some work. Would you consider her for a lady's maid?"

"Oh! Mrs. Coombes. Have you worked as a lady's maid before?"

"No, mum."

"My lady," prompted Mrs. Peterborough.

"No, my lady," Mrs. Coombes said immediately.

Well, she could learn. "But you're quite familiar with laundering and ironing?"

"Oh yes, mum! I make an excellent starch." She scrambled to correct herself. "My lady."

Eleanor told herself sternly not to let loose a barrage of questions. Surely this Mrs. Coombes could tie the laces of stays, and anyone could pin a hat. "How about hair? Have you arranged paper curls? Powder? Hot irons?"

"Irons for *hair*, mum?" This clearly flabbergasted the rustic Mrs. Coombes.

Ah well. Apparently Roseford would be a place to try some rustic, *simpler* hair styling. Eleanor glanced toward Mrs. Peterborough, whose face said that this was her only option. "Well. We'll try it, shall we? Perhaps beginning tomorrow."

"Oh, thank you, mum! My lady."

Mum my lady might get old after a while. Eleanor shrugged to herself. Or perhaps not. Everything was different at Roseford, but not necessarily horrible.

She hadn't swept up any spiders yet.

* * *

"Sir John awaits you."

Four terrifying words.

But Eleanor was ready. Determined to keep any hours *he* could, she'd been ready the entire evening, while her husband had disappeared again.

If he'd reappeared, it must be time.

She led the train of servants up the stairs to the door Mrs. Peterborough indicated.

Sir John paced inside, whipping around at her entrance as though expecting a firing squad. His eyes only widened when he saw the stablemen trooping in after Eleanor.

A washbasin, steaming water in a bucket, a table, scissors, a low stool; all were placed in the middle of his bare room without so much as a by-your-leave. Mrs. Peterborough laid a small stack of clean linens atop the table, and then they were all gone.

Leaving them alone.

Eleanor thought that the best way to approach this was with confidence. She had seen a groomsman quiet a nervous horse once by simply speaking to him calmly, and leading him with a firm hand on the reins. Surely this would be the same way.

The horse had loomed over the groomsman, much as Sir John loomed over Eleanor now.

"Sir John." She gestured toward the stool.

* * *

HE EYED IT SUSPICIOUSLY. "I feel as if I am about to be beheaded."

"That *would* stain the carpets." She took an exaggerated survey of the bare room. "Is that why there are none in here?"

"Comical."

"You should have told me I married a monk."

He was drawn toward those cherry-red lips even on a woman armed with scissors. He stood toe-to-toe with his new wife. "I am no monk."

A lesser woman would have quailed, but Miss Henry—damn, why couldn't he think of her as Lady Grantley?—stood her ground.

Indeed, from the sparkle in her eye he imagined she rather enjoyed his challenge.

"Nor are you a gentleman. Sit."

"Nor am I a dog." But he sat, keeping one eye warily on her.

Until she foiled that by spinning him around.

She poked about his scalp.

"I thought you would just have at it." He waved to the scissors waiting on the table.

"I must know first what is afoot."

It was disconcerting, leaning back and letting her run her fingers through his hair when he couldn't see her. "What could be afoot? It's hair."

His ladylike wife actually snorted. It was a shame he couldn't see her. The warm softness of her fingertips continued to thread through his hair, parting it first this way and then that, smoothing back from his scalp and occasionally tugging on a tangled lock in a way that only made him wish she'd dig in with both hands.

"Have you washed it again since yesterday? With Mrs. Peterborough's soap?"

"I thought you preferred me clean. And how can you tell?"

"I smell the lavender. It wouldn't have lasted from yesterday."

She was close enough to smell him. And he still couldn't see her.

Perhaps that made her bolder, as her hands caressed his head and he heard her breathing close. He wanted to see her, smell her, *taste* her, and the more he contemplated that the more he realized he was in danger of shocking the lady.

A married woman must necessarily come to grips with the effect of such things on a man, but he didn't wish to startle her.

Fortunately, she didn't seem to notice. "That soap is rough, certainly too rough to use on hair every day."

"Why? It's hair."

"Hair is meant to be soft and smooth. Yours is brittle as broom straw. Oh." She made a little noise and fell silent.

CHAPTER 20

"What? Did you cut yourself on my hair? What's happened?" Spinning on the stool, he gave up the luxurious sensation of her hands in his hair to see what had made her stop so short.

"I'm trying not to be so critical," she told him, and bit her lip.

The way she worried her lip gave him a childish urge to push her limits. Even barricaded behind ruffles and bows, there was something raw and wild in her. Why wouldn't she set it free?

"Here, let me get that for you," he said, sliding a hand under her cap-ribbons to stroke her neck and pull her down so he could bite her lip too.

It was just the smallest taste, and it left him hungrier.

Yet, like in hunting wild animals, even the smallest movement had given him away. She looked wary now, and ready to bolt.

Slowly he reached out and took her hand and drew her between his knees. All her formidable attention was watching him, every flick of his eyelash, but she came.

He said, "Does a lady know how to arrange all that wire and tinsel you're wearing so you can sit on a man's knee?"

"Tinsel! Sir, this is England's finest flax!"

"I meant underneath." Some devil drove him to test her armor by rattling the panniers under her skirt, his hands on either side of her.

He expected her to slap his hands away, or make some cutting remark. He wanted that.

Instead, she just placed her hands over his, stilling him.

"I truly do not know how improper ladies behave," she said softly. "Would you prefer if I did?"

"I have no corrections." He had to take her however she was, if she was to become at least accustomed to his touch. His hands slid of their own free will up to her waist. He pulled her onto his knee. It worked perfectly well despite all the architecture under the skirt. "I like you just as you are."

She gasped, searching his eyes for the truth of what he'd said, or perhaps just to be sure he wasn't enjoying sarcasm at her expense.

Then quickly, as if startled by her own impulse, she put her hands on both his cheeks, and kissed him.

Had he told her once to kiss him so she'd feel better? He'd been wrong. *He* felt better, for the first time whole in a way he'd never felt before. Some loneliness he'd been carrying around his whole life faded into insignificance and he felt the richest he'd ever felt, his arms full of lovely Eleanor... Grantley.

Names faded away as they breathed in the scent of one another's skin, exploring with soft lips and nips and the unfamiliar tastes of one another.

She pulled away, searching his face as if for encouragement. He hoped pulling her close would be encouragement.

It was.

She kissed him again, and this time she lit a fire that wouldn't go out. It threatened to burn them both down to the ground, in fact.

And if he lost himself in the feel and taste of her, his body pushing him against her, *into* her with an unsubtle message of *go go go*, she seemed to feel the same. Her arms wrapped around his neck and crushed the damn bows and ruffles between them as she opened those luscious lips and let him have anything and everything he wanted from them.

When finally, slowly, they pulled apart, she looked unfocused at last, eyes wide, staring into his, when they'd been closed a moment before.

"Me too," he said, knowing his voice would be low and rough.

That was one rough thing about him she didn't seem to mind. He felt her push closer again.

"What is next?" Her voice was none too smooth either. Its waver made him listen as closely as he ever had in the woods for an animal of prey. "What must I do?"

"You don't *must* do anything." He sounded too harsh. But he couldn't help it. He didn't want her *compliance*.

Yes, they had a bargain and yes, they ought to work on the heir business immediately. But the whole idea of her coming to him because she *had* to felt... dirtier than any soap would wash away.

Gently he set her back on her feet, steadying her with hands at her waist.

She swayed. "You... don't want to."

"I *do* want to. But you don't *have* to."

"Of course I do! We're married!"

That cooled his blood. "Will you give me leave to call you by your first name?"

She gasped. "It is so improper!"

"Well, Lady Grantley, until you can cope with something far more improper, let's let it stand, shall we?" *Stand* was the right word. Fortunately, she still hadn't noticed, and age had one benefit: he could survive till the unwanted hardness subsided.

She didn't like the answer, that was obvious enough. But she'd kissed *him*; if she really wanted, she'd do it again. Instead, she stood inches away, looking more worried than anything else.

"Must it be improper?" she asked him with a seriousness that almost made him laugh.

He didn't, though, because they were new to each other and whatever her name, his lady needed more in her life than to be laughed at. "It's going to be very improper," he assured her, matching her seriousness. "Far more improper than anything you have ever done in those ridiculous clothes or out of them."

That made her blush, and he liked the color in her cheeks. But her hands dropped to her waist and its tightly laced stays where his hands had just been. "If you don't like my clothes, why didn't you tell me to change them?"

"Because they're *your* clothes. I don't want you to do things just because I say to do them. I need a partner, Lady Grantley. Isn't that what you promised to be?"

"A partner." One of her hands crept up and touched her lip, plump now from his kisses. He could see it flushed an even deeper rose color than it had been. "Is that what I am?"

"Well. The kind you kiss." He didn't want to sound gruff, but this hardness was rather uncomfortable, and she was still going to torture his hair, he knew that. He spun again on his stool. "Hadn't you better do whatever you're going to do to me?"

* * *

ELEANOR COULD BARELY STAND. That kiss had swept through her like a fever, making her shiver and sweat. How could he just go on... *doing* things with that kiss looming over them both?

Well, apparently he could.

And he seemed to mean it, that Eleanor should do as *she* liked. A novel idea, but welcome.

The only thing she was sure she wanted right now was to make his hair presentable.

"Very well." She'd asked Mrs. Peterborough to find her husband's combs and hairbrush. It felt odd to think of anything as *her husband's*, but there they were. And per her instructions, those had been washed as well.

The smell of lavender and coriander pulled her attention as she took up the comb. It was settling into her core, that smell.

"I have never cut a man's hair before, but I've trimmed my own," she said, trying to sound like in-public Eleanor and not puddle-on-the-floor Eleanor. "The reassuring thing is, I can't make it worse."

His choked laugh reassured her. She tried not to yank, working the comb through the last of the knots. Honestly, they weren't as bad as she'd feared; his hair was bushy and thick, but he had combed it in the distant past. It just liked to tangle.

Taking up the scissors, she circled him, surveying how the hair sprang away from his face. "Why didn't you cut it in London? Why don't you have a valet?"

"They couldn't decide what to do with it. And I don't need to look pretty."

"I can well imagine a barber's dismay." She could. But it wasn't hard to snip one side so that it wasn't longer than the other any more. The shape of his head naturally drew the cuts around, a little shorter here and there until it was still long, but almost the same length all over.

"I would argue, however," she added, "that you could look a little prettier." And she reached for the box of her own pomade.

That made him grab her wrist. "My pardon, Lady Grantley," he said as formally as anyone could wish, "but I don't want my head powdered."

He looked so alarmed she had to smile a little. Such a big strong man afraid of hair powder. "Very well," she said, trying to look serious, "but I hadn't intended to try."

Slowly he let go her wrist.

Eleanor took a little of the pomade and warmed it in the palm of her hands. The sweet, earthy scent rose between them as it warmed, and Eleanor reached up to stroke her palms along the strands of his hair. Warily, he relaxed.

It was soothing, stroking her fingers through the thick strands of hair, her fingernails lightly scraping his scalp. The tinctures of plants and sweet oil, along with the pomade's tiny touch of beeswax, melted from the heat of her hands, and smoothed down his wild tufts until they formed, not ringlets, but at least gentle waves.

The color, too, settled from a dry brown to a burnished dark gold, one that brought forward the bright green of his eyes till he looked like an unsettlingly beautiful lion.

"What?" He was constantly in conversation with her expression; Eleanor wasn't used to being so closely watched without criticism.

The bronze of his skin shone dark against the hair, and Eleanor tucked one lock behind his ear just to touch it again. "It looks nice," was all she said.

She needed far more practice in giving compliments, and a much steadier idea of the duties of a wife, before she told him how handsome he looked.

CHAPTER 21

*H*e tried shaking his head. The waves moved a little, but not enough to brush his eyes. "It's all right," he said grudgingly.

"I'm not done." She knew the man would never stand for her to curl his hair at the sides as the older men in London did, and she didn't intend to try. She could plait his hair tightly against his scalp; but that would look too feminine, even on a man like him.

She had seen once in the street a man with a long queue behind, the sides twisted back to fit into the queue in place of the more usual curling buckles. It would come loose, but why not try the experiment?

He wanted her to do as she wished.

Carefully she twisted back each side, holding one in place with a comb while she did the other. He made grumbling noises all the while about "Can't I move?" and "You don't expect to do this every day, do you?"

"Such whining," she muttered, but let her fingers caress the last strands as she brought the sides into the back in a tight braid that barely brushed the back of his neck.

The end immediately disappeared into the loose collar, inviting

Eleanor to search for it there. But one look at the hard brown muscle, and she couldn't do it.

"How does it feel?" Her breath had grown fast for some reason. It hadn't been that much work. "I've just tied the end with thread."

"It tickles," he grumped, then pulled the queue out of his collar and settled his coat more closely against his neck. Eleanor immediately regretted the loss of her view. "But it will do."

Then he stood, and looked as tall as ever, but somehow more imposing, more manly, now that his hair was burnished and snug to his head.

His eyes showed more, with those appealing furrows in the corners, and the white at his temples made his skin look even darker. His nose was straight and regal as any king's, and his mouth looked as hard and masculine as his jaw and the rest of him.

Even though Eleanor secretly knew it could be quite soft.

Gruffly he asked, "Are you happier with it?"

Did he want her approval? He did. It showed in his eyes. It didn't matter how large a person was, thought Eleanor; they must all want compliments sometimes.

Her first thought was to say something to diminish the moment, and how ruggedly beautiful he did look.

But then she remembered her joke about a spiral of compliments turning this marriage into its own sort of hell and decided the new version of Eleanor was kinder.

"It is surprisingly handsome," she admitted, and the glow in his eyes was all the reward she needed for her new behavior. "Thank you."

"I suppose I should be thanking you..." He clearly didn't want to, but clearly didn't wish to return ill for a compliment. "So I do," he finally said like a sulking little boy.

She laughed. It was easier to do at Roseford than it had ever been before. "You're welcome," she said, and curtsied more sincerely than she had ever done in a London ballroom.

* * *

JESPER FELT STUPID, lying down to sleep that evening with his hair all done up.

Done up despite a lack of parties, or Ranelagh affairs. He'd only spent a quiet evening hour introducing his wife to the library.

He preferred it.

The shock on her face when she saw the library, and its books, made him pretend affront. "I've been known to purchase a book."

In fact, he'd bought several. His father might not have visited London, but he'd taken a London advertiser, and Jesper did the same. When an advertisement for a book caught his eye, sometimes he subscribed. A new book's arrival was the only thing that kept him indoors for any length of time, though often the volumes simply had to survive being carried out of doors in pockets.

"Obviously, there's the desk," he'd said, unsure where to look if he couldn't stare at his wife.

He wanted to find out what was under those steel pins and stays. He had a strong suspicion that Lady Grantley had softer parts. Besides those lips that had, honestly, bewitched him.

"There isn't a desk in my room," she said, turning in place to survey the motley collection of volumes. Opposite the parlor, the library was tall, warmed by decades of polish and candle smoke. He was conscious that it lay below her chamber.

"Use this one." Dammit, why couldn't he sound more gracious?

She laid a hand on its silken ancient wood. He wanted that touch for himself. "We can share?"

The swearing in his head grew so loud he was afraid she could hear it. This was why he couldn't just sweep her up in his arms and have at it; she was like a timid deer, really. Why hadn't any of those London men seen *that*?

"Yes, Lady Grantley. We can share."

"Thank you." Her look was wary, wondering.

"For the use of a desk in your own house? Roseford is yours. Take it. Use it." *Take me. Use me.* She wouldn't understand if he said it. He wasn't sure what it meant himself.

The thoughts were powerful, and new.

So powerful they must have leaked into his voice. He'd said nothing untoward, but she had blushed again.

"Do you—sit in here? Of an evening?"

No, he didn't. "I can. I can use a chair, and everything."

Now why had he said that?

Perhaps to make her more comfortable. Sarcasm, she understood. "Let me see you do it," she said with a slight roll of her eyes that made her seem more herself.

So he picked a book and sat on the other side of the Argand lamp, hoping she appreciated it was the latest design and very bright, and she did the same.

And for a whole hour, they'd been pleasant, if silent, company.

So why was he turning now in his bed, wishing that they were back in the same room together? To read, if that was all he could do. To tease. To listen.

To kiss. And everything that came after that. He wanted her free of those stays. He wanted to see what passion would do to her. He wanted to *hear* it.

He'd told her the heir could wait, but *he* couldn't wait, not much longer.

* * *

"MRS. COOMBES, what keeps Sir John in the village?"

Eleanor was up at an hour that in London would have been the middle of the night.

She needed chocolate, Mrs. Willowby's bracing presence, and something to look forward to besides lying abed with her husband.

Just the thought of it had kept her up all night. He was so *large*. Surely they could not sleep in the same bed. But wouldn't she rather sleep than try... anything else?

The right clothes protected Eleanor from her father's critiques, but also from roving hands. She'd been in many a lascivious ballroom, but in bed with her husband, she'd be *bare*. What kind of protection would she have then? For anything soft?

For her heart?

That Sir John would suddenly turn into her father had grown less likely with every passing hour. But if he did, his criticisms would *hurt*.

She *liked* him, Eleanor realized. And she had never liked her father.

She needed news to distract her.

Fortunately, Mrs. Coombes could arrange braids *and* gossip. And she seemed to know what kept Sir John so busy in the village. "Two men—I won't say gentlemen 'cause they ain't—just flamin' up constantly. Seems they can't stand the sight of each other and they take it out on the geese and pigs what wander back and forth. I think they'll keep going till we build a fence so high they can't see each other."

"That takes all Sir John's time?" Eleanor wanted to learn a great deal more about that story; Mrs. Coombes clearly knew something she wasn't saying. But it seemed too little to be the only thing that occupied Sir John while he was out of the house.

"Not at all. He checks in on folks, like, makin' sure everyone's got food and all, especially with no spring greens to stretch the winter."

"And you're doing well enough?"

Eleanor felt Mrs. Coombes stiffen. But she said nothing.

Well, Eleanor was always ready to tease out more information slowly, and with new connections. Mrs. Coombes didn't need to reveal everything right away.

And she *was* very good at making Eleanor's hair snug and ready for whatever lay ahead.

CHAPTER 22

The last thing Jesper expected to see first thing the next morning was his wife in a riding habit, waiting by the mounting block.

If that hat was a public hat, it was a restrained one. Flat straw with only one bow, it was pinned to her still-powdered hair, which had been woven into a tight circlet on the back of her head. In the dappled morning sun, her face looked fresh. Perhaps she'd had more sleep than him, or simply wore less powder than usual.

"Where are you going?" was his ungracious way of saying good morning.

"With you, as we agreed." She gave her gloves a no-nonsense tug.

"You can't go with me." His visions of the night before, of a soft, bare Lady Grantley twisting in his arms, badly fit his goal today of riding hard through wild forest.

"Of course I can. As you can see, I have a riding habit. I asked the stable for a calm horse."

"You belong—"

She raised an eyebrow, waiting for him to finish that sentence.

Well, she belonged here now. And he needed her here, though he'd pictured her less in the woods and more in his bed.

She was supposed to give him a *son* to be company. He hadn't pictured his wife being the company.

There was his stablemaster, bringing his quietest gelding himself. Everyone seemed to be aboard this plan but himself.

"Right." She had a point, it was prudent not to go alone. He'd never thought of taking anyone; his father had taken *him*.

The massive wrongness hit him, that *he* was the lord of the manor; his father would never beckon him outside again. It was a lonely thought. One that reminded him of the ticking clock his heart had become.

Well, his wife had offered her company. He could be selfish and take it.

"Let's be off." Stepping in front of his stablemaster, he put out his hands himself to help his lady into the saddle.

Was this what one did with a wife?

Well, she was *his* wife. He would do this for her as long as he could.

She settled herself confidently in the saddle, one knee around the pommel, and Jesper thought to himself that this wouldn't be bad at all.

* * *

THIS WAS TERRIBLE.

Eleanor was not used to the way country mud and chopped grass flew up from her horse's hooves if they went any speed at all—and Sir John seemed never to go slowly.

She'd ridden only occasionally, decoratively, as it were, in London, and today was a muddle of constantly minding her hands on the reins, her knee on the pommel, her balance, her skirts, and whether to follow Sir John's tracks, denting the sparse spring grass, or make fresh ones.

But the air was fine, and if she must constantly search her mind for what Sir John had already told her (borders, tenants, how he might change the flow of the streams), she was at least not sitting about the house, bored.

She was determined not to complain or demand he go slower.

When he finally did slow as they approached the woods, however, Eleanor breathed a silent sigh of relief.

"What are these woods for?"

His look held amusement, puzzlement, pride all at once. "To be woods."

That made no sense, for him to hold lands for no purpose other than to be lands. But she was here to learn, not critique.

And just because the forest was wild didn't mean there was nothing to see.

"Look up," he told her as she ducked below a branch, and she did, twisting backward in the saddle.

In the limb's elbow, in its smaller branches, was a fat patch of twigs and straw. A nest.

As Eleanor's horse moved past it, following Sir John's, tiny yellow bills popped out and the chicks began a fearful squeaking clamor.

A glossy black bird with sparkling-dot wings landed out of nowhere on the edge of the nest. It cocked its tail under to keep its balance and gave its baby something from its mouth. Then it flew away.

"Oh! Was that their mother?" *That was a stupid question*, she immediately thought to herself.

But Sir John didn't think so. "Father, I think." He turned his horse back to the nest. Tall as he was, he could stand in the stirrups and look inside it.

Carefully, the big man reached into the tangle of twigs.

His bare hand drew out a smooth blue little egg.

Eleanor couldn't stop her gasp as his horse drew neck and neck with hers again, and he showed her the tiny thing in his hand. "It hasn't hatched?"

"Some don't," but the careless way he said it was belied by the gentle way he cradled the pale blue shell.

"How did you know to look up?"

"Look everywhere," he said simply, those light green eyes boring into hers with a clarity that was rattling even in the light of day.

"Sometimes you'll see shells on the ground. Hatchlings push them out of the nest, or predators."

"Who would prey on such a tiny helpless thing?" Her indignance was followed by her own eyes darting everywhere through the branches and trees.

He chuckled. "A hawk. A falcon. That's the nature of the forest. The birds who nest on the ground needn't fear falcons, but may be prey to a snake. Animals seldom make friends."

"I cannot approve." Eleanor scanned the skies for signs of larger wings. These tiny birds were hers now!

The intensity of her feeling of ownership surprised her. She'd taken on his challenge, she could see that, caring not only for the tenants and their affairs, but for every little denizen of these woods.

"Would you like it?" Sir John offered her the egg.

Such a heartfelt, delicate gift. It touched Eleanor as no gift had ever touched her before. How could she explain she had no good way of carrying such a fragile thing, but treasured the gesture far more than the shell?

"Haven't you already given me all your eggs, and birds' nests too? At the altar?" And with his gesture in the library last night.

A multitude of expressions chased themselves over his face, too many thoughts for her to read. "So I did," he said, and placed the little egg in the crook of a tree, but Eleanor thought something had passed between them that was just as fine and perhaps more lasting.

* * *

JESPER FELT foolish even as he put aside the unhatched egg.

He hadn't given her rubies and diamonds because they weren't fine enough; why had he just offered her a dead egg?

Because she seemed to understand. She was spattered in mud, her elegant habit raked by brambles, and under her hat, her nose was turning pink. He'd have to take care to ensure she didn't hurt herself, as she seemed determined to follow him everywhere, through ditches and brooks and along the muddy edges of plowed land.

When Jesper stopped to hollow out a dry ditch that had collapsed, using his bare hands and a little spade he kept tied to his saddle, she stood beside the road, watching his every movement with the same intense focus she'd spent on his narration of his accounts. Jesper doubted she could lift the spade over her head, but didn't doubt that she would try.

He hadn't known when he'd barged into her room and insisted she marry him what a good choice he'd made. She would care for these lands and the tenants, as well as the house. She'd even asked one farmer if his new hay barn would catch the breeze. She had a sensible head for the way things worked, even so far from London.

But no amount of sensibility erased the real human understanding of life's fleeting, precious nature. She might have never seen a forest before, but she grasped something of its great complexity, and its beauty, and the fragile temporary lives of everything inside it.

Those thoughts didn't fade as he led her deeper, showing her where the old trails led, the little bridge that must be rebuilt, the edge of the truly wild places.

His lady still seemed reluctant to volunteer thoughts, a reluctance that led Jesper to curse her father inwardly several times a day. But she couldn't hold back her noises—murmuring with pleasure at a musical little fall of water, or gasping at the height of an ancient tree.

He loved those noises.

"There is a tree far to the north," he told her, "have you heard of it? So old and vast that the squire has hollowed it out to make a dining room inside. Mrs. Peterborough says that it can hold twenty people—"

The scent of blood cut off his words.

Jesper knew every hillock and branch in these woods, and the animals that came and went. Nothing that large should be bleeding so freely this time of year, not unless something unnatural had caused it.

He plunged into the brush, not caring if the bushes scratched at his clothing, only taking care not to run his horse into anything too harsh, trusting faintly his lady would do the same.

It wasn't far. It couldn't be, for the scent to reach him. "Stay back," he said absently, going closer to look. She wouldn't want to see this.

He didn't want to see it either. But there it was, the body of a doe slumped in the way that told him she was dead, buzzing insects already beginning the work of returning the body to earth.

Holding his hand over his nose, he let his horse stand and, dismounting, walked just close enough to see what he needed to know.

The arrow had hit her low, a killing shot, but not quick. She must have run; but what dastardly hunter hadn't bothered to follow? For here she was, dead, and for more than a few hours.

Someone had been on his land. Someone had killed his deer.

A doe, and a pregnant one, he realized by the state of her. Killed not only her, but her fawn. Or fawns.

A few hundred yards from the place where his father's horse had stumbled, tossing his frail body to the ground like a rag-doll. A death Jesper had witnessed.

A soft, slender hand crept into his. She hadn't waited. She stood next to him, taking in the sad sight.

"No one should be hunting now. Or here," he heard himself say, trying to think only of today. "A doe, and her fawns. Senseless. Stupid. Someone bothered to kill, but not cleanly."

What a waste, he thought to himself, *and how cruel.*

"There's nothing we can do, is there?" It wasn't a question. She was only saying aloud what they both knew: him from experience, and her from obvious deduction.

Bending to lead her away, Jesper realized tears were running down her face. They dripped from her chin, unheeded, speaking to him of the same helplessness he felt.

The woods were wide and wild, but this hadn't had to happen. She felt that too.

He walked her back to the horses, shifting and nervous at the smell of death. When he put his arms around her, he felt the silence of her sobs shaking her.

Even this she wouldn't let out?

"You don't have to be quiet," he whispered, and held her closer, one hand cradling her head against his chest as one choking sob, then another, finally broke free.

The sound of her honest sadness, so basic and real, wrapped itself around something inside him and yanked it free. He held her, but she held him too, two arms twined around his waist hugging him tight. He could be sad too, with her, perhaps because she had been sad first.

The feeling inside him swelled, choking him, till he laid his cheek against her hat and let it out. His sob echoed over hers, and the release of the tears and the noise let go of things he'd held clenched inside him since his father's death.

A secret fear of being alone; the burden of responsibility for so much, even things he couldn't fix; and most of all the terror and solitude of watching his father's light die out in his arms.

They must move the horses, but for now, he could stand here and be sad with his wife and no one would know but her and him. A new little family of two.

CHAPTER 23

*E*leanor had a peculiar wish to hold Sir John's hand all the way back to Roseford.

It was impossible to do, mounted as they were on two different horses; but she was loath to give up the closeness she had felt to him in the forest.

She could see now what kept him absorbed out of doors every day. It was an engrossing world, and a rich one, far more varied in its way than London.

She was exhausted, scratched, sore, and famished, and still didn't really wish to go back indoors herself.

Even as Sir John dismounted at Roseford's front door and she eyed the mounting-block, wondering how wobbly her legs would be, the noise she heard in the distance made her say, "Is that too something we ought to see?"

She never made it to the mounting-block. Sir John simply reached up, his big hands round her waist, and plucked her down to her feet.

She had an urge to check and see if he was laughing at her, or displeased somehow. The urge, she finally realized, had nothing to do with her new husband. It was only a habit, one perhaps safe to shed.

Still she waited for him to answer, "Nothing dangerous," before he put her hand on his arm and led her around the side of the manor house.

She only had time to wonder if he too had wanted that connection before they came on a scene that would have been familiar even within the boundaries of London.

Behind a long stretch of the manor Eleanor had not yet seen, the servants had stood great tubs of water. Piles of wet linen stacked in one told the story; it was washing day.

Rebby Coombes, her new ladies' maid, worked among the rest of the house's women, pounding and stirring soapy liquid.

She turned red and ran towards her the moment she spotted Eleanor.

"I'm so sorry, mum—my lady! Such a disaster. I started right in to work the moment I could, and pressed them and everything, but I never expected it! The house needs more cats!"

She was practically in tears, her face growing more and more red by the moment, and Sir John was uncharacteristically at a loss, standing by while Eleanor called over Mrs. Peterborough and tried to put together the story.

Finally, with the help of both women, and interjections from the kitchen maid, whose unlikely name was Willa, Eleanor pieced together that Mrs. Coombes had laundered her pocket panniers, the hip baskets that held her skirts aloft.

Stymied as to how to press them, she'd hung them out the windowsill, thinking herself clever to keep them so near the chest where they were stored.

By the time she'd returned to check on them, she'd found one of the little cloth-and-boning cages had been taken over by an interloper.

"It had twigs and leaves all in there! Building a nest!" Mrs. Coombes was clearly annoyed by the bird's sheer effrontery.

"And Sir John's instructions are that animals aren't to be disturbed unless they must." Mrs. Peterborough looked unperturbed.

"Well, it must! The lady needs her wire underthings!"

Mrs. Peterborough just closed her eyes, obviously wishing for forbearance from Eleanor, or perhaps from fate.

Eleanor's impulse was immediate. "Don't disturb it, Mrs. Coombes! I can spare the panniers." She turned back to Sir John. "Will the eggs be the same blue color?"

The soft expression in his eyes made him look younger. "If it is starlings. I doubt it is."

"Well, we must go look. Mrs. Coombes, never mind it. And look how well my hair has survived the day. Your skills." Then she remembered the state of her riding habit. "Mrs. Peterborough. Should I too change behind the stables?"

"Allow me, my lady." Sir John stepped forward. "A novel proposal. Willa, if you'll run ahead and ask everyone to stay where they are and close their doors for a quarter of an hour, I'll escort Lady Grantley to her chambers."

That made little sense, but the girl ran toward the nearest door, and Mrs. Peterborough only nodded.

Sir John offered his arm. "If I may escort you to the far side of the gallery wing, Lady Grantley?"

Intrigued, she took it. Their excursions today had been enlightening.

Around the far edge of the wing it was quiet, the sounds of laundering distant again. Sir John began to unbutton his coat.

"What are you doing?"

He had a crooked smile that said he was just waiting for her critique. "Leaving my clothes here. Mrs. Peterborough will collect them."

"You cannot be serious!"

"You don't want me to muddy the carpets." He'd bent down and pulled off one boot, then the other, leaning them against one another, his bare stocking feet on the stone threshold.

"Sir John! This is shocking behavior."

He just shrugged, the coat falling off his massive shoulders as he did so. "This isn't London."

No, Eleanor had never seen anything like this in London.

Right there in broad daylight he slid out of his coat, his waistcoat following it in a heap over the boots. "You are muddy too," he said with obvious delight.

The fluttering linen of his shirt came down over his breeches, but there was little between him and the air, and Eleanor did not know where to look.

He really meant to do this.

Clapping her hands over her face, she whirled and showed him her back.

"Give me a moment to unbutton," she said, avoiding his face.

It took more than a moment, Eleanor fumbling the buttons in her fingers, which seemed to have multiplied until there were hundreds.

Once the riding waistcoat was open, she peeled it away, feeling a rush of cool air as the layer left her.

It was peculiarly intimate, undressing before him, and more so here in the open air. Every touch of the cool breeze on her skin reminded her that his eyes might fall there too, and her heart beat faster with every untied ribbon.

Once she'd slid the voluminous riding skirt down over her hips, she was down to her stays, with under-petticoat below and chemise sleeves above. She turned to face him.

When her eyes met his, she found them nothing like she'd expected. They weren't soft anymore. They were *hot*.

When she bent a little to drape her skirt over the heap of his things, it felt like leaving behind a chain, and taking a leap.

But Sir John just offered her his arm, as if they were both fully clothed. She took it.

"This gallery was started by a grandfather of mine. I don't recall how many *greats*," he said casually as he led her past portraits featuring any number of Grantleys gone before. "I wish I could have talked to him. Did he have a taste for art, or was he only copying the fashions of the time collecting valuable baubles?"

"These don't seem to be baubles." Eleanor could hardly see them, she was so aware of the warmth of Sir John's big body next to hers.

"Family faces I never met. They look different to me now. Lucky.

Lucky enough to make me possible." His thoughtful expression seemed to hold something back.

Eleanor didn't know what luck had to do with it; they had no doubt found wives, as he had, and planned to have their children. There wasn't much accidental about it.

Sir John went on. "Because of them, I know I have a place here. I think my father wanted the villagers to feel like that. He enclosed the fields to rotate crops, you know, because of Turnip Townshend."

Eleanor nodded; Lord Townshend's legacy was well known.

Sir John said, "I think it was also to let them know what they had coming to them. Allotments of their own. It mattered to him, so much that he cut a piece out of the forest he loved to make a plot for the Shore family. They'd just planted wherever they could before."

"So." She just kept discovering him. "Your father was less a secret Parliamentarian than a soft heart?"

"Can't a good man be both?"

She envied his calm certainty that his father had been a good man.

Eleanor would never have that, but she hoped to give that to her children.

The gallery emptied into a hall that was far older, with time-stained stone. Sir John craned his head to make sure it was empty, then helped her over the ancient step. "I should have shown you the house. Or perhaps Mrs. Peterborough has already done it?"

The way he said it sounded as though he hoped not. That he wished to do it. That he wanted to stay *indoors*. With *her*.

"She hasn't." They passed a low door that smelled like a kitchen. Eleanor had not even wondered about this side of the house, only stayed in the parlor to which visitors might come.

Sir John probably never used that room.

Every door they passed was closed, with no disrespectful peeking. "You've done this before!" accused Eleanor.

"I am not *entirely* unaware of the carpets," he muttered as they passed the one he'd stained to go upstairs.

Eager to discover the nest, Eleanor pulled away at the threshold of her chamber, rushing to her window.

There were her panniers, hanging below the paned glass. As she put her head out to see, a flutter of gray and red disappeared out of sight with a soft *flap-flap* noise. And yes, there were twigs and leaves gathered together inside one capacious pocket - it would have looked like litter to her a few hours ago.

Eleanor whirled around to find Sir John already leaning out to see, right at her elbow.

His eyes met hers from only inches away, and Eleanor thought her heart might stop.

Then it was pounding so hard she could barely hear. "Do you—will it come back?"

He was looking at her, not the nest. His eyes looked even brighter, here, and so close. "I think he will get on with his main affair. A home, a wife, babies."

Was he looking at her lips? Eleanor had been watched all her life but not quite this way. "Such a lot of work."

Sir John reached up and brushed back a loose hair above her ear that had escaped its moorings. Just as she had done to him the night before. "He might like it."

The rush of things Eleanor felt was confusing, to say the least.

She wanted to cover up; she wanted to be bare. She wanted him to go; she wanted him to close the door. She wanted his touch; she wanted to touch *him*, and that shocked her the most of all.

If he kissed her here, now, the way he had earlier...

Oh no. "Sir John, I've realized the most appalling thing."

"Lady Grantley, you've just walked through the house with me in your underclothes. I wonder what you find *appalling* now."

"We've just returned in time for dinner. *Scheduled* dinner."

When she looked up at him again, his eyes showed every laugh-line in the corners, for he was smiling. No, he was *laughing*.

As she watched, he broke into loud, hearty laughter.

"Sshhh!" She didn't know why she shushed him; this all just seemed so *personal*.

"You are hoist by your own petard, my lady," he said as he wiped away tears of laughter. "Scuppered by your own steering. Hung with your own rope."

He felt it too. He wanted to stay. He wanted *her*.

He was also enjoying laughing at her discomfiture.

"I hate you."

"No, you don't. And what a miracle." In a second she was caught up in those hard-muscled arms, pulled against him. The light linen between them did nothing to spare her chest from the heat of his. "You like me, Lady Grantley, I can tell."

He'd feel her heart pound like this. He'd feel *everything* she felt. Even the things she didn't understand.

"You needn't be *smug*." Her hands slid of their own accord up onto his shoulders.

"I think I will." And with that, he planted a huge smacking kiss right on her lips, and then dropped her.

She didn't want to be dropped. She followed him out the door.

Whistling, he strode away down the hall, completely comfortable with shirt bared to the world. "Looking forward to our dinner, my lady."

Unable to think of a cutting remark for the first time in her life, Eleanor simply shoved herself backwards and slammed the door.

She could hear him whistling and laughing all the way down the hall.

CHAPTER 24

*J*esper couldn't tell if dinner had been so delicious because of the morning with his lady, or his frustrated desire, or if his cook really had that much of a way with turnips.

When he bid Lady Grantley goodbye after dinner, saying he would look forward to supper, it felt like they were planning a much longer separation.

But surely that connection hung by a thread of good luck. He didn't want to risk snapping it. The lady was clearly exhausted, her riding habit now seized as laundry; she should rest before they ventured forth together again.

Perhaps he could manage looking out for someone a little more fragile after all. The lady was different from his father, or a villager, or a servant. She was something so new it didn't even have a name.

Besides, he'd promised his afternoon to the local magistrate. Jesper didn't believe in others waiting for him, though he considered breaking his own rules.

The turnips had been delicious, he thought as he swung himself up into the saddle, beat smooth and baked with butter and cream until they were a sweet delight that melted in his mouth.

But he would rather have had Eleanor for his dinner.

The wave of feelings, fine and rough, when he thought of her had him doubting his plan. She was *so* young. It didn't feel right to hope that she could raise their son here and tend to all Roseford's affairs by herself. She'd have a lot of work, and a lonely life, now that he imagined it from the point of view of a beautiful young woman who could have been a countess, a marchioness, a duchess.

And if he did *not* leave her with an heir...

She'd lose her new home. He had absolutely no idea what distant relative would inherit the estate, if any. The lands might simply revert to the King, who might gift them to anyone he pleased. Or keep them.

Had he made her life precarious through a short-sighted plan to protect his own?

Looking ahead had not been his father's strength, Jesper realized now. Even to talk in spring of the fall's planting was too much. He'd wanted now, today, and nothing else.

Did Jesper have to live that way too?

And if he should not, what was he to do now that he had lured a lovely young wife to Roseford after all?

Not just a pleasant wife; Eleanor.

He yearned to go back to her room, tear off whatever she was wearing and throw her into the nearest bed. Perhaps they'd never leave. The hunger to touch her, taste her, be inside her had seized him like no other urge he'd ever had. It was ridiculous, at his age.

It was also inescapable.

He was going to bed her. But he ought to tell her why he'd been so urgent to wed. He ought to tell her about his heart. That she had married a man who couldn't guarantee not to leave her alone.

He'd keep every vow he'd made to her in that drafty old cathedral.

But he should have promised more.

* * *

EVERY INCH of Eleanor's skin prickled with the awareness of Sir John even though he was out of the house. She wasn't quite sure what would happen when he returned, yet wanted it so badly she could think of nothing else.

There was needlework in the parlor and ribbon embroidery by her bed. Perhaps she did some of them. She couldn't remember.

There were lion eyes in all the carpet patterns, and all the balustrades shone the color of burnished hair. She wasn't just living in his house; she was living in *him*. He was inescapable.

She had the bone-deep conviction that her husband was finally going to share her bed. And she didn't feel ready.

"Mrs. Peterborough." When she pulled that woman aside, there were still hours to go until supper. Her husband had gone she knew not where. But the evening was all she could think about, every tick of the clock taking both hours and no time at all.

"Yes, Lady Grantley."

"I'd like a deep bath in my room before supper."

"Of course."

"And, Mrs. Peterborough..." She had not thought long and hard about this. She had no strategy in mind, and it had come to her all of her own thought, not through any chain of news. "I'd like to wash my hair."

That made Mrs. Peterborough, her arms full of pressed linens, pause. "My lady?"

"I don't wish to use the washing soap you make up for the men, but... Powder and pomade won't really do for me here, will they? Yet that's all I know."

Mrs. Peterborough looked thoughtful. "Hmm. Well, all the wash-tubs are out, and I have a trick that might work. If you trust me. The potions for washing hair can be tricky."

If her hair were all scorched away by lye, she wouldn't have to sleep with Sir John.

That seemed terribly sad, and also to be wished.

"I have mixed feelings about nearly everything right now," she told the housekeeper with simple honesty. "Lay on."

* * *

Sir John wanted to swear at his reflection in his mirror.

He'd never had a mirror before. He'd bought one in the village. It was a horrible device. He could see every white hair, every groove in his face, and all the marks of a life lived out of doors.

If he could just remember how his lady had dressed his hair, he would at least know that she liked *that*. But his fingers wouldn't do it.

Some urge to make up for his badly twisted hair made him slip on his London coat. If she didn't like the look of him, perhaps she'd like the clothes.

He arrived to supper feeling as sheepish as a little boy, as decrepit as an old man, and very at odds with himself for a decision made late at night after a terrible discovery.

He trailed into the room with his eyes on his boot-tips, the carpet, anything but her. "Lady Grantley. I hope I have not kept you waiting, I—"

When he saw her, he had no more to say.

She wore another of those dresses, but this one had only a little lace, and few ruffles. It billowed a little at her hips, but not wide like a door, because she wore no panniers; she'd loaned those to a robin also in search of a wife and an heir.

Her nose was pink from their day outside, above deep rose-colored lips that had begun to haunt his dreams.

And her dark eyes watched him, focused, wary, under a curtain of glossy hair that softly curled around her face and tumbled past her shoulders.

It transfixed him. He wanted to dive into it, to bury his face in it. He'd never seen such a glorious color before, burnished darkness with a touch of red-gold.

"You're beautiful." It was out before he realized he should make a prettier speech.

Her eyes widened a little as she nodded. "It's good to know, sir, that all it takes for a woman to be beautiful is to wash her hair."

It wasn't just the hair. She seemed softer all over, less architecture and more of nature. She looked like someone who belonged here.

Someone he could know.

"Lady Grantley," and he pulled out her chair for her, fighting the urge to nibble her neck.

"Thank you." She seated herself with the same little hitch she always used. She hadn't changed.

But she had. And it wasn't just the hair.

She said, "You look like a baronet. Like a respectable gentleman with more to say to a lady than just to look down her dress."

He went to his chair. He ought to keep his mouth shut; if ever there was a moment, this was it.

He couldn't.

"I looked down your dress; I just didn't mention it."

Jesper very carefully did not meet her eyes as he scooted in his own chair. She ought to have a moment to decide if she disliked him after that remark; he thought it only fair. It was cruder than he should be. Certainly to his lady.

But when he looked, she had one of those little smiles playing around the edges of her mouth, as if she weren't sure if she should laugh or not.

Free of powder and paint and wire, she looked, she *smelled* as delicious as a cherry. He had to remind himself that cherries were rare and bruised easily.

But he had twin urgencies pushing him to taste those lips. One was that he had no idea how many days he had left.

The other was that he hungered for her as he'd never hungered for anyone or anything in his life.

It was madness to sit at supper and pretend that food was what he needed.

"What possible reason is there to joke at the table?" Her voice had that little rhythm to it that told Jesper he was listening to something memorized from her father. "Supper should feature serious discussion, or none at all."

"Now on that, Lady Grantley, you are wrong."

Slowly, letting her see what he was doing, Jesper picked up his muffin...

...and tossed it at her head.

He felt a moment of panic, wondering what he'd just done, *why*— when his lady caught the muffin in one hand.

She was perfect for Roseford. She was perfect for *him*.

He wasn't going to make it through this supper.

CHAPTER 25

She just sat there, staring at the muffin in her hand. "Why did you do that?"

"A surprise. You *look* surprised."

Her astonishment turned toward him. "You're an animal."

But she wasn't truly shocked. She said the things she should say, but she didn't feel them. He didn't know how he knew. But he did.

Every lonely scar inside him melted away. It ought to have healed his heart. How had he known she was just what he needed?

Pushing away from the table he took the step and a half that was all there was between them, then dropped to one knee beside her.

"Hmm." He took the hand still gripping the muffin and pretended to inspect it.

Then he reached for the pot of butter.

"I am an animal," he agreed, while carefully removing the silver top from the pot. He scooped up a fingertip of butter, aiming as if to pat it onto her bread.

Then, at the last minute, he dabbed it onto her nose.

Her shocked gasp made him grin from ear to ear.

He licked his fingertip clean, wishing it was her. "The question is, Lady Grantley, how do you correct the animal you married?"

Keeping her gaze locked with his, using precise motions of her slender fingers, the new Lady Grantley patted her own nose with the muffin, thriftily saving the butter.

Then she leaned close. "I just let him wander about," she said, and he lost all control.

Her lips *were* as sweet and luscious as they looked. The tip of her nose tasted of fresh, salty butter. Her cheeks flushed as he pulled her to the edge of her chair, pressing her thigh into his belly; the low growling noise he made was instinctive.

And she was *kissing him back*. Her hands clutched his shoulders and pulled him close, and for every kiss that tasted that sweetly grinning mouth—he had *never* seen the lady look like that—she gave him two in return.

They found themselves standing, bodies intertwining, mouths melting into one another, and Jesper knew that to wait another moment was foolish.

Sweeping an arm under her legs, he carried her right out of the room.

"What of supper?" She was gasping. From his kisses. Wanting his kisses more than air.

"Mrs. Peterborough may keep it for us. Or we may just have to wait until we break our fast in the morning." Someone would eat their untouched dishes; everyone in the house had the same, after all.

Silently, he thanked his heart for beating strong as he carried her up the stairs and into the lady's chamber.

"I have something to tell you," she whispered. He heard her over the roaring in his ears, the sound of his hot blood and the panting of her own breath.

"Yes." If it killed him, he would listen.

He slid her to her feet.

She said, "I still have the muffin." She showed him the muffin still clenched in her hand.

Roaring with laughter, Jesper kicked her door shut.

* * *

HE WAS LAUGHING. He thought she was *funny*.

No one ever laughed because she *amused* them, thought Eleanor.

Well, except Hortense. It was one of Hortense's most delightful features.

But this wasn't Hortense. This was sixteen stone of huge crashing man. Throwing his fine coat aside like a piece of paper.

It was too shocking to talk at a moment like this, but impossible to stay silent.

She watched him toss away his clean neckcloth. He *had* dressed for her. "Should I undress too?" She couldn't catch her breath, and it was not the tightness of her stays.

Those shoulders, gnarled with muscle like tree roots, emerged as he hastily tore off his waistcoat and shirt as well. "If we wish to do this," he told her with what looked like seriousness, "it won't matter at all."

"How can that be so?" *He* certainly wanted to be bare; in moments he had pulled off boots, stockings, and unbuttoned his breeches at the knee. "After all, you—"

He made that growling noise again, the one that made him sound like an animal but which Eleanor found bizarrely appealing. "My lady, you are wearing skirts."

Sweeping her up in his arms again, her husband buried his face at the base of her throat, nuzzled, and *bit* her there!

Her jolt did not stop him, though she knew he would stop if she used that word. Teetering on the edge of an *abyss* of impropriety, she watched, touched, tasted, and listened. He had yet to tell her what to do, but he made suggestions with his teeth, and hot mouth, that she was very inclined to take.

She shied away from crushing herself against his bare chest. How was he so brown all the way down to the waist of his trousers? She blushed to think of him sweating in the sun; yet he must have.

The pull was too much and Eleanor found herself flattening her hand, which looked small and frail against the curve of his chest, against that skin.

It must have absorbed the sun's heat as well to give off so much fire.

His hands slid up into the mass of her hair, apparently reveling in its new sleekness. Murmuring against her temple, wrapping her hair around his fist and touching it to his lips, he muttered, "Beautiful."

Eleanor heard *that*.

"Tell me what to do."

He pulled away, and she made an unhappy noise. But he cupped her face in his hands. He made her feel so small and so powerful at the same time. "Whatever you wish."

"But I don't know how to do it correctly!"

"My lady," and he lifted her off her feet to pull her against him, then sank backwards with both of them onto her bed, "there are no wrong answers."

He seemed to mean it. He stayed still and let her explore the muscles of his chest, finding them strange and somehow familiar at the same time. After all, he'd held her against him before.

It was so odd how a touch here and there added up to make such new, such intimate familiarity.

Her hair slid down across them both. He buried his face in it as she followed his lead, kissing her way across his sun-browned jaw to his ear, delighting in how that made him shudder, then down his throat to nip at the base as he had.

He rasped, "I've got to have more."

He flipped the two of them over so fast Eleanor was dizzy. *This is it*, she thought, waiting for the weight that would surely come. She might be innocent, but everyone knew how this worked.

As it turned out, no one could possibly know how Sir John worked. Because against all expectation, he tossed away both her slippers and dug his thumbs into the base of her stockinged feet.

"*Oof.*" The pleasure knocked her off her elbows. She couldn't sit up to see what he was doing any more; she also didn't care. It would happen by touch.

And it did. She hid her face behind her hands while his big, knuckle-scarred hands kneaded, stroked, *possessed* and progressed over Eleanor's feet to her ankles and upward. Every fingertip seemed to find some knot of clenched muscle in her being and to release it, so that by the time his big hands spread over the tops of her thighs, pushing up the edge of her skirts, she felt boneless.

She ruthlessly squashed the instinct to fling her arms wide open and let him see everything he was doing to her. There was improper, then there was humiliating. If she lowered every guard, what might he see that he didn't like?

He tried to coax words from her. "Would you rather be bare?" The deep hoarseness of his voice cut through the fog of her pleasure. Her hands closed over his. "Would you rather I could see all of you? Your belly? Your breasts?" He heaved himself upwards, and Eleanor felt a moment of fear, his shaggy head looming over her. Then she melted again, her fingers sinking into his hair as he murmured against the slope of one of her breasts. "I want the small of your back. I want your knees. I want your elbows, just as badly. I want all of you. I want to touch you and mark you with kisses."

Her husband did not believe in covering things up.

Her breath came as hard as his did. "I thought... men simply... got on with it."

"Oh, my lady." Reaching up to guide her chin till her eyes locked with his, he let his other hand slip higher, one callused thumb stroking the soft skin at the top of her thigh. "Only the fools."

And then both his hands slid even higher, and Eleanor felt his fingers *there*.

It was nothing like touching herself. Not even the way she did sometimes at night, dreamily. He was strong and sure and well able to slide his hands beneath her and pull her toward the light. Which he did.

She had a moment's respite from the intensity of his eyes when his gaze tore away from hers and slid lower down. Then tensed again when he pushed up her skirts and turned his gaze *there*.

"Such beautiful curls," and indeed he seemed swept away by the sight of them, because before Eleanor knew what he was doing, he had kissed them too.

The soft, stunning motion of his mouth against her curls, her lips, the softer brink inside brought Eleanor up on her elbows again in a near-scream.

Fighting her impulse, she fell back on the bed, one hand covering her mouth to smother her own cry as she arched herself toward him, wanting more of that fiery, silky pleasure.

She could *feel* his growl as he pushed up on his arms, one hand pulling her hand away from her mouth.

"Don't be quiet," he said with a fierce intensity she didn't understand but had to believe.

CHAPTER 26

$\mathcal{E}$leanor had never imagined a man who *wanted* to hear her, much less touch her like this. She felt something flutter inside her like the wings of her wild birds. Perhaps it took flight.

And when his mouth came to her again, she tried to let loose her moans, soft as they were, and her cries of pure pleasure.

So much she had never known she wanted.

Surely there was something she could give *him*.

Barely able to lift her shaking hands, she nonetheless felt along the edge of her dress front, sliding out the pins and threading them back into the cloth so they would not be lost, and tossed the thing out of the bed as soon as she was sure, with her half-formed thoughts, that it was all of a piece.

She clutched at his hair as his tongue did a deft little move that made it impossible to breathe, the pleasure that surged through her was so sharp and so deep.

"Tell me. What you like, what you don't like. Tell me everything," he murmured into the flesh of her thigh, then fell to feasting on her again.

Babbling, words fell from her lips she didn't even know she was saying. "It's alarming. Unbearable." The sparkling pleasure he lit here, there, everywhere with his touches turned to flames. "Yet I want more too."

Sounding more like a hungry bear than a man, he rolled off the bed, confusing her more; then he drug her sharply to the bed's edge, throwing her legs over her shoulders, and Eleanor wondered if she could die of this.

It wasn't possible to breathe, yet air rasped in and out of a throat grown dry with her cries. It wasn't possible to withstand the wave after crashing wave of pleasure that clutched her, clenched her, drove her hands twisting into the sheets, but she did. Ever more intensely the pleasure swirled tighter and tighter, her nipples sharp against the soft cloth of her stays, her skin flushed hot everywhere, and just as one coherent thought—*would she die from pleasure?*—pierced the hot fog of her mind.

She pressed herself against him and the tightening of her muscles set off a cannon shot.

Nothing so intensely, burningly pleasurable had ever happened to Eleanor. It seemed to go on and on, with him urging it on, until she fell, shaking and limp, back against the bed. How high had she flown?

He was nuzzling her thigh, her stockinged calf, his face still hungry and drawn as he looked up her body to fix her with those unearthly eyes.

"So fast," she gasped, though it had also felt like hours.

"Our evening's just begun," he promised her, and the last of Eleanor's fear fled.

He came higher on his knees, surveying every inch of her with obvious interest. "You unpinned your gown."

She still couldn't really catch a full breath. "I thought you would like it... if I untied my stays." She looked down at herself. "I didn't manage it."

The very thought made his eyes go darker. It looked both less like him and more intoxicating. "I do like it," he said simply, his nimble fingers taking over where hers were shaking too hard to move. "Thank you."

Surely that couldn't count as a gift—he was doing all the work!—

but the look in his eyes once her stays slid away, her belly fluttering as he pulled her chemise free of her skirts and over her head, said that he counted it a gift indeed.

"You make a beautiful vision." His voice held wonder. And knowing every beautiful natural thing he had seen, Eleanor felt honored by that.

"You are very beautiful too, Sir John." She slid one hand up the column of his arm where he held himself still braced above her. "Would that I could pleasure you the same way."

She felt him shudder.

"You can, my lady, but tonight I lack patience. My wish to be inside you is outweighed only by my wish that you not find it abhorrent."

* * *

He saw her consider this in that serious, contemplative way of hers. "Then go slowly," she advised him, as if it wouldn't tear him apart.

He had planned to do just that. But her sweet invitation made it impossible to wait any longer.

"How slowly?"

Her dark eyes were trusting. "As slowly as you can."

Christ. She would kill him.

But there was nothing on earth more worth savoring, and as soon as Jesper pushed the rest of his clothes away, he was poised, and she was waiting.

"Please," he said, pleading, "call me Jesper. We are alone, here."

He so wanted that silly little intimacy; but he could see how improper she felt it was. Even now, when he was between her thighs, about to possess her completely.

"Very well," she said, and God help him, the little primness to her tone just made him harder.

Every quarter inch of him throbbed with urgent ache as he did indeed sink himself into her slowly, as slowly as he possibly could. Which was very, very slowly.

She was so incredibly hot, so slick from his attentions, that his mind and body were howling at him to *thrust*.

But since she'd asked him for something, such a small thing, he would do it for her. For his wife. His lady.

All his, he thought with wonder as he felt himself slowly slide into her all, all the way.

"*Mmph.*" Her little noise made him instantly worry that he'd hurt her. She slapped a hand over her eyes.

"Are you well, my lady?"

"Fine," she managed to say. "Just... it's very startling. Wait but a moment. Please."

That soft *please* made him throb. She peeked through her fingers. She'd felt it.

"Jesper," she murmured, and held out her arms.

It was heaven; it was home, as he sank into her softness, careful to keep her free of all his weight and yet diving into her as deeply as he could. He needed this; he needed *her*.

And giving her leave to be free had freed something in him, too. "Please," he told her in return, "my lady. Let me move."

"Y-yes," her catching voice whispered in his ear. "Just—gently. If you can."

If she needed it, he could.

His seemingly delicate wife gripped him with a silky ripple that was surprisingly strong, and when he moaned, he knew she felt that too.

Smoother than the butter he could still taste when he kissed her nose, they developed a rhythm between them, both giving and taking and giving again till Jesper knew they'd both lost track of where one stopped and the other began.

He pressed his arms closer, wanting to cage her in, and reveling in the stroke of her skin against his chest. *She was so unexpectedly strong*, he thought, as her arms looped around his shoulders and held on tight.

It was absurd to expect her to reach her peak again so soon, in an arena she had never played in before, but he wanted it. The same unreasoning way she'd appealed to him the moment he saw her. The same way he'd married her. *Because he wanted her.*

"Let me hear everything," he grunted into her hair, that amazingly rich mass spread over the pillows. "What you feel. What you want."

"I want this." Her head turned away, pushed into the pillow, as if she were fighting for her pleasure to peak again. That was his lady, ever ready for a struggle, no matter how sweet. "I want it. I want *you.*"

Every little moan and gasp was like a honey-drop: rich and golden, hard-won treasure that only he would ever know how to find.

"I want you to feel it again. The peak. You can do it, can't you, Eleanor?"

And when he felt her arch against him he realized he'd called her by her unbearably intimate name too.

"I can call you Eleanor if it will take you over the edge, but I must confess."

Her eyes popped open, just like her lips.

Those *lips.*

"I just think of you as *my lady.*"

And when he captured her mouth again, driving faster and faster into her, she cried out into his kiss and he felt her peak.

He should never have doubted her. She was perfection.

With a long, low groan he let himself go, his own pleasure climbing through him like a firebolt and shaking him so hard he had to collapse.

Careful still not to crush her, beside her he lay on his chest, heaving for air, and let his arm drape across her waist.

She still had her petticoat on.

"If I took off your petticoat, would you make more noise?" he managed to ask, and reveled in the sound of his lady laughing and slapping at his arm, no harder than she would at a fly, until he could catch his breath and roll over, pulling her against him to fall asleep with her hair tickling his cheek.

He never once thought about an heir.

CHAPTER 27

*H*is worry about an heir was, however, his first thought upon waking.

Said heir might already be on the way. With Eleanor. The spitfire who had lectured him for daring to talk to her in the street. Just days ago.

Who lay next to him, sweetly sleeping, with a pink flush on her cheek that might have been from the sun or might be the remnant of their pleasure the night before. Just looking at her, he hardened.

If she woke now and looked at him, if she opened those luscious lips and asked him one question, he would confess all his selfish actions.

What would she say then? He wouldn't enjoy being privy to *those* emotions. He'd stolen her chance to be a cow-eyed merchant's wife. Would she have preferred that to raising his son alone?

Or to being a homeless widow?

He had to be elsewhere when she woke up.

* * *

THE SUN WAS HIGH. That was Eleanor's first waking thought.

Her second was that she still thrummed with pleasure from the night before.

She squeezed her eyes shut. She had to be calm when she faced the man she'd... well, *he'd... they* had done some surprising things together last night.

She wasn't *embarrassed*. No, yes she was. There was improper, and then there was completely abandoned. He'd nearly unhinged her senses, and he'd seemed to want *more*.

She didn't think she could give him more without losing her last shred of dignity. She didn't want to look him in the eye; yet she desperately wanted to be in his arms.

Finally, the latter wish won out.

Only to be thwarted. The bed was empty.

She was up before she thought about it, shedding her last petticoat with a blush before washing at the basin. Remembering how carelessly he had brushed aside the idea of skirts. Then her actual skirts.

Had he *gone?*

Had she done something to break him away?

Of course gentlemen retired to their own rooms; but he'd slept here. She vividly remembered his chest, solid and hot, against her back.

Had he gone to the woods? The village? Back to *London?*

Her mind swam with terrible visions of him deciding once and for all that she was the wrong wife. That she had said or done something appalling, and he wanted rid of her. Perhaps husbands could banish wives to French nunneries too.

He'd never given her any warnings, but that didn't mean there were no traps.

She had to find him. She had to dress. If she couldn't pull her stays quite tight, it wouldn't show; she pulled on a fresh *robe à l'anglaise,* tied each bow with shaking fingers. She could picture a dozen, twenty ways he would tell her she had to go, the dread growing and growing until it felt like it might crush her. More than it had when her father had told her not to come home.

It felt foolish, childish, to look in room after room for him; but she couldn't stop.

She nodded to each servant she passed, as if nothing was wrong, as if she meant to be searching for her husband with nothing on her hair and evening slippers instead of walking shoes.

At the end of the portrait gallery, with generations of disapproving Grantleys staring at her bare head, she gathered up her skirts and ran out the door.

If anyone saw her, she had no explanation. Nothing made this appropriate. She simply needed to find him.

* * *

MORNING SUN WAS BRUTAL. It showed everything bright and clear, and it did Jesper's soul no favors.

The night had flayed him open. He could see faults in himself he'd never imagined, not least that he had bandaged his loneliness with a woman's life.

Yes, it had appealed to his budding gallantry to rescue a woman without a home; but beyond that, he'd offered for her because she might be good for Roseford, not because Roseford would be good for her.

Why couldn't he tell her what he'd done? Was he only a wild animal, as she said?

No. His life might have been small, but it had been full and rich. He had never known a moment's fear that he wasn't wanted.

And that was the problem now. He had never before needed someone's approval, someone's *forgiveness*, and been afraid that he might not get it.

His father had been everything to him. He was gone now, and if Eleanor wasn't his family, then he had no one.

And beyond that, a darker voice said that if he kept melting for her, she could cut him. Badly.

It might not be her that broke open. It might be him.

Jesper had *never* imagined that lying with a woman could feel *dangerous*.

There she was now, on the other side of the rosemary, both blushing and angry. Her hands gripped each other at her waist and her icy stare sliced.

He winced, hoping he could keep her from finding out what he'd done to her for one more day.

* * *

He winced as she came. What was wrong with *her* appearance? *He* couldn't care about the lack of a hat.

Eleanor had tried to be perfect every moment, and even so, even after the most soul-shifting night of her life, the man couldn't meet her eyes.

"I didn't intend to bother you this morning," he said swiftly, quietly, even as a stableman approached.

He would not *bother* her?

They'd *bothered* each other last night?

"Sir John." The stableman stood awkwardly at the edge of the garden, juggling his rough hat because of Eleanor's presence, not meeting her eyes either.

And yes, her husband turned away. "Peter?"

"There's another dead deer. A buck."

The baronet stood as still as stone, and Eleanor didn't know what he was thinking. Of course it had to be about his lands. His inheritance. His duty. It wouldn't be about her, even on a morning like this.

He might at least have bothered to tease her, if she'd worn a cap.

"I'll come." Sir John was clearly perturbed. About the deer, not her.

Her mind was racing. What should she have done differently? How was she to know?

Or was it, as the disillusioned brides of London said, a losing proposition? That men simply wanted the bedding and then their interest waned?

Surely it shouldn't have happened so fast.

"It comforts me to know you'll be well on your own," Sir John tossed back over his shoulder as he started to leave.

To *leave.*

She might be unlikeable, but she was by God not going to be ignored. She had put everything she was at risk the night before, and gambled that she could trust him. She might have lost, but she would have her cards back.

"I was perfectly fine on my own before we married, Sir John, and nothing has happened to change that."

She saw the cut hit. She might not have a weapon in hand, but she knew he felt its slice.

"Peter, I'll be along." The stableman ran so fast Eleanor knew he had only been waiting his chance.

Sir John straightened, no trace of a smile on his sun-weathered features now.

He said, "That's a comfort to hear, too."

"We made a bargain. I don't expect society out here. No Lady Hortense, or braggarts, or Taggarts." *Just you,* she thought, but that clearly wasn't what he wanted to hear.

Well, trying to please him had accomplished little.

He frowned. "There's a name that came quickly. So you miss him." Hair flying, his eyes stayed down as he bent over and picked up a small snake, glowing green in the morning light.

He slipped it into his brocade pocket.

He looked like a bear, or a little boy. Not a baronet.

What words could keep her afloat among the shreds of etiquette and failure? "I miss civil life. People who respect themselves, and others, enough to brush their hair. And address people as they deserve," she added quickly, reaching for a suitable barb.

"I address people as they deserve." The light of his eyes matched the color of the pocketed snake, and they looked oddly intense. Eleanor remembered him calling her his lady.

They stared at each other across thorny plants and soft ones, the fresh spring earth too tender for either to step closer.

"Lord Burden at least made clear that all he wanted from me was obedience." Her words came straight from deep inside. "Looking back, I can see a simple honesty to that I never appreciated before."

She saw *that* dart hit.

It didn't make her feel better.

Nearly twenty-five years of holding in check not just her temper, but her heart. And she'd tumbled into marriage with the first man who'd said nice words to her. Four.

She thought she'd left humiliation behind her in the trees with Mr. Taggart. She was wrong.

He said heavily, "Not all actions are yours. I should not have dragged you from London. I should not have made you come here."

Her heart, which she'd feared he could hear, slowed and seemed to frost over. "You mean we should not have married."

He fixed her with one eye. "Can you say that we should have? You don't miss London? You'd prefer to be in a garden at dawn without a public hat?"

She stopped herself from checking her hair. She wore no hat at all.

The most devastating critiques, Eleanor knew, were the true ones.

She said, "There is nothing discomforting about Roseford but you."

And with that, she left him to it.

CHAPTER 28

*M*rs. Peterborough had taken heart from the untouched suppers. It had been easy to see from the first the distance between her baronet and his London lady; but also to see how they wished to be charitable to one another, the effort they made to span the distance.

Perhaps they had fires between them that just needed tending. Perhaps she would see another little Grantley here one day after all. And she could feel that she had done one last favor for the old Sir John, who had let her bring her little ones here, far from her home, and begin life anew as a widow. A task he well understood.

When the new Lady Grantley marched in past the kitchen from the garden, hair flying, no hat, and wearing dancing slippers, Mrs. Peterborough's hopes crumbled.

"Will you break your fast, Lady Grantley?"

"Yes." It was not a good sign that, dressed as she was, she turned toward the breakfast room.

"And Sir John?"

"Sir John can eat what he finds in the woods," Lady Grantley muttered as she marched into the depths of Roseford manor alone.

* * *

ALL THE SERVANTS noted that after such a promising start, things did not seem to be going well in the new Grantley marriage.

For days, their new Sir John did just the same as the old one did, leaving at all hours of the day to ride wherever, returning whenever he pleased. He ate cold plates in the kitchen, whatever the cook kept for him, and spoke little.

None of the servants had ever seen a Lady Grantley before. Now that they had one, they saw how she stayed indoors among the library books, doing ribbon embroidery and writing letters.

The situation did not look likely to produce any heirs, but more importantly, it made things at Roseford stiff and thorny. None of them were used to Roseford being stiff and thorny.

Some of them, mostly the maids, blamed Sir John. Many, mostly the stablemen, muttered dark things about the lady. The old steward, who had spoken little since the day he'd dug a grave in the village churchyard for the old Sir John, stumped about his usual tasks and left everyone to it.

But Mrs. Peterborough didn't allow arguing in the house, and kept things amongst the household civil.

She wished she could do the same for her baronet and his lady.

* * *

ELEANOR DRIFTED out of doors at every opportunity.

She wouldn't ride the lands without Sir John, and he had given up any attempt at punctuality. Or speaking. Human tasks were apparently beyond him.

But in just their few short days together, he'd shown her how much life teemed out of doors, and she couldn't bear to lock herself in again.

She found herself standing by the garden while Mrs. Peterborough used a long stick to make holes in the ground to drop things in.

"What are those?" Eleanor pointed to a delicate cluster of deep violet flowers huddled at the edge of the garden.

Mrs. Peterborough looked surprised. "Bluebells. Nothing more English than that. You don't know them?"

Eleanor stared almost hungrily at the little flowers. So much she didn't know. She'd just begun to learn. And Sir John had taught her so little before he'd disappeared from her days. And nights.

He'd told her to speak then walked away. Perhaps she should have shed the last remnants of her pride when they were alone together, but Eleanor did *not* think this was her fault.

"I've seen them embroidered," was all she said.

Then she bestirred herself to say more. If Mrs. Peterborough were to be her only company for the rest of her life, she ought to make conversation.

"I'm surprised you don't have a flower garden at Roseford as well," she said, then bit her lip. Would that, too, sound like a critique? Could she make no conversation at all?

Mrs. Peterborough just gave her a long look, long enough for Eleanor to wish that she'd said something different.

Then she untied her apron full of whatever it was she was planting and drove her stick into the ground to stand upright, like a spear.

"Come with me," she said.

They walked in the soft grass along the edge of the drive, following its slow turn around the hill to the road.

At the bottom, bushes grew so thick along both sides of the road that the light turned to shade.

Look everywhere, Eleanor heard her husband's voice in her head.

"There you are." Mrs. Peterborough pointed. "There's Roseford's garden. In two months the place will be so thick with roses no one can move. The air will be full of them."

Carefully pushing aside a thorny little branch, Eleanor saw it was true.

Fat buds were pushing their way out on all sides, their delicate tenderness protected by the brambles.

There were indeed plenty of roses. All of Roseford would bloom.

"I see."

Was it the nature of such a place, half-groomed, half-wild, to surprise her at every turn?

Or had her London life lacked something she'd found here?

It wasn't only her ghost of a husband.

"Mrs. Peterborough, do you like me?"

Mrs. Peterborough made some sort of noise. Disapproving? Startled? "You're the mistress of the house, Lady Grantley. You don't need servants to like you."

"I do, though." Eleanor turned on the housekeeper with a betraying urgency. "I don't wish to live surrounded by people who don't like me. I had two true friends in London, one a servant." Realizing whom she was addressing, Eleanor fumbled. "I mean—Mrs. Willowby was my governess. She kept her position with me as long as she could, but of course when it came time to choose between me and her family, she chose her family. And Lady Hortense—"

Silly, laughing Lady Hortense, who loved everyone. Because she had been loved.

The unfamiliar thought was also unwelcome. It would be pleasant to blame her social failings on her unfeeling father. Once done, though, it was still Eleanor who had to work out how to change.

Not that she wanted her husband to love her.

She *didn't*, even though she dreamed every night that Sir John would come to her window—or the dining room, or even the lawns— and say something sweet to make her forget his boorish silence. Perhaps he'd bring a musician to strum on a lute while he asked her to dance because he couldn't live without his arms around her one more moment.

She had wonderful skills at imagining things; she just couldn't make them happen. Perhaps people who'd been loved knew those secrets. If so, she'd never learn them.

Mrs. Peterborough didn't wait for her to finish her thought. "Roseford is like anywhere. There's all kinds of people here. Some may like you, some won't. But for what it's worth, yes, my lady, I do like you."

"Really?" Eleanor spoke before she thought. "Why?"

With a laugh and a shake of her head, Mrs. Peterborough gestured they should walk back toward the house. "Don't ask *why*, just let people like you," she said half under her breath as if not wanting to be too forward with the lady.

But Eleanor heard every word.

* * *

THAT NIGHT, Mrs. Peterborough walked down to the stables in the dark. Her grandson would soon visit, and she wanted a groomsman to show him the horses.

"She's a bucket of ice, that one."

"Ghastly."

In a pool of light shed by the lantern, the stablemen—boys, really, most of them—sat on the floor or piles of hay, chewing over the day.

And apparently, the character of Roseford's new lady.

"It only makes sense." One of them was gesturing with a plait of straw he'd woven to keep his hands busy. "If you want somethin', you want the nicest one you can get, right?"

"I don't call a bucket of ice *nice*," muttered the first.

"But she's a *kind* of nice, she's all—" the fellow waved his straw as if to indicate frills and furbelows. "Fancy. If you hadta go to London and get a wife, you'd get a fancy one, wouldn't you?"

"He don't like her."

Do you like me, Mrs. Peterborough? Remembering the words, Mrs. Peterborough could hear the wistful loneliness under Lady Grantley's crisp tones.

A wistfulness that said that perhaps Lady Grantley liked Sir John and wished he were here.

"Matchmaking takes more sense than any of you have." She stepped into the circle of light, and the grooms scrambled to stand.

Looking them up and down she put as much starch in her voice as she could muster. "Marriage is a serious business. I can't help noticing none of you know that." One of them flushed; the others looked down at their toes. "You let Sir John manage his own affairs, and you keep to yours. But don't forget." She stopped in front of the first fellow and stared at him till he lifted his eyes to meet hers. He did, and flinched. "She is the *lady* of Roseford now. She deserves your respect. You don't have to like her, though you might. I do." She did, she realized. She'd told the lady the truth. "You've *no* right to heap coals on her head. You've barely met her. And your work here doesn't involve gossip."

She stopped in the middle of the ragged circle, giving them all a glare they could feel even if they couldn't meet her eyes. "If I hear one more slight against the lady of the house, I'll have the steward turn you out the same day. This is *her* house. It is her *home*."

Leaving them to contemplate how they'd feel if someone smeared their reputation in their own homes, Mrs. Peterborough, rubbed too raw to talk about horses, stomped out.

* * *

NIGHT WAS FALLING, the air chill and blue, and instead of dealing with his wife Jesper drove deeper into the woods, each thin black branch that whipped at him studded with fresh leaves trying to grow despite the lack of rain.

If he couldn't sort out his marriage, perhaps he could find out who was hunting his deer.

When Jesper hadn't known what to say to his wife, it had seemed sensible to say nothing. But hours had turned into days, and he still didn't know.

"There's a branch broken." Mr. Price, his father's old steward, rode beside him. He knew how to read the signs of the woods as well as Jesper did. "Maybe we can follow the trail."

Riding a-horse, even with dour Mr. Price as company, felt familiar. Simple.

Underfoot, little animals scurried under the skeletons of leaves fallen in winter. Overhead, budding branches fought their way to the sunlight. They all knew what to do. They had simple lives. Few options. Each little vole and dormouse knew how to make a home and get on with life, making more voles and dormice for a future they'd never know.

He'd rather be a man. He'd rather have Eleanor. But he envied voles, who never had to talk.

"Who would kill my deer?" Jesper muttered.

"Someone desperate for food?" Mr. Price had never seemed inclined to think well of people, and his mood had declined since the old baronet's death. "Someone listening to his wife nag day in and day out, who finally snapped?"

No, the man wasn't half the good company Eleanor was.

"No villager could bring home that much meat without someone seeing. And a traveler alone won't kill a large animal."

"Women can drive a man to do almost anything."

Clearly, Mr. Price missed the Sir John who'd been wifeless. Perhaps he'd taken the old man's solitude for shared animosity toward ladies.

Jesper didn't think his father had felt like that at all. The old baronet never remarried, but he'd been unfailingly polite to Mrs. Peterborough, and all the women of the house. His actions had spoken like words.

Just as he hadn't talked over his plans; he just kept the woods wild, all the way north. Following the interloper's trail that way, Jesper realized he might have to cover that whole distance. If he did, he wouldn't be back to the manor house before morning.

He'd done it many times. But he didn't want to cross the physicians. And he didn't want to go that far from Eleanor. He felt the pull now, not just to her bed, but to her. Her focus, her truth, her secretly giving heart.

His gelding tipped his head up, then dropped it, upper lip rolling as he sniffed the night air. He'd be willing to go as far as Jesper wanted.

"Let's go another mile, if the trail lasts, then sleep."

Mr. Price looked offended. "Sleep? So that's how it goes. Marriage makes you soft even when your wife ain't here."

"It will be dark in the woods, Mr. Price. And since when have you been such a barrel of complaints?"

Tonight, Jesper would do what he knew how to do. Stay in his role, do as his father would have done, what anyone in England would expect.

Perhaps tomorrow would show him the path back into his wife's good graces. She was vastly better company than Price.

* * *

HE CREDITED the sleep for his ability to keep his mouth shut when he crossed his wife's path the next morning, on her way to the breakfast room.

She took in the state of his stained, rumpled clothes. Perhaps he should have checked his hair for leaves.

Then, saying nothing, she started back toward her breakfast, back ramrod-straight among all those ruffles.

"Lady Grantley."

That stopped her in her tracks. She raised an eyebrow.

Before he could stifle himself, Jesper said in a rush, "We've been cordial. Surely marriage is better that way. Can't we be cordial again?"

Her jaw dropped, then closed again, but she clearly could not find words, though her expression threatened that he had better stop using that word. "You've just come from the woods?"

"Yes."

"You should go back there." And she turned her back on him, and went out.

CHAPTER 29

*C*ordial.

She ached inside for reasons she couldn't entirely name as she watched Sir John lifting his end of a beam poised to expand the stable roof.

Apparently he had plans for things besides walls that he'd never explained.

He'd stripped to the waist, his brown skin glowing in the sun with sweat. Eleanor would have swooned from the inappropriateness of it all, but she was too hungry for the sight of him.

She could just barely see the muscles of his back bunching as he lifted the heavy beam. It took three stablehands to relieve him of it and hoist it into its final spot.

Self-respect was beginning to feel like a luxury. She could all too easily imagine simply going out there, placing a hand on his arm (which would be slick with sweat—another shocking idea that made her shiver, some of it from anticipation), and informing him when supper would be served.

Could she pretend that his cut had never happened? For she'd long pretended that her father was a decent, reasonable man. She saw that now. If she could pretend that, why not ignore that her husband was happy to bed her but despised her company?

There were no cold baths. No spiders. Roseford was, to every extent, pure luxury compared to what might have been her fate.

Why couldn't she just be grateful? And silent?

Because the great oaf couldn't have it both ways. The burst of anger that came with that thought staved off tears, and Eleanor was glad of it. He'd told her to speak. To forget etiquette. To take off her clothes and let him into her every secret space and to let him see, let him hear how he could take her apart.

And then he reserved the right to walk away?

No. Eleanor had never learned to manage actions *that* far apart. She hoped she never would.

* * *

WERE those drapes fluttering at the lady's window?

Jesper almost dropped the heavy beam. Swearing, he heaved it back up, feeling its splinters dig into his shoulder.

What had he thought, that she would fly out the window and come to him?

This was foolish. He was the same man who had marched into her chambers and demanded she marry him. Why didn't he just march up to her chambers now, unburden his conscience, and take whatever her temper dealt?

At least, he *hoped* she'd be angry. If she were simply quiet, it would be worse. Why didn't he do it?

Because, it came to him as he heaved upwards, letting the men take the rafter. His muscles hummed with the effort, and the blood pumping through his veins told him new things these days. Now, he had more to lose.

* * *

"YOU HAVE TAKEN MORE than you know."

Eleanor couldn't bring herself to scold the servants. According to

Mrs. Peterborough, some of them might even like her.

So she safely took it out on the robin, who had built a fine nest in her panniers, still hanging out her bedroom window.

His livelihood kept her from closing the window tight, and the cool air at night kept her awake in a lonely bed. Surely it was safe to lambast *him*.

"I'll never be able to wear those panniers again. And when will I get to London to buy more?" Eleanor did have another pair, but it felt good to complain. No one would hear.

Sir John had no valet. The stablemen did not like Eleanor. She had no way of learning more about what he liked, what he didn't, or reaching him with a secret message. If only Mrs. Peterborough would tell the maid Molly to ask the magistrate's cook what Sir John ate when he visited. Perhaps she could find out something, anything to *use*.

But Mrs. Peterborough just looked at her blankly when she suggested it.

At the big desk in the library, Eleanor wrote to Lady Hortense, letters that she kept carefully vague. She spoke of Roseford, and of unspecific dissatisfactions, but not of Sir John—*Jesper*, as she sometimes thought of him now—or what had passed between them.

It did not surprise Hortense to hear that married life at Roseford was less than congenial; she wrote Eleanor soothing homilies. Many of their friends had not found marriage to be what they'd hoped. Lady Ashford was positively miserable, even after presenting her husband with three sons! *There is no way to predict men*, Hortense wrote with the sage certainty of someone who was not married. Even as she contemplated the suit of Lord Dunsby, who, along with the dancing Lord Overburg, had become her most ardent suitor.

Eleanor had never had a suitor. No one had ever come to court her. She was happy for Hortense, and jealous of the feeling of being wanted. Her chances for that seemed to be over.

She had been the fool, she told herself over and over. That hairy beast had charged into her room and insisted she marry him, and she *had*. What had she been thinking? What had she *hoped* would happen?

She'd escaped London, yes, and the men she hadn't wanted. But she also had to admit that somewhere deep inside she'd wanted *this* one, and she was most disappointed in herself.

"You're a silly optimist," she told the robin, who had become quite accustomed to her standing at the window watching him tuck bits of leaves into his nest. "You'll find a lady robin, and, what? Bed her and leave her sitting lonely in this nest? You think this nest is so fine that she'll simply sit there and await your return? Hatching *your* eggs?"

For Eleanor knew she could be with child even now and not know it, and the prospect gave her no joy. She hadn't been happy in London, and she wouldn't be happy here either, it seemed. The problem wasn't the rest of England. It was her.

If she finished her letter to Hortense, a groom would take it to the village tonight. It might reach her the day after tomorrow. The mail carriages traveled faster every day.

But it didn't seem to matter. She would still be here, spending the rest of her days, apparently, letting Mrs. Coombes find new ways to dress her hair. Eating alone, breathing alone, and sleeping every night alone.

Wherever her husband was, it wasn't with her.

So she stood by the window, watched the robin, and when he fluttered off, hoped he might do better in choosing a mate than she had.

* * *

JESPER HAD WALKED these halls his entire life, many of those years as a child; he knew where to step to stay silent. He walked back down the hall, avoiding the creaking boards that would tell Eleanor he'd been outside her room.

She'd been very bitter to the bird. Or birds. There must be two by now, building that nest; he suspected that would only make her more bitter. She sounded lonely. Maybe even enough to miss *him*.

This was all his fault. He shouldn't have married her, but he had. She had no chance now of a more advantageous marriage; she was stuck with him. A hairy boor. He'd tried *not* being a hairy boor, but it hadn't helped because it wasn't the problem.

The problem was that *he'd* gambled with *her* life.

That life had beautiful facets, like a cut-glass field of flowers. He could see now exactly how Roseford, with its ancient beams and trespassing robins, was too rough a setting for her.

Yet she'd fit, shaping herself to match her surroundings far better than he had shaped himself to admit a wife. He'd let her cut his hair as if that were sufficient sacrifice, when she had given up everything of the life she knew and lived under a shadow without knowing it.

Forget how she might treat him. How could he make this right for her? How could he warn her without making her feel the precariousness of her position?

She was clever. She might find a way to prepare. Perhaps she could write to Hortense and arrange to be her companion, if nothing else. London society would never take Eleanor back.

No. Everything in him rebelled at the thought of his Eleanor, *his*, back in those hideous stiff clothes, hiding her colors to be a gray widow. If he died tonight, she should get to stay here, at Roseford, discovering everything there was in the manor and how much more there was in the woods.

But how to manage that with no heir?

There was nothing simple about the situation in which he'd put them, and Jesper had no practice with things that weren't, ultimately, simple. In his life before Eleanor, crops, animals, people lived or died. There was no question of whether they were in the right setting, living the right life; they simply existed.

He might have disliked London life, but it had given Jesper a window into a more complex world. His way, his father's way, wasn't the only way to live, and carting Eleanor away to Roseford to serve as a propping beam in his life had cost her. He'd picked her pocket. Robbed her. He'd pilfered her future, and beyond explaining that to her, he needed to fix it.

CHAPTER 30

$\mathcal{T}$he urge to fix *something* sent him back down to the village, even though he was in no mood for goose arguments.

He found himself walking past the village church, the new little shops, even the mill.

Mrs. Wright was in her yard, in a fit of spring cleaning despite having to reach around her own belly. Little Susie Shore was helping her.

As he drew closer, he was reminded how fast time could go by, for little Susie Shore was seventeen if she was a day and cast longing looks his way the second he came into view.

Good God. His wife was closer to Susie's age than his. How had he ever considered himself a fair bargain?

He kept his distance from Susie, giving her only a faint nod. "Mrs. Wright. Should you be working like this?"

"You think I can *stop*?" She laughed as she straightened, pushing back a lock of hair. She nodded toward her little boy and girl, happily rubbing sand round her biggest iron pot to absolutely no effect.

His wry nod admitted her point. "I assume Mr. Beardsley and Mr. Hatch are in the fields? I wanted to see if they'd cooled on Hatch's geese."

A shadow crept over her face and her smile faded. She was fairly young, but in that shadow, looked older. "Not yet," was all she said.

Susie just kept quiet.

Jesper tried again. "I thought I'd speak to Mrs. Beardsley, see if she'd talk her husband into some sense. I suppose she's at home?"

Now Mrs. Wright looked positively strained. "She's not, no. I think she went into the woods to find some greens to stretch her dinner."

That was how people more commonly stretched their winter food. Jesper still saw no signs that anyone near here had killed his deer, even though this year, the drought kept the world barren, and food scarcer still.

"I'll lay in an extra store of wheat to sell—to you, or anyone, if there's need." He'd give it away, but some stubborn villagers wouldn't take it; he'd sell it for a few pennies and find ways to slip some to families with more children.

"Oh, that's not the p—" But Mrs. Wright cut off her words.

Little Susie stopped gawking at Jesper and scrubbed the pan in her hands fiercely.

Jesper waited, hoping one of them would say something, but inwardly shrugged when they didn't. Food shortages he could fix; secrets he couldn't.

"Very well. Good day, ladies," he said with a slight bow of his head, which was all it took to make Susie blush.

It wasn't lost on him that secrets didn't make anything better.

* * *

BACK AT ROSEFORD, Jesper was prowling round the house, considering whether he could bear sending Eleanor north to live in a cottage and start a new life, when he saw her.

She wore a gown like a fluffy cake, with a shawl tucked into the front where he most wanted to untuck it; and, wearing a very public hat, she thrust her arm into a hedge and pulled it out. Repeatedly.

He couldn't send her away. What was he thinking? Just the sight of her drew him closer. He wanted that hair across his chest again. Even if she snapped at him while he buried his face in that cherry-bronze glory. He wanted *her*.

When he drew close enough to see her slide something through the folds of her dress into the pannier-pocket beneath, he froze.

Well, his heart stopped; his feet moved like lightning.

"Take off your skirt."

"*What?!*" Her back, ramrod straight, tightened; she pulled away from his rushing approach. "What are you doing? What do you *mean*, sir?"

"Take off your skirt. Now."

* * *

THIS WAS TOO MUCH. She couldn't spend a life here, moping about for days, waiting for brief interruptions when her husband rushed at her and demanded she undress.

All her bitter anger gathered in her, and she took a deep breath, ready to let it out as words she would *not* regret.

Then she saw his face. He'd paled under the sun-brown of his skin. The hand he'd half-extended her way was shaking.

"What are you afraid of?" For he was clearly afraid of something, and it wasn't of ordering her out of her clothes. Though he should be.

"My lady, *please*. I beg you. Step out of your skirt and those basket-things. Now. *Please*."

Well. He meant it.

Perhaps he was mad. She hadn't thought of it before, but it would explain so much. She didn't think so, though.

And for the sake of a delicate blue egg and the way his kisses melted her knees, she put her hands to her waist, slowly, and untied the ribbons that held on her overskirt.

It was the work of a moment to lay it, then her panniers, on the grass.

He adores undressing in public, she thought wildly to herself, not even sure what was happening.

"Back away."

No more gentle words than that; but she did.

Slowly he advanced and picked up the panniers from under her skirt.

He tipped one out toward the hedge, the one she'd been using as a pocket.

Not one, but three little snakes wiggled out of it.

"Jesus Christ." His voice crossed the line between swear and prayer.

Grabbing her skirt with one hand and her with the other, he backed away from the hedge, keeping his eyes on it until there were yards and yards of open, sheep-cropped grass between them and the shadowy hedge.

Then he dropped her clothes, and yanking her into his arms, crushed her close.

She could feel his trembling. It was more than startling in such a big man; it was sobering. "What's wrong? I only did what you did. I was moving them farther from the house." Perhaps if she asked her questions softly enough, while he was holding her—*thank God he was holding her again*—he would answer.

"My lady, you filled your pocket with *venomous* snakes." His arms crushed her even closer. She could feel his heart pounding in her chest.

"*Oh*." Suddenly happy he held her so close, in case her knees gave way, Eleanor wrapped her arms around his waist and just hung on.

Even so, she could still speak. "Why didn't you just *say* so?"

"I didn't want you to panic. I didn't want you to grab them and try to throw them away and startle them."

"Have you ever seen me panic?"

"No. No." He admitted the truth of her words but didn't let her go.

Not that she wanted him to.

After a long, long time, he drew in a shuddering breath. "I should not have let you roam the grounds alone. I should not have made you leave London."

That pulled Eleanor's spine straight. "You did not force me to leave London. I had had quite enough of it."

178

Then she sank against him again. He might not care about her any more than those horrid London men, but it felt so good to be in his arms. "You *could* show me which are the venomous snakes."

Her words seemed to break something in him. From just holding her close, he pulled her into him, his big body seeming to surround her. She felt his breath along the edge of her ear, at her temple, even burying into her neck. His hands went everywhere.

"The bite is mortal for very few," he said, sounding calmer than his actions, "but you are so *thin*."

"I'm perfectly healthy!"

"Oh, Eleanor." The way he said her name banished any thought of letting go.

Finally she lost an argument with herself and pulled him down to press his cheek to hers the way she wanted to do.

One of his hands gathered up her hair where it fell down her back, so much longer now that it was no longer styled fashionably. "If you were hurt. If you suffered. I could not bear to cause that."

Should she stay quiet?

Not this time.

"I *am* hurt, and you *are* the cause." Her tone was softer than usual, but the words were sharp.

If he suggested being *cordial*, she'd scream.

CHAPTER 31

$\mathcal{H}$e didn't pretend not to know what she meant.

"I know." Cradling her in strong hands, he rocked her close. "I know. I'm sorry. It's my fault. I've made a mistake."

Thinking that he was about to put her aside made Eleanor's arms tighten. "Marrying me?"

"*Eleanor.*" He surged against her, lifting her bodily off the ground and carrying her to a little stand of trees away, far away from the hedges.

There he sank down to his knees with her still in his arms, and before she knew it she was astride his lap, reveling in his kisses, with his arms around her.

She had never imagined two people could wrap themselves around each other this way, much less one so tall and one smaller. But they fit perfectly. Shockingly well. Till the distance between them was gone, in every way.

It was frenzied, even more than what she had felt was a wild night together. His hands were even more hungry. Starving to touch her.

Yet that was all he did.

She could feel his hardening, his body cradling hers, surrounding her, yet he gave her only sweet, drugging, hungry kisses, his thumbs caressing the line of her jaw till his fingers sank into her hair.

Eleanor had a vision of long lonely nights punctuated by this kind of desperate longing.

She'd take it.

"We *are* married," she reminded him. "I agreed to learn about Roseford, and provide you an heir. You have shirked your duties on both."

* * *

SHE SHOULD DESPISE HIM, and instead she said that.

He wanted to throw her over his shoulder and lock her in a high, strong room. He wanted to cry out with horror just at the thought that *she* might have died. She might have died right there, in his arms, as his father had done. He might have lost the little sense he had left.

She would know his worst weaknesses if he put any of that into words.

Thanking every fate he'd once cursed, he wrapped her hips in his hands and pulled her against him, tight. He wasn't the man she wanted, but he was desperate for her, for this.

His body reacted to her closeness with a hunger that only echoed what he felt inside. He didn't intend that. His hunger for her was *his* problem.

But they were married. She was his. And if her invocation of their bargain wasn't eager, at least it wasn't indifferent.

"Are you saying that you're willing to do something else improper?" Surely she saw how desperately he wanted her. With his body, with all of him.

Her eyes looking down into his were sober, but when he rocked her against him, he could see fire light in them. "Are you going to be a boor afterwards?"

"I'll try not."

She put out her tiny, *commanding* hand and pressed it against his chest. "Not good enough. I didn't make you court me, sir, but neither am I rubbish to toss aside. Perhaps this means no more to you than sneezing, but I find it... personal. Convince me to risk it again."

Well. Some might rule by the finery of their clothes, and some by the quality of their actions; his lady did it with a clear, ringing voice.

His movements stopped.

His mind, such a hurricane these last few days, produced only one thought that might convince her. She thought this wasn't personal for him? He had no other way of showing it than the way he held her right now. But he did have one argument he could say in words that might convince her.

"My lady, I will be an excellent father."

He saw that melt some of her ice. He knew what that meant to her. She knew what a gift to her possible child a good father would be. She knew.

"Well-aimed," she murmured. "Almost unfairly so. As I would expect from a fraud, and a bear-boy."

What in hell was a bear-boy? "My lady, I will find a way to mend my actions."

He knew she would take that to mean his clothes and hair, when he meant he would find some solution to the problem of her life that he had created. She could not be ripped from her home again if he died. He would do something. He would fix it.

He saw himself clutching at the thought because he had to believe it, and hated himself for it.

She still held space between them. And those dark focused eyes held him pinned, as much as the sudden piercing honest vulnerability in her voice. "Can't you just promise me you won't leave afterwards?"

God. He was a *nightmare*. The one promise she wanted hear was the one thing he couldn't say for certain.

"I wish I could promise that, my lady. I *regret* that I can't."

If she pushed, he'd have to tell her everything.

But apparently she didn't want to know what he was keeping from her, not badly enough to stop this. *Perhaps his height had done something for him after all,* he thought with a leaping heart when he felt her relent, and sink gracefully against him, letting his back against a tree support them both.

He wanted to believe that she wanted this.

For himself, *want* was a wholly inadequate word. He needed this, craved this, was starving for this.

"Do you understand what we can do like this?" His hands stroked upward, smoothing along her ribs toward her breasts. The stays shielded their softness from his touch; he palmed her through them anyway, trying not to squeeze but still feel their weight, their pointed peaks.

"The basic arrangement is obvious." Her expression was still haughty, but she rocked *herself* against him, and he nearly spent in his clothes like an untried youth.

"Are you willing?"

She did not look about. They were in public, with no one in sight, but the open road lay beyond the hedge. "What *is* your fascination for disrobing out of doors?"

"Never had it before. It's new." He rocked against her again, felt a flood of gratitude that at least in this way he seemed to please her. He saw her eyes fog and lose their knifelike focus. "Is that a yes?"

"Yes."

His hands slid up over her thighs, one higher, and found the center of her. More gently than he touched anything, he touched her there, rewarded by her shudder and the way her head dropped back.

"Yes." He could tell her this. "I want to see everything you feel."

She sat straighter, drawing in a shaky breath.

"Then we should do this in private," she said, crisp as ever.

"My lady, the truth is..." He levered himself forward to touch his tongue to that fluttering spot at the base of her throat, dying for a taste of her. "That's just a challenge."

She might have qualms about him, or this, here, but she let him pull her closer. Let him nibble teeth against the edge of her soft little ear, let him help her balance so he could reach around her thighs and undo his displeasing-to-her clothes.

And for Jesper—she was food, and he was starving to death.

When she slid back, her eyes widened to feel him hot and hard against her bare backside, under her skirts.

Oddly, she seemed more confident, though letting no emotion loose.

Perhaps their one night had been enough to rub away the newness of this for her.

If so, it was only her. Because for Jesper this felt very new. He had never known this heat, this surrounding softness, this *rightness* as she wiggled a little back along his length, positioning herself to let him come home.

He didn't know when Eleanor had replaced Roseford as *home* for him. He only knew it was true.

There was just a flicker of something in her eyes. "Are we really going to do this?"

"Is that fear, or anticipation?"

"Both."

She was so painfully honest. She deserved someone younger, richer, *better.*

At least when he said, "I've got you," he meant it in every possible way.

She didn't nod, but the way her hands clenched on his shoulders conveyed agreement, though under tight control.

He wanted that control destroyed. Maybe he *was* despicable. How much more willingness, or trust, did he need than the way she let him stroke his hands under her skirts, along her open thighs?

Her eyes widened as she realized what *she* had. *She* was in control of this. That *she* had to sink down on what he gave her for this to work.

That *she* decided when to move.

He'd been a bad bargain, and didn't know how to make it right. But this he could give, and would, every chance he got.

"It's all you, my lady," he said with a choked noise as she sank lower.

"Obviously not," though the edges of her crispness were wearing away. She gasped as she hilted him in her completely.

Then, as he had done to her, she took his chin in one hand so he had to meet her eyes. Those beautiful, serious, heat-fired eyes.

"Is it just to fulfill our bargain?" she asked him then, holding him trapped where he most wanted to be.

"No," he half-roared, surging up to meet her and wrapping her in his arms, pulling her down with him into the soft spring grass because he had to have more of what only she could give. Now. *Now.*

He had to kiss her when she made those soft little cries of pleasure. He had to.

And when her soft strength gripped him with the fury of her pleasure, and he spent inside her, the two of them rocking together as one, he had to hope for an heir, not for him, but for her and everything she deserved.

CHAPTER 32

*L*ondon might be full of knives, but at least it made sense.

Roseford made no sense. Days of lonely silence, then swept away again by Sir John. Apparently open skies ignited his passion.

But perhaps they had also burned something away, because that fragile sweet something that had started to build between them was gone. She'd even ridden beside Sir John once, watching him search the woods for signs of the hunting interlopers, but they shared no confidences.

What confidences could there be? She'd seen a tree stump with deep roots, but still no branches. He'd had no thoughts to share, not since he'd offered her a starling's egg.

At least he wasn't a self-important lizard like Lord Burden.

And if he wasn't as gentle as she had imagined Mr. Taggart to be, at least he sometimes looked at her with an undeniable hunger.

Apparently that would have to be enough.

She'd found a desk in one of the unused rooms, of which there were many. Some Grantley had built Roseford to house a large family. She didn't think about that, just asked Mrs. Peterborough to have the little desk moved to her room.

She only wanted a place to write that didn't remind her of him and the tentative connection they'd had before she somehow broke it.

She was sitting at that desk when the note came, as if she had willed it. The only note not in Hortense's hand.

Perhaps one day I may call? There were a few more words than that, but she barely saw them. Only the signature below. *William Taggart.*

No, London didn't make any sense either.

She threw it away more quickly than she ever would a venomous snake. Then, standing, picked it back up and tossed it into the fire.

"Mrs. Coombes," she asked that worthy woman, "what would you say to visiting the village?"

"What, today? Some farmers are trying the new plow. Sir John bought it from a manufactory. It's got all its parts the same. No, its parts are like every other plow's parts. That's it. And the blacksmith can even make some if they break without sending all the way back to Rotheringham. Sir John says it's a marvel." Mrs. Coombes obviously grasped there was reason to be excited about the new plow, even if she herself didn't feel it. "The Hatch and Beardsley lands are right by each other, so them sharing a plow will be a sight to see."

She was far more excited about whatever conflict there was between the Hatch and Beardsley farmers than she was about the plow; Eleanor wanted to know more about *that.* But Mrs. Coombes didn't produce information easily.

So Eleanor said, "What would you think of a visit to the cobbler? I believe I ought to have higher boots for riding than I currently have, if the forest is going to grow more brambles."

"Everything grows brambles round here, mum—my lady, rather. The roses ain't begun to bloom, but when they do—"

Mrs. Coombes bent right over to peer at Eleanor's shoes, and her neck kerchief slipped up. Eleanor suspected that she didn't wear it at home.

Or perhaps she wore it now for other reasons.

Because under the kerchief were dark fingerprints on her skin.

It was frightening just to see them. Eleanor felt repulsed by them, horrified. A shock upon the previous shock.

Then she remembered how much more horrifying they must be for her kind Rebby Coombes.

"Mrs. Coombes," she said, steadying herself with a hand on her desk. "I have never asked you about Mr. Coombes."

Quick as a flash the round little woman shot upright, giving Eleanor a searching look that said clearly, even without words, *what do you know?*

Eleanor had to think. This wasn't a bit of news she wanted about where Mr. Taggart walked in the park, or who had flirted with whom at a Ranelagh masquerade. This was *important*.

And Mrs. Coombes, as much as any society lady, would not be likely to answer directly.

"Would Mr. Coombes be well enough on his own, do you think, if I asked you to stay some nights? It would be easier to have you live in the servants' quarters. But I am thinking only of my own comfort." She tried to meet Mrs. Coombes' eyes as evenly as she could, say what she could not say. "It would be up to you, of course."

The little woman fairly slumped with relief that she hadn't been asked a direct question that would force her to lie.

"I might well do, mum." She seemed reluctant to speak of Mr. Coombes directly. "If that'd suit you, I will do. I'll bring some things."

"Good." Eleanor put some starch into her tone. Perhaps that would make it easier for Mrs. Coombes to say, quite rightly, that her presence at the manor was what her mistress wanted. "I'd prefer it if you did."

"Did what?" Sir John had lurked about the house a bit more for days, but not in Eleanor's company; he just appeared and disappeared, rather like the robins outside her window, of which Eleanor suspected there were now two.

He'd chosen this moment to stick his undressed head into Eleanor's chambers. Because she hadn't been able to bring herself to dress his hair for him, and he clearly couldn't, or wouldn't, do it on his own.

Eleanor felt her insides lurch at the sight of him.

"What I asked her to do," was all she said. For really, if a husband only appeared from time to time, shared little, and ate apart, as he did? Such a person had no business knowing her affairs.

* * *

ELEANOR'S STARCH was for show. Jesper wanted to sweep her into his arms again, spread her over him like butter, let her sink into him until they became one. While they'd been wrapped in each other's arms under the trees, his mind had been blank and his insides peaceful. He wanted that. It would be so easy to seek it again. He thought she'd be willing.

But if the new Lady Grantley was anything, it was truthful to the point of cutting.

She knew something was off between them, and if he didn't find the right way to say it, her truth would flay him to the bone.

After two more days of loneliness, avoiding his own house and his own wife, Jesper was considering even consulting the vicar for advice. He'd never consulted the vicar on anything important in his life.

He walked all the way to the village, but stopped at the vicar's gate.

The men who ought to have been in the fields were standing in the vicar's yard. Not Coombes, likely drinking down at the inn; but every other village man was there, their wives with them. Big Will Carver was weeping, one hand pinching his eyes against the tears; his other arm gripped Mrs. Carver. Hatch was there, his bachelorhood painfully obvious, just looking lost; his neighbor Mr. Beardsley sat on a stump, head in his hands, with Mrs. Beardsley watching him sadly.

Jesper summoned Hatch with a wave of his hand. "Mr. Hatch." He kept his voice down. "What's happened?"

The young man looked stricken. "Mrs. Wright. She died."

The words opened up a black abyss inside Jesper. It was so wide and howling, he couldn't hear. "What?"

"Aye, the baby come, and she died. Last night. Too much blood."

Jesper didn't need to hear more. He didn't want to hear more.

Another death, so soon, so unexpected. How could he rely on the earth at his feet not to open him up and swallow him whole?

As baronet of Roseford he ought to find Mr. Wright. Do something. What, he didn't know, for he couldn't repair the man's wound.

"He's all at sea." Mr. Hatch clearly divined Jesper's thoughts. "Mrs. Hedges has took the new boy, it'll be all right." Mrs. Hedges had a baby only eight months old; she could feed the newest Wright. "But what about the other two? Who'll take care of them? He's in there wondering if he's got to marry Susie Shore, or—"

"Tell him not to panic." They were ironic words, because Jesper was swimming in panic right now. His lady might not panic, but he was finding himself well capable of it. "No one has to marry anyone. His children will be fed and have a roof. So will he. His only need is to grieve. Can someone tend his field?"

"Not much to tend till the rain comes," Hatch said wryly, "but I can."

"Good man. I'll pay you to do it." He waved away the young man's faint protest. It would be heavy work, managing two of the new strips divided by hedges, and Hatch had no wife. "I'll send over dinners from the manor. Stay with it."

Hatch just nodded, sandy eyebrows quavering, wondering if he'd just gotten himself in good with the baronet or taken on too much.

Jesper barely noticed.

Mrs. Wright had given her husband another son. And lost her life.

What must Mr. Wright be feeling? Hatch said he was only worried about taking care of his children, and half-ready to marry again to make the house whole.

As Jesper had tried to tell the Duke of Gravenshire, a wife wasn't a luxury in the country. All the mechanisms of life revolved around her force.

Now that Jesper had a wife of his own, he could imagine such a loss. Losing Eleanor wouldn't just leave a hole. It would crush his universe.

He'd brought her here to bear his heir. But that wasn't why he wanted her, not really. He wanted her for himself. To live with, lie with, breathe with.

And the very reason he'd brought her here was the last thing he could risk.

CHAPTER 33

Of course Eleanor noticed him staring over the supper table; he couldn't help it. The particular tilt of her nose, the color of her cheeks; even the way she buttered her muffin with neat, sharp strokes.

The life he'd given her was a bad bargain, unless she produced an heir. But now he could imagine something worse.

"I must visit London."

Jesper hadn't expected to say the words till he blurted them out.

Based on the way his wife paused in buttering her muffin, she hadn't imagined them either. "Why?"

Damning himself for a stupid liar, Jesper realized that of course he should have decided how to explain himself before he spoke. Of course she would ask why. He could hardly say that he had himself in a quagmire so deep that he needed help to find his way out.

It was a mark of how Mrs. Wright's death had rattled him. He barely recalled his own name, but he knew down to his bones that he couldn't bear to lose Eleanor like that. The Grantleys in the portrait gallery had already lived and gone. What Jesper needed was her.

"Business." He chose the shortest answer he could think of.

"What business?"

Twice stupid. He'd explained all his business affairs to her. Did he think she'd *forgotten?*

"A solicitor." Well, he'd pulled that out of some deep pocket. "His Grace's direction for one, at least. On the matter of whoever's hunting my deer."

"Have they killed more?"

The softness in her face, the worry, over his deer pulled at something in his chest. His ice-crystal Eleanor, worried over his deer.

Proving her brittleness was for show.

The idea of parting hurt him, actually pained him. He hated the idea of leaving her here. He couldn't take her with him; she was too clever, she'd soon divine there was more weighing on him than the hurt to his deer.

Yet the idea of traveling all the way to London without her stretched him thin inside in a way that was entirely new.

"Will you be well here?" Jesper didn't notice that he hadn't answered her question. He only saw her flinch, as if the news that she would be staying while he left pained her, too.

Did it?

"I expect so." She took a bite of her muffin. "I shan't put any snakes in my pocket while you're gone, at least."

He choked on an agonized snort. She raised an eyebrow.

"Don't ride in the woods," he told her. His need to get help fought with his newfound panic about her safety. Clarity, at least, might make her follow his orders. "Don't ride in the carriage without two footmen. Don't leave the Roseford lands."

"What about the garden? Is that safe?" There were her barbs back again, the bridge of her nose whitening as she clenched her teeth.

Christ. He would be worried for her every minute he was gone.

But telling her that would only make him sound like a schoolboy. Or a bear-boy. He never had discovered what she meant by that, but he could guess. "Should I bring you anything from London?"

He'd expected her to at least ask for more panniers, but his lady just shrugged. "I don't need anything."

But what about things you wanted? He wanted to ask, but couldn't.

She hadn't wanted this life, but now it was all she had. She wouldn't be safe unless she produced an heir; but how safe would she be if she did?

* * *

"The girl might bear your son right now." His Grace was blunt.

Jesper winced. "I realize to a man of your age, everyone seems young. But it's a poor choice of words."

The Duke of Gravenshire's eyebrows climbed. "What, *girl*? You've decided she's too young for you? *Now?*"

The Gravenshire house in London was vast, filling one entire side of Claremont Square. It did not pretend to be a country house, with a long drive for carriages; it hulked up to the street, eating as much city space as any house could.

Once Jesper would have found it merely interesting. Now it intimidated.

And the Duchess of Gravenshire, on a settee inside, even more so.

Her style bowed to no one, with no deference to her age. The Duke could have married a young girl just out of the schoolroom for his second wife, but he'd chosen a lady clearly his equal. Her piled-high hair was studded with yellow silk celandine blossoms, and her dress a confounding collection of lace ruffles and silk bows. What had Eleanor called it? A *robe à la polonaise*? Though Jesper did not know how to tell if this was one of those, or something different.

He didn't wish to argue with women in those, whatever it was.

"Do not tease him, Your Grace," she admonished her husband, and sipped from a delicate cup of tea. "It is a special complication, to fall in love with your wife."

Her words shook him harder than any large man could.

Was that what this feeling was? This hunger, this terror of losing his wife? Wasn't it all the fear of death brought about by burying his father, the only companion he'd ever had?

He'd loved his father, but this feeling wasn't like that. It was bigger than he was, powerful, ravenous. It was the feeling that he must do everything in his power, not for himself, but for Eleanor.

"Forgive my contradiction, Your Grace. But the problem isn't feelings. It's what I've done to my wife."

"Oh, la la." She waved a hand still graceful, though the joints were a bit knobbled by age. "Many London men do far worse."

"My wife is right." The Duke sat beside her, coat-tails spreading magnificence on both sides of him, one ankle comfortably crossed over the other. "Your problem isn't that you've done anything so terribly wrong. Your problem is that you feel badly about it."

Jesper couldn't sit. The ride to London alone had been fast, but taxing. His thighs warned him he was no longer twenty, and pacing was preferable to sitting.

Plus his father had the right idea. Thinking about the future was torture. And Their Graces weren't getting this at all.

He picked one fear to address first. "The law isn't just. She's my family. She ought to be my heir."

"But she won't be. I hope you're not asking me to introduce a bill to Parliament to change centuries of inheritance law." The Duke patted a pocket absently, perhaps searching for a pipe. Remembering he was in a drawing room with his wife, he desisted. "All of England would fall if men couldn't depend that their sons would inherit their legacy."

"My legacy right now is an old house, a fertile pig, and a village about to riot over some geese."

"Flim-flam." The Duke crossed his arms over his chest. "Roseford is a thriving estate. Don't tell me that girl has you thinking twice about your own inheritance. Sir John was a good man and did well by you. I won't hear it."

"My lady hasn't complained at all. On the contrary. That's not the issue. The issue is that if I die without an heir, she will not inherit Roseford."

"And so 'tis." The Duke shrugged, still-broad shoulders shifting his coat of fine silk embroidered with bluebells and hares. "Would you have the peers of the kingdom putting their lands in the hands of men who had done nothing but marry their daughters?"

"No. I'm talking about leaving them in the hands of their daughters."

The novelty of this idea so struck the Duke that he fell silent.

His Duchess, however, did not seem so flattened by it. "You can provide for your wife," she said softly, as if to soothe him. He knew if he drew closer she would pat his arm. She did things like that. "You cannot give her your estate; you know that."

"No different from any other man of property who marries," said the Duke, rallying.

"No?" Jesper stopped his pacing. "And if you died? I know, you have a son. But if you hadn't? You'd want your wife turned out into the streets?"

"She'd hardly be sleeping on the pavement! As dowager Duchess she would have a house in—never mind." Remembering the distance between a duke and a baronet, the Duke of Gravenshire changed his course. "Put some money in the five per cents for her and get on with life. That's all you can do. That's all any of us can do."

"It really is, my boy," said the Duchess kindly. "So why does it trouble you so?"

Sinking into a polished oak and embroidery chair opposite, Jesper faced what he ran from.

Eleanor had put three venomous snakes in her pocket without a moment's hesitation. Taking her cue from him.

She was following *him* down the marriage path.

All he'd asked of her was to bear him an heir. What if, with all her unblinking focus, she held to their bargain?

And it killed her?

How could he say that he shouldn't have married her *because* he loved her?

For he did. More than his generations of inheritance, more than Roseford. More than anything.

Him, the great ox. He'd married a delicate lady. Her temper might be more than a match for him, but the rest of her was small.

"Women die in childbirth all the time," he said heavily.

Confused by the turn from Jesper's mortality to that of his wife, the Duke sat up.

Jesper went on. "I can't lose her. I can't leave her. I can't be without her. If I tell her the truth of her situation now, she'll hate me."

"Not unless you die prematurely," the Duke pointed out. "And if you do, you won't hear about it."

His wife shot him a look pointed as a dart.

"Well, it's true," said His Grace.

"I don't want her to hate me. I want..."

He wanted to be with her every minute of every day. The idea of her living without him was abhorrent. The idea of living without *her* was torture.

He had indeed fallen in love with his wife, and he couldn't bear the idea of leaving *or* losing her.

"Very well, I will put some money for her in the five per cents." It was the right start, but not enough.

"Good man." The Duke slapped his own knee. "I'll give you my own solicitor."

"But what do I do if she does become with child?"

The Duchess' soft eyes understood. "You'll do what every man does. Pray for mercy and her life."

"I stand by my position that Eleanor would kick Death himself in the teeth." The Duke clearly kept his own emotions at bay with flippancy. "If it's any comfort," the Duke added, "London for a widow is quite different from London for a young unmarried girl. She'll be able to attend the theater, concerts. And even if society won't have her, there will be some invitations. Perhaps even another marriage. You don't need to worry."

Another *marriage*? Jesper had never thought of that for *her*. He wouldn't want her to be alone. But his whole body rejected the idea like poison.

"I should say," said the Duke, feeling absently for his pipe again, "all in all, better for you if you live."

CHAPTER 34

*J*esper shouldn't have let the Duke convince him to attend this ball.

"One must pass the time," said the Duke, looking out over the crowd with obvious satisfaction. He did love a party. "And obviously, my solicitor wasn't to be found. He must be in London; how far could he get?"

"I would have preferred a different solicitor to waiting."

"There are some areas of life where waiting for quality is worthwhile. One of those areas is the law. Have some punch."

And with that, His Grace left him to enjoy the scene.

Jesper wore a borrowed coat and breeches from His Grace that were too short, and that didn't help. He looked and felt even more awkward than when he had arrived in London the first time, and he knew everyone could see it.

On top of it, it was as though his eyes had become opened. So used to delicate things in the forest, and unused to ballrooms, he had barely seen what there was to see the first time.

Now he saw how men curled and tied back their own hair, if they didn't wear wigs. He saw how the widest gentleman was light on his high-heeled slippers when he wanted to impress a lady. He saw how those ladies cut a man dead if he did not meet their approval—and many didn't.

He had never had his pick of London ladies; likely none would ever have spoken to him but for Lady Hortense, and the Duke.

And Eleanor, *his* Eleanor, had only spoken to him to scold him on behalf of Lady Hortense.

Lady Hortense herself was still a magnet for all eyes.

She, however, only had eyes for him, darting to him the moment she saw him.

He braced for some unapproving words, but Hortense wasn't Eleanor.

"Sir John! How nice to see you!" She curtsied prettily, her panniered skirts swinging, bell-like, with the speed of her motion, and waved herself with her fan. It was warm in the ballroom, and she wore a foot-high wig, which bore many little tufts of wool besides.

"Lady Hortense." He bowed and gave all seriousness to deciphering what was in her hair. These things, he now knew, were important business for ladies. "May I ask, is your hair sporting sheep?"

"Rain clouds," she said with a dismissive wave. "My maid wishes to set a fashion. I doubt it will work. Tell me everything! Lady Grantley describes Roseford as very lovely. I wish to hear far more about the crockery and less about the birds."

His lady had written about the birds?

"I would answer anything you like, Lady Hortense, but I doubt I could guess what would interest you. You are welcome to question me." He had to think hard about the plates. He saw them every day, but he hadn't looked at them.

Look everywhere, he'd told his lady.

"The crockery is... plain whiteware, I believe you would call it. There isn't much of it. Roseford does not entertain."

Would Eleanor *like* to entertain?

A house party would cost him a small fortune. He'd do it if she wanted it. And buy the plates for it besides.

Lady Hortense seemed to have a similar thought. "Do try to convince Lady Grantley to host a small party. There are several people who would love to attend. And not all of them to gloat." She said this as naturally as breathing.

She wasn't unaware of London's darker emotions; she simply did not give them much time.

"I'll ask her, Lady Hortense. Thank you for the suggestion. She has been melancholy. A party might cheer her."

Lady Hortense's unsuspected conversational trap closed. "And what do *you* do to cheer her, if she is melancholy?"

He gave her a rueful half-smile. "I try to relieve her of the burden of my presence."

"Nonsense." For a moment, fluffy Lady Hortense showed steel like Eleanor's. "When she married *you*? Expecting *you* to keep her company in a new place? You wouldn't be that cruel." Her eyes shifted from kitten to killer. "Would you?"

No, he'd been wholly unequipped to handle real ladies all along.

"Lady Hortense." He didn't know what she knew, but she was under the impression—the *correct* impression, he told himself bitterly —that Eleanor was unhappy. "I haven't done Lady Grantley a kind-ness by marrying her. I've put her in a terrible position."

Her snort was all her own. "Have you wandered from your marriage vows? For half the men in here have. You are not displaying her on your arm like a watch-chain, nor are you insulting her half the day. I won't even speak of the men who beat their wives, or worse."

Big, strong Jesper felt his stomach turn. "You needn't."

"If my friend is in a *terrible position*, as you say, then make it better. She chose to marry *you*. You can prove that her choice wasn't foolish."

Lady Hortense could set a man back on his heels quite as well as her friend Eleanor.

Around him London society turned and danced, laughed and gossiped, painted and papered to look like dolls.

Eleanor hadn't given this up. She'd *escaped* it. She'd *wanted* to leave. And she'd left with him.

He needed to make her choice worthwhile.

"Lady Hortense." Could he humble himself before a very young, very bubbly young lady, and admit his faults at least to her? "I did not tell her before we married what a poor choice I was."

"You lied to her." Quick as a snake.

"A lie of omission."

Her eyes flashed with that fire again. "Then you had better tell her, and quickly. Because her letters are full of everything that isn't you. She either hates you or loves you, and if you make her miserable, then you are a miserable man."

He was. He had been. But he didn't think Eleanor hated him. And if she loved him...

He cursed the Duke's wandering solicitor. Jesper wanted to be at home. With Eleanor.

He wanted to find out if she loved him too.

"Lady Hortense, you are wiser than I knew." He reached for her hand when she hadn't offered it; she jumped as he kissed her fingers. "My eyes made a shrewd choice when they first settled on you."

"Oh!" Giggling, she waved him off with her fan, then used it to cool her pink cheeks. "I would have gotten in that carriage for Gretna Green, you know."

And with that, she laughed and left him there.

* * *

SEVERAL PEOPLE NOTICED Sir John's arrival, and several noticed him leave.

Few noticed that, like distant ripples, there were other arrivals and departures thus set in motion.

Jesper did not think of himself as a feature of any London circles, so he neither noticed, nor wondered if any of those movements pertained to him.

He knew to look everywhere, but he was not of a suspicious nature.

* * *

SILENT SUPPERS with her husband lurking outside were better than silent suppers entirely alone.

Eleanor had dined alone often at Roseford, but it was different with Sir John in London. It *felt* as though he were gone, and no amount of butter could give the food back its flavor.

She looked at the table, all the dishes arrayed in a square *à la française* and serving only her.

She'd had enough.

She pushed back her chair. "Mrs. Peterborough!" she called out the door.

Mrs. Peterborough bustled up the hall. "My lady?"

"We've all had enough of this. Sir John isn't here. Even if he is, when I eat alone, we needn't set the full table. You can have the kitchen prepare a tray."

"Ah—as you wish, Lady Grantley. But does that mean you won't eat?" Mrs. Peterborough's eyes glanced toward the table. "You should certainly eat some more."

"I'll eat." When had Eleanor become a liar? The idea of choking down food repulsed her. But Mrs. Peterborough looked so worried. "I'll be in the library." She didn't look back into the empty dining room, with its platters, lit candles, and no Sir John.

Jesper.

Had he been trying to tell her something with that name?

Mrs. Peterborough hurried ahead of her, lit the library's Argand lamp, and left. Presumably to put some of that food on a tray. Eleanor didn't even remember what it was. She ought to have simply brought her plate.

What did it matter where she ate her food? Where she wore her cap? Her panniers were hanging out her bedroom window. What, after all was said and done, did it matter?

The Argand lamp glowed on the shelves beside the desk. The newest books were kept there, the colors of their bindings making bright stripes against the wood.

She picked through them, settling on one and taking it to the spot where she'd read that night in here with her husband.

It had surprised her about him, the books. She wanted him to be a simple clod, but he kept confounding that idea. Plus, the Argand lamp was a new device, as novel as his manufactured plow. Even without trips to London, he'd acquired one.

He could have held house parties. Musicales, dances. Roseford was certainly large enough. From what he'd said, he could bear the cost.

He'd *chosen* how to live his life. Sir John was a grown man, seasoned.

Even so, he'd accepted her re-ordering of the dining schedule without a qualm.

And then ignored it, she reminded herself with some acid, *once it required him to spend time with her.*

What had sent him awry, when they'd started off so well?

She'd tried to stay as gentle as she could. She *had.* Even the robin now living in her skirt wires suffered no real bursts of her temper.

And Sir John—*Jesper*—had said over and over he wanted to hear her. Not to censor herself. Not to hold back.

Eleanor felt her face flame as she thought of the way they'd rocked together under the trees. What could she possibly have held back? She'd given him everything.

Not everything, said a snide little voice inside that might have been her father's, or might have been hers. *There are things you didn't tell him.*

She hadn't told him how happy he'd made her under those trees. With his desire for her.

She hadn't told him how she dreamed about him, his eyes, his big strong hands splaying over her skin and holding her close.

She hadn't told him about the distracting ache that no amount of touching herself could banish. How she woke searching for him in those bleary moments before full consciousness because some part of her wanted him. Around her, inside her, *with* her.

Wives admitted those things, perhaps.

Or women in love.

CHAPTER 35

*D*ropping the book on the table, Eleanor hid her face in her hands.

She didn't know if it was the worst possible thing that she loved her husband, or the best. It wasn't a public question. She simply didn't know how to handle such things appropriately. If it was unacceptable to call one's husband by a private name, how much more unacceptable was it to actually crave one's husband in one's bed?

That was most difficult to admit. She could tell anyone he was decent company, thorough and fair in his accounts and holdings. He even had a kind of gallantry to him, as long as it involved rescuing her from snakes and not combing his hair.

She could admit that his weathered face was more precious to her than any jewels could be, and that she was more glad she'd married him than of anything else in her life.

But it was difficult to admit that she craved him like the earth outside craved the rain.

And like the earth outside, craving didn't mean getting.

Mrs. Peterborough opened the door again, silently placing the tray on a low stool by Eleanor's feet.

Eleanor only nodded and picked up her book.

Trying to distract herself, as the housekeeper withdrew, she even tried to read it.

One essay caught Eleanor's eye. On manners, of all things. How was that meant to be amusing? For she'd picked the author for his wit.

Eyes tripping down the page in the bright Argand light, Eleanor decided people must have called him humorous because they did not wish to admit that he was also right.

She felt mocked by his trenchant observation that court was the worst place to learn manners, and his befuddlement at those who wanted niceties observed.

Absently Eleanor picked up her muffin with one hand while continuing to read. Mrs. Peterborough had thickly spread the muffin with butter, and topped it with jam. She too must worry that Eleanor was too thin.

Eleanor considered being offended.

Was extra jam good manners? Or taking offense at extra jam? She turned back to the essay's beginning. She should know more about this.

Pride, ill nature, and want of sense, are the three great sources of ill manners.

The author never mentioned emotions. What about craving her husband, was that rude? What if she *loved* him? Was it really ill-mannered to feel?

Jesper never made anyone uneasy, except through horror at his dress. He was never proud, and had no ill nature at all. As for want of sense, she only worried that he found their marriage less than sensible for some reason.

Had *Eleanor* treated him in an ill-mannered way?

Closing her eyes, she desperately grasped through all their past interactions wondering if she had.

She'd been sharp, but not cruel. She'd offered opinions; but he'd thought they were good ones, and he had *told* her to speak.

So she might not be ill-natured, and perhaps was sensible enough. But wasn't she guilty of pride?

Why had she bothered so, she wondered now, letting the book fall from her nerveless fingers, with what was *proper*? Lying with her husband wasn't necessarily *proper*, and those had been some of the dearest moments of her life.

That beautiful day they had ridden so far together, and shared moments of sympathy, and peace. Had she plodded through that mud because of pride?

Wanting to eat at set hours was only practical. Wincing at his threadbare clothing was pride.

Sitting alone in the front rooms of the house when the house was full of people was *definitely* pride.

Well, if this learned gentleman was right, then perhaps Eleanor had been guilty of poor manners without even knowing.

If so, she could repair the fault.

Sweeping up the tray, she carried it out herself, maneuvering it past the library door with some dangerous clinking. There, she'd already learned something new: carrying trays was harder than it looked.

When she arrived in the heavy-beamed kitchen, there was a scramble, surprised faces, and silence.

"Mrs. Walker." She greeted the cook by name. "I'm sorry not to have done your supper justice. The rolled potatoes were excellent, as was the partridge. Molly. Eliza. Thank you for tidying my room without disturbing that brash little robin."

The unexpected words rustled all the women. Mrs. Peterborough pulled the bench away from the kitchen table, gesturing for her to sit.

Suddenly unsure, Eleanor realized that she'd been taught dictates on how to behave from people who thought they were her betters. She was less sure how to speak to people without making that assumption.

They needn't be bosom friends. She thought to herself of Mrs. Willowby. They had lives of their own. But she simply could not sit here alone, miserable and missing Sir John for the rest of her life.

That poisonous note from Mr. Taggart flicked across her mind —*May I call on you?*—but Eleanor slapped that thought away. She was not interested in going backward. She'd come to Roseford to go forward.

"Thank you, Mrs. Peterborough." It had all gone through her mind so fast that only seconds had passed, but still all the kitchen was standing and waiting for her to do something. She set down her tray. "May I eat? I do apologize, I've only just discovered that I'm hungry." Another thought crossed her mind and instead of squashing it, Eleanor said with a smile, "Perhaps I've spent more time with Sir John than is good for me."

At that, everyone in the kitchen laughed, even the girl Willa who seemed a bit unsure why they were laughing.

"Ladies," she said, just as she would address the Duchess' drawing room. "What do *you* think I should do with my time tomorrow?"

* * *

IT WAS a long night of Jesper tossing and turning. It had been nearly impossible to sleep, and then worry that sleeplessness would push his health the wrong way had only made it worse.

He wasn't used to being fragile. Now that he was in London, where apparently his eyes had been opened in many ways, he could see that part of his inner turmoil was this new fear of being fragile. His sense of invulnerability was gone.

Well, some part of his mind told him, perhaps Mrs. Peterborough's voice, *about time*. He was thirty-eight. Only the young were foolish enough to think themselves invulnerable—to time, the elements, or the ravages of love.

He could see his father stomping along in front of him clear as day. The slight hump to his back speaking his age, the wiry muscles. He'd been slighter and shorter than Jesper, his hair cropped short, scalp slightly showing.

But Jesper had never read his father's expression. He'd seen it every day and hadn't known what it meant.

Look everywhere.

Thinking back with his new eyes, he saw a man ready to laugh, yet worn with sorrow. A man who'd given up on yesterday and tomorrow, and only lived for today.

A man who had survived losing his beloved wife.

Was that what he feared most? Truly following in his father's footsteps? He was Roseford's baronet now. He could too easily become his father's ghost.

Well, one couldn't avoid a ditch one couldn't see. Now that he felt that fear and named it, he could steer himself away. He would set things in motion to protect Eleanor's future as best he could. Then he could stop running from the past and perhaps live for today without being a copy of his father in every respect.

His wife was alive. And he wanted every possible minute with her.

Rising from the bed, Jesper pushed open the drapes, willing the sun to come up. He had to find this solicitor fellow and get back to Roseford. His wife. His life.

* * *

THE SKY HAD BARELY LIGHTENED when Jesper let himself out the front door. He'd heard some servants stirring, but the butler was still asleep.

Most of London was still asleep, so it surprised him to see a young man half-snoring, leaning against a tree opposite, in the Square.

As Jesper came down the steps, the boy snuffled himself awake.

Leaping forward with the quickness of the young, he accosted Jesper. "Sir."

"Your pardon." Jesper gave a little bow of his head. "I have an urgent appointment." With a solicitor, and then his horse. Riding so far again at speed would take its toll on him, he mused, but his heart would simply have to bear up.

"I've been awaiting your pleasure," the boy said. "Lord Faircombe wishes to speak with you."

Jesper frowned. "You don't want my *pleasure,* you want my *time.* And I don't wish to speak with him."

"He believes you do, sir."

"He believes a lot of things."

Then the thought took him that this might have something to do with Eleanor.

"All right," he said as the boy rubbed sleepy eyes, "lead on."

"Lord Faircombe won't rise till mid-morning, sir," the boy stammered.

"Yet here you are. And so am I. If this meeting is urgent, let's go."

Visibly juggling the instruction to bring his quarry immediately, and the knowledge that his master would be asleep, the boy seemed to have no better solution than to do as Jesper said.

CHAPTER 36

*I*t was with great restraint that Jesper didn't barge into the
Marquess' sleeping chamber.

He'd try to be polite, though it was wasted on this man.

"Grantley. You do tax a fellow," Faircombe mumbled as he finally
entered, blinking blearily, tucking in his collar.

"I understood your need was urgent."

"Nothing is urgent in London before noon. Sit."

Jesper stayed standing.

Lord Faircombe sighed. "Why do you have to be like this? So
piggish. Just like your father, when there's no need. Fine." He balanced
against the edge of his own carved desk, fixing Jesper with piercing,
bloodshot eyes. "Very well. Do not push the Duke to take action. It
won't help you at all."

The Duke? What action? Did the man know about the solicitor?

Jesper lowered himself into a chair, slowly, keeping his eyes on
Lord Faircombe.

Who took it as a good sign. "I'm glad you see reason. What's done
is done. And you don't want your wife to find out."

Veins running cold, Jesper stood up again.

Had this pinched little man with his little spies somehow learned about Jesper's heart?

He leaned close, ignoring the way Faircombe leaned away.

That part of Eleanor that had worked itself into his heart showed him things he didn't understand before. Faircombe's eyes were black with fear, but he was afraid of more than Jesper. Perhaps he'd been afraid all his life. Perhaps that was what London had done to *him*.

Jesper spoke slowly to be heard over the other man's no doubt pounding heart. "You're playing games. Don't."

Faircombe swallowed. "I only meant—Lady Grantley need never know that your northern lands are gone. After all, it's not like she would go there."

His *northern lands?*

Realizing that Faircombe was the sort of prey who would run right into a snare if left to do it, Jesper kept his stare level and did not move.

Faircombe fidgeted a little. He was clearly uncomfortable, leaning away from Jesper. But he didn't yield his ground. "I know what your tiny, tiny title means to your wife. Making it even smaller will cut her."

He didn't know Eleanor at all. True, she could lecture about what no titled lady would do. But then she did it. Titles didn't matter to her at all.

Any worries he had about his land or legacy would have to wait until he satisfied himself that this toad couldn't actually hurt Eleanor. "You know nothing about my wife. You're cut because she would have married a man with no title at all before your lizardy friend Burden."

Gathering himself, Faircombe stepped away. Space gave him courage. "She might have bedded Taggart; she wouldn't have married him. That kind of hot blood finds its outlets."

Jesper stepped close again, proving Faircombe's courage false. The man's face drooped.

Jesper leaned his own face even closer. "Never speak of my wife again."

The red in Jesper's vision surprised him. He might have worried for his heart, but it was beating strong.

Even if he died right now, he'd take this crawling little beast with him if he said one more thing about Eleanor.

When Faircombe raised a weakly warding hand, Jesper took it for capitulation.

Then the Marquess put his desk between them for good measure.

"Then let us speak of you," but he didn't meet Jesper's gaze. "You have not used your lands to the north, and I have. The Duke may proffer a solicitor, but I assure you I have the King's ear. My suit for your lands *will* succeed."

Jesper didn't have time to be clever. "*What* suit for my lands?"

Faircombe sucked his teeth, a sarcastic little sound. "It's open knowledge that you consulted His Grace for legal advice. How you found out about the suit I don't know, but I assure you it is well underway."

It was tempting to call this whole thing a charade—but Faircombe didn't play those sorts of games.

"You will not get my lands." On that, Jesper was clear.

"I will." Faircombe looked and sounded like he felt no uncertainty at all. "Your father made no use of the land, nor your grandfather. No houses, no mills, no roads—nothing. I have a hunting lodge that faces your grounds. My hunting has had no response from you."

"No *response?*" Much made sense and much more infuriated Jesper to a degree he had never thought possible. "You sneak onto my land and kill my deer, and blame me for having no *response?*"

"I don't *blame* you for anything. You clearly haven't a clue how land is to be managed. Very well, the Crown understands that can happen with one man—but your father and grandfather did not either. Your lands are by grant of the King, and if your family cannot use them for the benefit of England, then the lands must go to a family who can."

Emboldened by his righteous indignation, he was the one this time who stepped closer.

"You have shown all of London you are a pig farmer wearing a title."

Jesper's anger subsided. His desire to wipe Faircombe off the earth was now a simple urge to safeguard the world against a viper that was not only poisonous, but vicious.

But protecting Eleanor came first. This little man wanted to deprive any future Grantleys of their inheritance; but what were his plans for Eleanor?

Even Grantley land was not as important as Eleanor.

"All this," he said, controlling his breathing with deep effort, "because your friend Burden lost the opportunity to terrorize my wife?"

"No. But he doesn't like to be thwarted." Faircombe shrugged. "Neither do I."

So. Faircombe had pushed for Burden to have Eleanor as the prize he wanted, to get Burden's help for his own prize: the northern Grantley lands.

That settled one thing. Eleanor must have enough money that, if the worst happened, she need never come back *here*.

"I'm not going to kill you for two reasons." The certainty of his voice made it more than a threat, and Faircombe backed away again, startled. "One is that you've given me some clarity that I needed. And the other is that killing you... *here*... is a thing no titled gentleman would do."

He spread his hands, flexing his thick scarred fingers.

"But if you or any of your family ever set foot on my lands again, I will show you I can be a most proper lord, and kill trespassers with dispatch."

The man blanched, and Jesper knew his point was made.

"The King's Bench will decide if it's your land," Faircombe muttered, unwilling to let the matter drop without a parting blow.

"Until that happens, take care."

And with that line drawn, Jesper strode out.

* * *

ALL THE WINDOWS of Roseford were thrown open to the spring air.

"Am I doing this right?"

Mrs. Peterborough inspected Eleanor's attempt to polish her dressing table. "The work looks good enough, if I ignore that a lady like you shouldn't do it."

Eleanor felt lighter today, and happy with the sunshine. A new day was always easier than the end of an old one. Anything might happen. "I have our visit to the village inn to look forward to. How should I amuse myself until then?"

"A lady like you shouldn't visit the inn either. Till then... ribbon embroidery?"

Eleanor just laughed.

It felt good to move, too, and feel the blood pumping through her limbs. Admitting to herself how she felt about Jesper had cleared her mind, somehow. Little truths were clearer.

And big ones.

Molly clattered by her door, banging her wooden pail and mop. How many times had she climbed the rear stairs so as not to disturb the lady with the front ones? The whole house was full of life; Eleanor just hadn't been living it.

Perhaps better manners led to a better life.

What she'd tell her husband about that was an absorbing question.

Mrs. Coombes, sweeping the carpet, observed, "It'll be time soon to take the carpets out for a good beating."

"Should we do it today? I could do anything today."

Clearly wondering what had come over Eleanor, Mrs Peterborough said, "Lady Grantley—"

She stopped when the rattle of wheels clearly sounded from the road.

All three women crowded to look out the window without a robin nest.

"There's a fine carriage." The housekeeper peered hard, but clearly couldn't see inside it; neither could Eleanor. "Did you expect—" Just like that, she turned whippet-quick, a flash of something like suspicion in her eyes. "Lady Grantley. Did you *expect* visitors?"

"No." It couldn't be someone to see her, could it?

Though who would come in a carriage to see Jesper?

"Agh! I'll have to receive them." The idea of armoring up in all her clothes today was odious, but it would have to be done. "Mrs. Coombes, I'll have to have something that is ready, no time for pressing—I'll take the pink dress." It was sturdy linen, so it would at least have a reason not to look perfect in the middle of the day. And it had a bit of lace.

"Of course, my lady."

And where to receive them? She didn't want them in her library. She didn't want them at all. Why couldn't the outside world leave her alone?

Only the thought that it might, conceivably, be Hortense drove her to dress instead of sending them away.

"Please put them in the parlor, Mrs. Peterborough, and I'll be down directly," sighed Eleanor.

"You sound as if you'd rather clean the carpets!"

"I'd rather sweep up spiders, and that's the truth."

CHAPTER 37

*N*othing could have astonished Eleanor more than to find the man awaiting her in the parlor.

"Mr. Taggart! What an unpleasant surprise."

That couldn't be good manners; but then, why waste good manners on him?

She had another surprise when he smiled. She'd never seen him do that. "I've always admired your wit, Lady Grantley. Did I ever tell you that?"

He certainly had not. "It isn't wit. It's annoyance. Why are you here?"

"I wrote you a note; you didn't answer."

"Because I didn't wish to." Well, she couldn't smooth all her edges in a day.

"I had to see you."

"I've no similar urgency. Truly, Mr. Taggart. What could have possessed you to ride all the way here? Have you come from London?"

"I rode all night."

On second look she could see the signs of wear on him; he had circles under those soft brown eyes. "Whatever for?"

"I wanted to see you, Lady Grantley. I did write you that note. Then when I saw your husband, I realized—"

"You saw my husband?" Her heart leaped even at the mention. A cynical, sharp part of her mind called that foolish; the rest of her told the sharp part to hush. "In London?"

Her interest in the mere mention of her husband disconcerted him. "Yes. He looked even more poorly put together than usual. It was clear he'd borrowed a coat, and we need not speak about his grooming."

"We need not. Well, Mr. Taggart, thank you for telling me. When he returns, he may wish to receive you."

"Lady Grantley, I'm here to see *you*." He swept toward her in a rush, and took her hands.

She took them back. "Then I'll say what I would have written, had I been interested enough to bother. Why? You had an entire season to stare at me and say nothing, Mr. Taggart. You made your cowardice quite clear in our last conversation. I am *married* now. What else could you possibly have to say?"

"Don't you see how your marriage changes things?"

"Not for you."

"I wasn't meant to be your husband, clearly. But I could have been your heart."

"What on *earth* are you talking about?"

More emotion animated his face than she had ever seen in him. "You wouldn't have wanted to marry me, not really. But I had always hoped—even if a title was your match, that we might have some stolen hours together one day, where I could show you how I truly feel."

She had a feeling he meant he wished to show her parts of him she did *not* wish to see. "You make no sense at all."

"Our marriage was never meant to be. But our *affaire*—that has yet to begin, surely?"

He was making her head spin. She hated it.

"Marriages aren't *fated*, Mr. Taggart. If you propose to a woman, she has the chance to say yes or no. You bowed to pressure from bad men. How is that fate?"

He clearly chose not to see it that way. "You wouldn't truly have wished to marry someone without a title. I know you may have felt that way in some particular moment, but not really."

"How can you say that? Did you not see Miss Pritchard marry Mr. Cullen just last month? There's a cabinetmaker, for goodness' sake, marrying a viscount's daughter!"

"And is she happy? Her father disowned her, and she isn't admitted to society."

Eleanor suspected she was deliriously happy. There was a great deal more to do in a day, she now realized, than anything permitted by society.

"Regardless, Mr. Taggart. You made that decision for both of us. And as it turns out, I quite agree."

He moved close, tried to take her hand again. She pushed his away. How had she ever thought him lovely? Those mopey eyes weren't appealing now. "We have time now, don't you see? I could even return tonight. Use the servants' stairs." Persistent the way he'd never been before, he captured one of her hands in both of his. "I just want to talk."

His breath, hot against her cheek, said he did not want to just talk.

Eleanor yanked her hand away, then *shoved*.

It had an admirable effect. He was so startled that he stumbled.

"You give the class of men a bad name. Now I wonder what you were doing all last season, Mr. Taggart. Shopping for a wife, or for targets?" Wishing now they were in the library where there were heavier weapons to hand, she put a chair between them, not wanting to look weak, but edging toward the door. "I don't know whether you think me fair game now because you don't have Lord Burden breathing down your neck, or because you really are too much of a coward for a wife of your own, and only want those of other men. Regardless, I haven't spared you one thought since we parted in the park except to wonder about my taste, and despise it."

"Really?" Did he think that cow-eyed look romantic? "Not one?"

Well, she used to find that look romantic. How desperate she'd been. "Not one. You're ruining my new determination to be polite. Get out, Mr. Taggart. And don't ever come back."

Glad she'd never closed the parlor door, Eleanor backed out.

Molly and Willa were packed one overtop the other just behind the door. Molly waved wildly toward the stables. Eleanor took it to be a question as to whether she should fetch more men.

"No thank you, Molly." Eleanor wouldn't keep silent, not in her own house. "Mr. Taggart was just leaving. I think he has plans to fall off the edge of the earth into a deep dark abyss and never be seen again."

Mr. Taggart seemed to finally realize he could stay alone in that room all day, or follow her out.

He stepped out with his head held high, tugged his waistcoat down in an expression of great affront. "Lady Grantley."

She cut off what might be another speech. "Goodbye, Mr. Taggart. Goodbye. *Goodbye.*"

"Yes, I'm leaving."

"Not fast enough. Good-*bye.*"

Finally giving in, Mr. Taggart opened the front door of Roseford himself, and left.

Molly dissolved into giggles. Willa, wide-eyed, just stared first at her, then at the mistress of the house, then back again.

Conscious of the girl's eyes on her, Eleanor bent over a little to meet them directly. "A man who only wants what he can get from you isn't worth your time."

"What's my time worth?" Willa seemed to want a price.

"More than that. Every woman's time is worth more than that."

* * *

THE SOLICITOR MUST BE ACCUSTOMED to pressure from a duke. Jesper couldn't understand why one baronet in a hurry dismayed the man so.

Though Jesper was large.

"If you put all this money into funds for Lady Grantley, what will you use to run your estate?" The man had clearly never seen a proposal like Jesper's.

"Probably the same money. What, you think she won't fund her own house?"

"This isn't the way it's done. You want to leave her a sizeable widow's portion—"

"With respect," Jesper just managed to keep himself from growling, "don't tell me what I want."

The solicitor must have seen the Duke's note to humor Jesper with whatever he wanted. He was used to the whims of the gentry; his fine blue coat and gold buttons announced that. He just hadn't seen a whim like this.

"Very well, if you will not be dissuaded. On this other matter, the suit of adverse possession..."

The man just shook his head.

Jesper was finding it hard to care about anything but making things right for Eleanor. Some part of him was appalled at himself; or maybe it was all those Grantley portraits scolding him at a distance. They were enough to keep him in his chair when he'd rather sprint for Roseford.

"What about it?"

"These things seldom carry. But there is a danger. You've not used this land. Nor did your father or grandfather. Lord Faircombe might make a good case that he *has*, especially if he has further plans for it."

"All he's done is hunt it. I've done that."

"Are you sure that's all he's done?" The solicitor wasn't an old fellow, but he had old eyes. Eyes that had seen people behave badly a lot. "Have you seen every inch of these acres?"

Not lately. "Yes. And it has a purpose. To keep wild."

"The Crown won't consider that *use*." Leaning back in his worn leather chair, the fellow didn't look like he thought it was a use either. "When every British acre is stretched to hold more and more crops?

When every farmer grows turnips because it will, oddly enough, grow more wheat? What have your lands done for Britain?"

"It's not as though the King still hunts in St. James' Park."

"No one is challenging him for that."

Jesper stared at the man's ink-stained fingers. "His Grace has great confidence in you."

"My thanks." The man looked unmoved.

"So on that basis, I assume you are good at this work."

"I am good at my work," the man said in utter calmness, "because I do not worry myself with what is right or wrong; only with what the law will decide."

Jesper didn't think that charming, but he didn't need charm.

"Then I will leave you to it, Mr. Highland. I must return home, but when I can, I will come back to London; and if you will, have any papers ready for both."

"I can have a letter ready for you in an hour for the handling of your money in the five per cents. Finding and answering the writ will take more time."

This was agony. He *had* to see Eleanor. He was hollow without her.

But if he could sign something that would at least give her the power to direct her own fate should he drop dead on the ride home, he must do it.

"Very well. In an hour, Mr. Highland."

"If you please, Sir John," the solicitor said, watching Jesper pace along one end of the room, "allow me to call my carriage for you. You will be more comfortable with His Grace until I have papers to sign."

"Thank you. Do that."

Mr. Highland never rushed. Outside his library, he found one of his footmen. "Send for the carriage and bring up some tea. Pointless work is thirsty work."

Then he turned back to his seat, ignoring that Jesper must have heard the whole exchange.

"Wonderful confidence," muttered Jesper.

But standing over the man would accomplish nothing; muscles

had no effect on legal proceedings. And if he returned to the Gravenshire house, he might pack and prepare to ride home.

Jesper scratched his chin. Too bad the journey was so long; his lady would probably prefer to see him smooth-shaven, if she was glad to see him at all.

CHAPTER 38

"So you're saying that the cobbler won't make shoes for the Carvers, because Mrs. Carver accused his wife of stealing a sheet."

Resolutely not thinking about how much she missed Jesper, Eleanor was managing to have tremendous fun. She had worn her second most exciting hat, the one patterned after the French Queen's garden fancy.

Rebby Coombes had put ribbons in her hair, and Eleanor felt daring, and quite fashionable.

She was far too fine for just the Roseford inn, but that was where she was enjoying a plate of stew and listening to gossip. If her bed was lonely, she'd simply avoid it. And the inn was full of news.

"Gossip is an awful habit," Mrs. Peterborough put in beside her. Probably for Willa's benefit.

"Yes, it is," Eleanor nodded soberly. "Now, Mrs. Coombes. If the magistrate ruled in favor of Mrs. Shore, then why is Mr. Shore holding a grudge?"

"He's ashamed, isn't he? What an awful thing to say about his wife. They're too poor to have much, and the Carvers as much as hung out a handbill saying so."

The innkeeper maintained as much of the wide, straw-scattered, mud-scraped floor between him and the table of women as possible. The day had grown long, and a farmer or two had put in his head for a pint, including the unmarried Mr. Hatch.

Most of the villagers, Eleanor thought, would be at home. Which meant it was the perfect chance for her to learn all about them.

But her fun was cut short when the iron-bound door swung open and admitted a crew full of Roseford stablehands.

"We can go," said Mrs. Peterborough, sensing Eleanor's mood shift.

"Not at all. They can be here; I can be here." She might be taking this new Parliamentarianism too far, thought Eleanor; but then she wanted to try as much as possible.

She could be what Sir John wanted. She *would* be what Sir John wanted. As soon as he came home. And she told him she loved him.

The feeling among the stablehands seemed to be one of little enthusiasm for her presence as well. None of them nodded to her, just threw themselves down at a table where the innkeeper gave them tankards with no words spoken.

"Men here don't say much, do they?" Eleanor asked under her breath.

"Do the men in London talk more?" asked Mrs. Coombes, all astonishment. She looked ready to depart for London this minute.

About to expound on the failings of London men, Eleanor's opportunity was squashed when the door opened again and admitted one.

"Pox and perdition," Eleanor muttered. It was Mr. Taggart.

He stopped dramatically just inside the door, openly staring at her. Mrs. Peterborough *shooed* him on his way.

He went as far as a table in the shadows where he could lurk and watch Eleanor as he sipped his ale.

What a stage actor he is, Eleanor thought.

He made his way through half a plate of the admirable stew, and an entire tankard of ale, his baleful glances growing more and more obvious till Eleanor was in danger of laughing aloud.

She looked his way once, and immediately knew it was a mistake. He took it for a signal.

"You must wonder," he said, pushing himself off his bench, "why I'm still here."

Ugh. The women around her stared, wide-eyed, at the effrontery of the man; the men in the inn were silent. Especially the stablehands, all studying the inside of their tankards, while this unwanted man spoke to her *in public.*

It was more than Eleanor's newfound Parliamentarianism would allow.

"Absolutely no one here is wondering that," she said without rising, hoping he'd quiet himself.

He didn't. "Everyone *must* wonder," he went on, slowly moving to the center of the smoky, thatched-roof room.

To Eleanor's shock, it was a Roseford stablehand who answered. "Nope," loud enough for all to hear. The fellow took a deep drink from his tankard while his mates laughed.

"I'm not ashamed of my feelings anymore." What had Taggart been drinking before he'd come here? "You've taught me that, Lady Grantley. Your feelings have freed mine."

Eleanor would *have* to say something.

"Unintended, I assure you." She tried to turn back to her food.

"We can't hide how we feel," he hissed from his spot in the middle of the room.

"You have astonishing faith in your charm. It's unfounded."

Most of the inn sat frozen, silent.

One stablehand snickered into his ale.

Mr. Taggart turned his way, eyes widened in the gloom. "Passion is no reason to laugh, young man. Lady Grantley's feelings toward me behind closed doors earlier today were very different."

Eleanor felt herself go pale. And the stomach-aches that had plagued her in London made a return appearance.

Men like this, she realized. She'd had stomach-aches because of men like this.

Before she knew *what* to say to the villagers who had all just heard this London gentleman accuse her of cuckolding her husband—

—to her greater shock, another stablehand leaned back in his chair.

"Nah, that don't sound like her," he rocked his chair on two legs thoughtfully and announced to Mr. Taggart and the room.

"Aye, it really don't," and their agreement went round the table. "Can't picture it." "Don't *want* to picture it." "Oh la, don't touch my hat, love you madly though, London man," one said in a high falsetto voice, and they all laughed.

Despite wanting to hit that last one with a fan she didn't have, Eleanor felt her insides calm.

They were laughing at Mr. Taggart, not *her*.

She was so relieved she laid her hand over Mrs. Coombes'. It had felt for a moment like nowhere in the world was safe from the type of judgment she thought she'd left behind in London society.

Sir John—Jesper—had been right. She didn't have to hold everything in. Not all the time. Not among the right sort of people.

When the inn's door opened and a red-eyed, greasy-haired man staggered in, the laughter died down and Mrs. Coombes' hand clenched under hers.

"Mr. Coombes?" Eleanor guessed under her breath. The woman beside her just nodded.

* * *

WHEN JESPER RODE his horse into the stable, there was no one there but the old steward.

"Mr. Price." Jesper's horse was nearly lathered, he'd ridden so far so fast. He winced as he dismounted. To hell with his heart; it was his knees that would be the end of him. "Where is everyone?"

"The lads went down t' th' inn," said the steward with the kind of shrug he'd given to everything since Jesper's father had died.

"What about Lady Grantley?"

"What about her?"

He was a grizzled old man, but built like a wall. Jesper had to heave to turn him around. "Mr. Price. What about Lady Grantley? Is she in the house?"

"Don't know. Haven't seen her since she had that London gentleman caller." Price's stubbled lip curled, saying *caller* like *dropping.*

"What caller? Was she all right?" Had Faircombe ignored his warning? Surely it wasn't Burden.

"Didn't catch his name. 'Spose I should have, if his bastard is going to be getting your father's house," the steward grumbled.

Jesper had to stop himself with the man splayed against the side of a horse's stall.

He took a deep breath.

"For the sake of thirty years' service to my father," he said, "you have one chance to say that differently."

"Look," said the steward, disgust splaying all his features, "I know a man's gotta marry and all, but why couldn't you have picked a nice, quiet woman you'd know wouldn't stray?"

"Wrong answer." Swinging down a fresh saddle, Jesper heaved it onto the back of the quiet gelding Eleanor had ridden. "You'll need a new position, Mr. Price."

"I'm done." His shrug made clear he knew he'd been done for a long while. "But your father must spin in his grave to see a woman carrying on with a cow-eyed puppet, right in his own home."

Cow eyes?

"Taggart," muttered Jesper, backing the gelding out of his box and swinging himself astride without another word to the discharged steward.

CHAPTER 39

$\mathcal{N}$o one was laughing now.

Coombes had stopped by the women's table, his glare fixed on his wife. "Get home, ya corn-faced fussock."

Rebby hadn't budged. She sat next to Eleanor with her lips so tight they were a thin line, and didn't even acknowledge her husband.

That seemed to enrage him. "I said get home, ya rag pot!"

He tried to reach across the table to grab Rebby's arm. Across *Eleanor*.

Eleanor shot to her feet.

"Mr. Coombes," she said with the sort of tone that cut glass in a London parlor, "you are not welcome or wanted."

He had trouble focusing his eyes on her. It was not coincidence, apparently, that he smelled like a brewery. "Don't care what ya want," he managed to string together. "You! Get home."

"Mrs. Coombes doesn't have to go home if she doesn't wish." Out of the corner of her eye Eleanor could see the flush on Mrs. Coombes' neck. This was embarrassing for her.

Eleanor wouldn't claim to have been in her shoes, but she understood humiliation.

Mrs. Coombes looked up at Eleanor and mouthed *I'm sorry, my lady*, just as the drunken man leaned over to grab her upper arm. He had a habit, noted the detail-gathering part of Eleanor's mind, of leaving marks where they wouldn't show.

On sweet Rebby Coombes who worked hard, protected her robin's nest, and never hurt a soul.

Eleanor leaned as close as she could into that smelly, sticky face, and tried to let the inner rage show that had rattled her father.

"Let go. Now."

Whether startled or frightened, his hand slipped loose, Mrs. Coombes made a little noise, and the idea that she'd been hurt ratcheted Eleanor's temper higher.

"I have had *enough* of all you men who think people must do as you say because of the contents of your breeches!"

Mrs. Peterborough put her hands over Willa's ears.

The table of stablehands gave each other another round of chuckles and shoves.

Eleanor, shoulders squared, took another step forward; Coombes stepped back.

"You callous, beer-soaked brute. Take your fat hands and your greasy face and *get—out!*"

Some part of her words penetrated his beer-fuddled brain, and slowly, like a brick crumbling, Coombes' face crumbled from astonishment into fury.

His curse startled Eleanor, as did the way he grabbed *her* by the arm, and tossed her out of his path.

Everyone in the inn gasped.

Mrs. Peterborough shot to her feet. And Rebby Coombes.

And the entire table of stablehands, knocking their benches backwards.

Coombes moved fast, clearly from habit, raising a hand to swat it backwards across her face.

Eleanor's fist clenched from some instinct. She gave that instinct free rein. Rage felt clean; it felt *good*. She'd drive a fist right into that belly if she had to. For herself, for Rebby. She had had *enough*.

She saw his hand lift, but Eleanor wasn't afraid anymore. Not of spiders, or cold baths, or being tossed away. She knew she didn't deserve it.

Before she could swing, she felt a big, warm hand close around her hand, making her fist huge. And a slab of hard warmth at her back that could only be—

"You're back!"

Forgetting to strike, she spun in her husband's arms, and threw her arms round his neck, right there in public view of the entire inn.

"Aren't we brawling? I always wanted to see you let go," he murmured, in that voice she loved.

"Jesper," she whispered against his neck, huddled under her hat, where only he would hear. She felt the softness in his face, the smile just for her.

And she clung to him with all her might, barely registering the mutterings of the stablemen at their table. "Wasn't expecting that." "Of her, you mean." "Yah, that's a shock."

With one arm around her, Jesper looked over her shoulder at Coombes. "I'm in a good mood, Coombes. Lucky for you, by the time I can attend to you, you'll be gone. Likely, oh, five minutes."

Coombes' face went through a remarkable set of expressions, Eleanor saw out of the corner of her eye.

With her rage subsiding, she felt a little wobbly. Rage was a wonderful thing, she mused, but a husband like hers was even better.

"Four minutes," said her husband, and beckoned his stablehands. "See that he goes. He takes nothing. My lady, I must speak to you."

"That's a short minute!" Coombes sputtered as the baronet led his lady to the inn's low door.

"I don't have a watch," he said, and led out his wife.

* * *

MOLLY TOOK a step toward the door as Roseford's baronet and lady went out, hands locked together.

"Sit down," said Mrs. Peterborough.

Molly looked torn, though probably half from an interest in

serving her lady, half from an interest in what would happen next. "But what if my lady wants—"

"You've no sense at all," said Mrs. Peterborough with disgust. "Sit down. We're all going to stay *right* here."

* * *

"You're not hurt." Jesper said it so he'd believe it.

Eleanor seemed well enough, and the way she had lit from within at the sight of him would stay with him all his life. She'd glowed, and melted into him as though she'd been waiting for him every second he'd been gone, the way he'd been waiting for her.

He hoped he wasn't about to put that light out. He had to talk to her. Now.

As long as she wasn't hurt.

"Not at all. Jesper!" He loved the sound of that. She said it like a secret. "I'm so glad you came home."

"Of course. I didn't leave you for long." It hit him what that must have felt like. Of course she would be alarmed by her only family *leaving* her. "I'm back. I came back as soon as I could."

Cuddling her against him as they walked, he nonetheless took her a few steps away from the inn, out along the road. This conversation was only for them.

"I missed you so." The words just flew out of her, and Jesper wanted to catch and keep all of them. "And that Mr. Taggart. Pox and perdition! He called at Roseford, can you imagine? You were right about him all along, I must tell you."

"I know." He'd seen Taggart slipping out the back door as soon as he'd come in. Not helping Eleanor, Jesper couldn't help but notice, even in extreme need. "That must have been alarming."

"Annoying! And even after I threw him out—wait, you know?" Eleanor steadied her wide-brimmed hat, looked back up the dusty road down which she and the other Roseford women had brought a wagon. "Someone at the house told you? Is that why you came to the inn? You must know I had no interest—"

"Ssh, ssh, of course I know." Any vague thoughts that she might have preferred Taggart disappeared the moment she'd wrapped her arms around Jesper in public. "I'm simply agreeing with you, my lady. I said from the start he was cow-eyed and useless."

"You were right." She covered her mouth with one hand, but went ahead and said it. "With no balls at all."

Unable to be even an inch apart from her for another second, Jesper swept her up in his arms and swung her around, laughing so hard he shook them both. "Much more vehement agreement, my lady, and this marriage will spiral into a hell for both—"

"*Jesper.*" She flung her arms tight around his neck again, this time simply holding onto him for dear life.

He'd thought himself overpowered with feeling when he'd seen that man raising his fist to Eleanor. It was dwarfed by the feeling of her arms around him, and all her emotion in his name.

"I'm glad I arrived when I did." Though it would have been a sight to see if she'd gotten into a brawl with Coombes and his stable-hands. Gravenshire was right; Eleanor would kick Death himself in the teeth. Letting her slide to her feet, he kissed her temple.

She undid the ribbon that tied under her chin.

"Whoa, madam." He was not prepared for such precipitous action. "Are you taking off your public hat? In public?"

She tried to make a joke, those rosebud lips wobbling a little. "I know how you love it when I undress out of doors—"

He swept her close again. He couldn't resist her. Her hat billowed against his back.

She whispered against his shoulder this time. "Jesper, I never told you I lo—"

"My lady," he cut her off, though the hurt places she'd patched inside him hungered for her to say it. "I must tell you what I've done to you."

She shook her head against his shoulder. "Nothing bad."

"Yes, bad."

He tried to put her away, just a few inches, so they could speak. Eleanor just held on tighter.

The feathers on her hat tickled the back of his neck. His eyes closed. He would have to confess like this.

"Eleanor, that night at Ranelagh—afterwards, that is, at Gravenshire House. I—" How to explain how he'd charged out of the Duke's rooms, head swimming at their conversation, and found himself waking at the bottom of the stairs? "His Grace called physicians. I had a fever, you see, years ago, but sometimes the room spins, sometimes I cannot stand. It's my heart, my love. It isn't quite... whole."

CHAPTER 40

Slowly she loosened herself from clinging around his neck. Withdrew until she could see his face.

He had no idea what she was thinking, or if she was thinking. So many shocks one after the other, it was too much. But he couldn't wait another minute. He'd waited too long.

"I ought to have died already, they thought." The color left her face at that, and her mouth fell open. He rushed on. "But I haven't, obviously. I just—I went right to you. I had this driving need, I didn't even think, I just felt, *marry her*. As though I had to do it. And you agreed— you *agreed*. But I wasn't—It wasn't honest, Eleanor. You're *always* honest. You didn't know, and you should have. You might have married some London gentleman—"

"Who?" she said in a voice like an icy whip. "A ball-less wonder like Mr. Taggart?"

She did cut to the truth. "Someone who wasn't *me*, Eleanor." He took her hands in his; they felt cold. "No titled lady deserves a husband who could die and leave her homeless at any moment."

He could see her heart pounding in her throat.

Could see her reaching to understand.

"Doesn't every woman have that?" she said slowly, one hand sliding up to stroke the streak of white at his temple.

His own heart started to pound, treacherous thing, at the idea that she might find a way to live with this. With him. "Plenty of ladies with husbands even older than me," he agreed, "but not without knowing the odds they faced."

"Some of whom have dowries," Eleanor nodded, "which I did not have. But that was hardly your fault."

"It was my *fault* that I didn't give you the *choice!* You might have found a husband—not Taggart—" he would forever hear her words for *that* one, "someone with much tidier hair and better clothes who keeps more distance from the cows."

Those dark eyes focused on him until he felt that, like under Lord Dunsby's microscope, every part and piece of him had been minutely inspected. He fell quiet, waiting for her slicing sentence.

"I might have liked the choice," Eleanor finally nodded, "but what good would it have done? I was always going to fall in love with you."

Yes, she could deliver a lightning strike like no one else. And she didn't even have a fan.

"I want to believe that." Hoarse, hopeful, he let himself gather her into his arms again.

The sunlight had dimmed, he vaguely realized, because clouds had covered the sun. Gray clouds, neither light nor dark, with the barest promise of life-giving rain.

Her arms clung around his waist, and Jesper thought how familiar that had become, and how desperately dear.

"Are you all right?" He whispered it into her hair.

"I wish *you* were all right." She wouldn't let go of him enough to let him see her face.

"I should have told you before." Could he make this lighter for her? "Even like this. On a public road."

"Anywhere. You are all that matters to me. And the idea that I could lose you, lose everything—"

"I went to London to settle money on you. You'll never want for a home."

At that she pulled back a little, moved a slender fist to pound his chest. Then clearly thought better of it, as if her tiny fist could hurt his heart.

"*You're* my home, you great oaf."

Hearing his own thoughts come back to him this way made Jesper wonder how one man could possibly get so lucky. Three days in London, and he'd literally run into the woman who made him feel whole.

"But I know you mean Roseford." She pulled away a little, looking back toward the manor, hiding her face even without the hat.

"I mean you. You're everything to me, Eleanor. But about my heart —for you, whatever time we have... even if it's only one more day. Will it be enough?"

The warm, damp air wrapped around them like a kiss, delivered a raindrop. Then another.

No one had followed them out of the inn; they were alone in the dusty road, her looking back toward their house, him looking at her.

The raindrops spattered her hair, her shoulders, leaving stains here and there. When she turned back, he didn't know what was rain and what was tears.

"It's not enough," she told him, "but it's like the rain, Jesper. It's what we have."

* * *

THEY TOOK advantage of the long, slow walk back to the manor to look in the trees beside the road, and the ditches.

"What's interesting about a dry ditch?" Eleanor wouldn't let go of his hand. No one could make her. And why should she care if someone could see?

"It's what's not there. The frogs," Jesper said, a little grimly. "There's no water for them. And those few raindrops won't have helped."

Perhaps not, but they had helped steady Eleanor. Perhaps she'd learned something other London ladies her age had not. With any luck, droughts ended, birds made new nests, and time ticked on. What mattered more than any one moment was the overall color of life. She wished her husband had confided in her, but he wasn't perfect, and she'd known that all along. She'd wanted kindness; she'd wanted to be loved. She could see that now. And he'd given her that. She could forgive him anything.

Though by the time they had reached Roseford's kitchen door, she also realized that no one else was coming, and that her husband looked gray and worn.

"You must want to bathe. Here, the washing tubs are in the laundry room. You can bathe in there."

"Out behind the stables there's a—"

The buzzing under Eleanor's skin was new. Was this how panic felt? Just at the idea of him leaving her again. She wasn't having it.

"No. And I won't have you carrying buckets up and down stairs," she told him, "yet clearly all the men are occupied in the village."

"The women too." He stretched and sighed, his big bones cracking in his shoulders. "I have been riding *so long*, Eleanor."

The little silver thrill she got from hearing him say her name hadn't gone away. She hoped it never would.

She hoped she had long, long years to find out.

"Yes. You smell like you have," she said in her crisp way, trying to get herself back on course.

On the one hand, she felt foolish fussing over such a big, strong man; on the other, she wanted to wrap him in quilts and not let him out.

Would she ever be of just one mind about her husband?

Right now, for instance, she both wanted to wash away the horse smell, and wanted to climb in the barrel with him.

The latter urge would have won, but she wouldn't have fit.

He barely seemed to notice her flaming cheeks as he stripped out of his clothes, heaping them to one side before unselfconsciously lowering himself into the half-barrel of wash water.

"*Yaggh*," he groaned as the water hit his tender parts. "Cold baths for the wicked, I see."

"Soon I'll have you sweeping up spiders."

"Is there any of Mrs. Peterborough's soap?" He yawned, and Eleanor felt the return of her rising panic.

This time, it threatened to swamp her.

She clutched the edge of the barrel, offering him the bowl of soap in a shaking hand.

"Whoa. My lady." Water sluiced off his skin as he half-rose. "Are you not well?"

"Are *you* well?" Her fingers itched to check his breathing. "How do I know? Will you tell me?"

"What, every minute of the day?" His voice was gentle, even if the words weren't.

His beautiful eyes. It would only be good manners to tell him the truth. "When I look at you, I can't bear the thought that it could be the last time."

He didn't owe her apologies. She could not constantly flutter about after him. He would still do what he did, his strong body in service to his lands and tenants, and she would simply have to cope.

She didn't expect him to nod, his eyes still locked on hers. For a moment, the wear in his features looked like age. "My lady, I feel the same way."

"What? How many times must I tell you I'm perfectly healthy?"

"So was Mrs. Wright."

The heavy weight in his body as he sloshed backwards in the water told Eleanor how the village woman's death pressed him.

"Mrs. Wright." Eleanor had had a busy few days of gathering all the village news. "Mrs. Hedges took the baby, isn't that right? And Mr. Hatch is plowing his fields. I thought the widower was well."

"He isn't *well*, his wife is dead!" Jesper scooped a handful of water through his hair, shook the droplets all over. "He can't be well. How could he?"

Eleanor took a deep breath. This marriage business was a constant cavalcade of challenges, but at least they were sharing them now.

She gave him the soap, and leaned against the barrel's wet edge, chin on her hands. Her gown was already damp.

"But I'm not going to die. Well, eventually."

"And I'm not going to die either," Jesper matched her tone, "other than eventually."

"That's not the same! Women do die sometimes, from childbirth. I suppose no one ever thinks it will be them, but we know."

"And I could not bear to lose you. Eleanor, I truly think I couldn't bear it." He fixed her with a lion eye, water dripping from its lashes. "I think just the idea drove me a little senseless."

"Yes. I can easily imagine." She could. "But I think... I would feel better now, than I would have a week ago, because I know Mrs. Peterborough and everyone else would be here to help me bear it. I have been too much alone in my life, and everything just seems... easier, with other people. Does that sound foolish?"

He was silent so long Eleanor might have thought him judging her again, except that she could see in his face how seriously he was listening.

"You're right," he finally said, and she let out the breath she was holding. He needn't always agree, but it was still new, and still bliss. And on this, it was important. "I couldn't bear the loneliness when my father died. So much so, I charged off to London. But it was easier, with people to help. Though I never had to bear what you bore. It made me furious from the start, the way those men spoke to you. And that Burden pustule."

"Oh, *pustule!*" Eleanor had to grin. "You *have* been spending too much time with me."

"Never enough, my lady." He stroked her cheek with a dripping hand. "That is my point. It will never be enough."

CHAPTER 41

S
he closed her eyes and pressed his hand closer.

"Then a new line to our bargain." Each crease of his palm made its own pattern on her face. Nothing else would ever be like it. "We agree to care for Roseford, to produce an heir, and to survive no matter what comes."

"We do agree. How does that help?"

"I don't know how it helps," she said as honestly as she could. "But it does."

"Mmm." His thumb stroking over her lower lip soothed her inner worries, a little. "You seem to know more about it. I'm willing to follow your lead. I find myself more complicated than I thought. I never expected to so fear for you, and still crave you."

He craved her? "Sir, it would be extremely inappropriate for me to explain how I have been dreaming about you, night and day, since you left."

"Then do it!" He shoved himself upright and, as soon as he was out of the tub and on his feet, with water still running off his bare body, swept her up in his arms. "I would very much like to hear all about the inappropriateness."

"Jesper, you can't!" Eleanor's genuine worry spilled out past the way her arm clutched around his neck. "What if you—"

"My lady, imagine that you conceive a child of ours in the next thirty minutes."

"Thirty minutes?"

"Maybe sixty. Seems fast. Then do I have your leave to tell you *you can't* for the nine months after?"

He was carrying her straight through the empty house and up the stairs.

His heart thudded, evenly, strongly, just under her cheek. She felt his comparison wasn't fair, but had a hard time finding the flaw in his reasoning when he hitched her higher in his arms so he could kiss her nose, her forehead, even her lips as he carried her up. "I don't think it's the same," was all she could manage, a little breathless as he deposited her on her floor.

"I think it is," and he kicked closed the door.

A fluttering flash of color caught his eye. Two birds flew up into the gray sky from the nest hung at the window.

"He did find a mate," Jesper said with a little smile.

He was so beautiful standing in her room with the sunlight on him. It took Eleanor's breath away to think he loved her too.

She had to look down to pick at the ties to her bodice. So she was surprised when his hands covered hers.

"Let me," and she was enthralled by the look of his long, strong fingers, so worn by rocks and trees, delicately unraveling the ties to her bodice, then her stays.

The noise he made in the back of his throat as her chemise came free and his hands reached to cup her softness made Eleanor think he was through playing the ladies'-maid. But instead his hands spun her in place, untied the ribbons to her overskirt, then petticoat.

Shyly she ducked, one hand across her chest, to pick up the skirts.

He made the noise again. "My lady," he said with a true quiet pain, "I've waited so long to see you like this. Please. For me?"

She felt her cheeks flame. Why did she let him do this to her? Or why couldn't she simply ease into the comfort of being a simple bare animal, as he did?

"I... don't think I will ever have your comfort with being brazen," she confessed, even as she tried, sliding her hand up her neck, ignoring how it bared her breasts.

"Perhaps. I do like to see you try."

Her reward was that he wrapped her again in his arms, tempting her with intoxicating kiss after kiss that tasted just like their first one.

"What is it you want from me?" He wanted to reward her effort, clearly, his hands spreading across her bare back to hold her close.

"Not to leave," she said instantly.

That shadow crossed his face again, and she realized why she'd seen it before.

"I don't mean for you to promise what you can't," she rushed to add. "But if you're alive and with me, be *with* me. Sleep here. Wake here."

A shred of a smile came back. "I suppose it would be asking too much for you to sleep one night under the trees with me."

"You know I'll try if you wish."

"Because we made a bargain?"

"Because I love you." She pulled him down to have one of those soul-stealing kisses again.

His hungry hands took over then, lifting her onto the bed, shoving aside her coverlets, rolling her over him, under, everywhere as he touched, tasted, explored every inch of her body. His kisses brushed the insides of her elbows, the small of her back, even the tips of her toes. She was so swept away by his eager open hunger that she returned touch for touch, brushing her lips against his chin, his navel, the complex interlocking bones of his knees, and in an especially brave moment, the hardness he'd shown for her since the moment they'd laid down.

She wasn't expecting his indrawn breath, the way he froze in anticipation, telling her without words that there was more, that she could give him more. She found herself kissing him there the way she kissed his lips, giving her softness to his hardness, cradling him in her soft lower lip until the noise he made sounded like an animal ready to charge.

"Please," he said, putting his hands under her arms and drawing her up with a harsh, guttural rasp. "Please, my lady. I need more."

"Have I ever told you no?"

Wrapping himself in her arms, her hair, her legs around his waist, he sank into her with a groan that seemed to echo in her ears. Relief from hunger, from loneliness, from the hopelessness he'd been carrying—she heard it in his voice, and finally understood why he wanted to hear her.

They weren't completely alike. She wouldn't walk through the house wet and naked. But alone, here, in an empty house?

Encouraging him deeper with the press of her feet, she raised her hips to his and tried to meet him thrust for thrust. When he braced himself over her, arms locking in muscled pillars, his face harsh with the hunger she felt too, she pushed into him again, and again, rolling herself against him until she felt like the pleasure might burn her up from the inside out.

And while words weren't possible, she let out her breath, her voice, and her moans, soft as they were, seemed to hit him like anvils.

Every little moan drew an answering groan from him, and a thrust that would be punishing if she hadn't wanted it so. When she threw her head back, a cry wrenched from her by a particularly deep, perfect thrust, he gasped as if the air had been punched out of him.

"Please," he whispered with the desperation of a starving man, and as he wrapped the two of them closer, she tried to give him everything he needed.

"Jesper!" Her eyes flew open as he thrust deeply, over and over, the two of them working as hard as they could to make one body for as long as it could last.

"My lady. There's no one to hear."

His rough, urgent whisper and the way he slid his hands under her hips to pull her tightly to him was like the hearth fire had exploded to engulf the entire room. The heat of him, and the burning core of her, struck so perfectly again, and again, and again, that Eleanor was lost.

Her cry was loud enough even for his ears, the sound keening and rising until with a little scream, she gave in to the pulsing, burning explosion inside her.

Dimly she heard his wrenching moan as she forced him to join her.

It seemed like wave after wave of creation and destruction, fire and coals and more fire till Eleanor was wrung out, limp in his arms, and he collapsed half over her, gasping heavily.

Her hand crept around his throat to feel for his pulse.

With an exhausted, understanding smile, his tangled hair tossed back and she could see his open lion eyes again. "Still here," he assured her, knowing what she was doing.

"Me too," she gasped, wondering when she would be able to breathe again even as she drifted into sleep.

CHAPTER 42

"There's a peculiar lack of servants," Jesper noted later as the two of them, bathed again and mostly properly dressed, ventured again into the kitchen.

"Yes, it's almost as though they wanted us to be alone," Eleanor observed drily as Jesper dug in a covered basket for the day's bread.

He made a little noise of satisfaction as he uncovered four fresh muffins.

"I begin to see the appeal," Eleanor said as she ladled out two dishes of the porridge at the side of the hearth.

"Of this?" Jesper felt guilty for subjecting anyone to more meals like this. What a coward he'd been, unable to face the woman even to eat. Those London lords, they'd made finding a wife sound like picking up a pebble. Jesper had found it to change his life.

"Of listening to you make those noises," Eleanor said, biting into a muffin and chewing it with a bold little grin that Jesper knew no one else would ever get to see.

Her hair tumbled forward over her shoulder; she not only had no hat, her hair wasn't even dressed. It was a shocking display of inappropriateness and Jesper loved it.

He grinned back.

"I think," she said after swallowing a delicate bite, "that we should eat, then go back to our room—" apparently that room was theirs now, "—and I will listen to many more of those noises until we both fall asleep. And then the same tomorrow."

Staying in the house had never sounded so appealing.

"As long as you wish," he said, touching his fingertip to her buttered bread and then to the tip of her nose. "Though within a few days, I must return to London."

"Why must we go to London?" Her dark eyes and all their focus turned to this new bit of news.

Well. Apparently *they* were going to London.

Loneliness had no chance against his lady.

"Eh, only Faircombe." When she sat up straighter, he waved her still. "Some tussle of law. He has been hunting our land and thinks to claim it. The solicitor says we've an even chance; they might think him frivolous, or the court might grant his claims. Says we haven't done anything with the land."

"What? You have done *everything* with the land!" Eleanor was clearly paying no heed to his false calm. "You keep it safe!"

"Not safe enough." Her faith was cheering, but courts weren't swayed by faith. "I wouldn't mind it, my lady, but it makes me feel like I've failed my family. My father."

"You have failed *no* one!" Yes, her temper was definitely cheering.

"Even you." She also brought out his honesty. "Faircombe made out to London that I am just a pig farmer in a borrowed coat, and I've shown him right." How wise had it been to ignore advice that came from Mrs. Peterborough *and* a duke?

"You haven't failed me by being a pig farmer. My love isn't that fragile." She had that edge back to her tone that told Jesper that some London men might be in for a few words, and her eyes shot sparks. "I thought I was to be your partner? Or was that just flowery courting?"

He swallowed. "I meant it!"

"Then let me help with this! When it comes to battles of words, I ought to be able to help, or my life's been wasted. Who decides this case?"

Jesper waved his muffin. "There's a court, but it may go to the King. I hope not."

"I hope not too." Her eyes glittered with all the things she thought as she looked into the distance. "A court is just a collection of judges, sir. Judges who care about their position, and like to be right. I think I can help, if you'll trust me."

"I always have. Well, once I got over you warning me away from Lady Hortense."

She brushed that thought away as if beneath notice. "Hortense would have been a bad match for you. That was obvious. We must take a house in London, quickly, and Mrs. Peterborough will have to arrange for many of the servants to come as well. Have you the money to hire a carriage?"

Leaning forward on his elbows, he grinned. "*You* have. Nearly all my money is now in your possession."

"What?" That startled her enough to come back from wherever her mind had gone. "I cannot have property that is solely mine, not as long as we're married."

"But I can give you control of the funds, and leave them to you in my will. And I have."

Her mouth open with surprise, she grasped his hand. He squeezed hers back. "You were thinking of me that entire trip to London. I'm truly honored."

"And a long time before that."

"You have a nobility, Sir John, that... doesn't show." She let go to wave her hand around his person in a way that indicated his general inadequate appearance. "We can change London's view of that, if you're willing to do a few things you won't like."

Jesper saw exactly where this was going. "I won't like them."

"As I just said."

"Are these changes supposed to be permanent?"

"How suspicious." She reached for a pot of jam. "They haven't even happened yet."

"I have too much to do here. And I've discharged the steward."

She didn't question that. "I think your men in the stables will keep control of things for a while." Her bite dropped no crumbs, and the way she wiped her fingers afterward somehow questioned why his elbows were on the table.

He moved them. "I can't even turn my back for a day without Beardsley and Hatch barking at each other, and now Hatch is looking after Mr. Wright's field too."

"Perhaps Mr. and Mrs. Beardsley would like to come to London and help us. Mrs. Coombes may need help, and Mr. Beardsley has never been to London." She laid down the little silver spoon beside her teacup.

"How would it serve anything for Beardsley to come to London?"

His wife's eyes glittered again, this time with amusement. "Because his wife is dallying with Mr. Hatch, which is why Mr. Hatch and Mr. Beardsley are constantly at one another's throats. If the Beardsleys have a little time to themselves, perhaps they can come to some understanding regarding their marital ties."

Jesper gaped at her. "How in hell do you know that?"

He was wrong; her eyes weren't glittering, they twinkled. "The barmaid at the inn overheard the vicar lecturing Susie Shore to mind her own business when she asked him how she was expected to keep quiet about it. Molly's married sister shares a flock of chickens with that barmaid, so Molly could blame the indiscretion on the vicar, in a way, when she told me. And that, sir, is a solid chain of information."

Jesper slowly shook his head. "I was never equipped to deal with women. I never will be."

"That's all right, you do well enough with me." She patted his hand again. "And we agreed to be partners. The kind you kiss. So I'll manage this sort of thing for you."

* * *

JESPER HAD BEEN MANAGED to within an inch of his life by the time they reached Gravenshire House for a late supper.

It had been only a few short weeks, but less hurried than his first or second trip to London, and far more detailed in preparation.

By *late*, the Duke meant nine o'clock, and Jesper, used to working during daylight hours, had already eaten. Eleanor had eaten too, partly to keep him company.

And partly to keep Mrs. Willowby company.

"You'll enjoy the carriage ride?" She squeezed Mrs. Willowby's hand.

"Will we!" Mrs. Willowby's eyes fairly sparkled, and it was delightful to see the sparkle echoed in the two little girls with her.

Eleanor could see a little of their grandmother in both of them. What fun, if she could someday see a little of Jesper in a child.

"Do just as you like with it," she assured Mrs. Willowby, "and I'll see you again tomorrow for dinner."

"That you will, pet."

Eleanor smiled her gratitude, ready to face the evening knowing that her social calendar for tomorrow would be much more fulfilling.

Sir John, as she preferred to think of him in public because thinking of him as Jesper made her blush, handed her down from the coach.

She congratulated herself every day on her luck in finding him to marry; and she reminded herself to think more than twice before she made judgments. For she never would have guessed, when she was desperately looking for a man to save her from a French nunnery, that she would find him in the form of a raggedy farmer.

Who, tonight, wasn't raggedy at all.

"I thought the powder would be uncomfortable."

"How could it be uncomfortable? It's powder." Eleanor brushed away a few specks. His deep wine-purple coat had no braid, and no gold-embroidered trim; but it fit him flawlessly, from the breadth of his shoulders to the snowy cuffs at his wrists.

It was clearly *his* coat.

She preferred him without the powder, but she'd enjoyed every second of dressing his hair herself, arranging curls beside his face and then ruffling them apart with her hands, giving him the look of a harried young courtier straight from the King's palace on serious business.

His low shoes were plain, but perfectly polished, and Eleanor had the feeling that when London saw her husband's muscled thighs encased in his breeches, there would be a fashion for plainer footwear on very well-turned male legs.

"We should have bought silver buckles." She couldn't stop fussing over him. She always wanted to touch him, and now, framed as he was for London consumption, the urge was worse. If the judges did not see him as Eleanor wished them to see him, she'd feel like those generations of Grantleys in the portraits were scowling at her all the rest of her life.

"I'm already weighed down by the extravagance of the sleeve-buttons. Eleanor."

"Shh!" At the foot of the stairs into Gravenshire house, there was no time left to lecture him in proper etiquette.

"My lady." He seemed uneasy about something besides his hair. "I know our wedding wasn't all you wished—"

"I was so perturbed that day. Did I say something awful? Don't think of it now!"

"Eleanor." He took both her hands in his, and she settled before him, looking up into his beautiful eyes. "I know you could have been a duchess. A queen. You gave up a great deal to marry me."

Why did he look so serious, and at a moment like this? About their wedding? "Nothing worth having," she assured him. It was as far as she would go in a place this public, but surely he could see in her eyes that she had no regrets.

"You gave up a place in society," he said grimly. "To the point where we have no invitations, only a supper."

"In the home of a duke!" No larger affair would do. Eleanor had planned this with the Duchess of Gravenshire as carefully as any war campaign. Those gentlemen whom they most needed to think of Jesper as civilized would be here tonight, judging her husband on everything from his fingernails to his ability to eat soup.

"Nonetheless. I gave you everything I own that day, as you said, right down to my starlings' eggs. But I didn't give you this."

From his coat pocket he slipped a small pouch, and from its inky depths slid a sparkling jewel, recognizably a sheaf of good English wheat.

Each fat kernel of corn, as the farmers called it, was formed of a clear sweet ruby, and diamonds outlined its husk.

"I'm not sure what I meant it to say," her husband faltered, the stones flashing in his work-worn hand. "I wanted you to have it."

"I want to have it." Though it might be too much for public view, Eleanor brought his hands to the edge of her neckline, urging him to fasten it among the ruffles. It would stand out from the pink-and-gold pattern of her gown. It would look magnificent. "It will look as though I am married to a farmer who is not shabby at all."

"Well, you're married to a farmer, of sorts." The tension around his eyes lifted, and his fingers fastened it nimbly just where she wanted it, the back of his hand lingering only one inappropriate second against her skin. "It ought to have roses."

"Your waistcoat has roses. So do the carpets at home, and the drapes. It is good to have one—" she leaned close so only he could hear, "—*blasted* thing that doesn't have roses on it."

"My lady." He spread a hand across his chest, pretending to be shocked. "And where anyone could hear!" He wanted to kiss her, she could see it. He was only restraining himself for her.

"Don't make me laugh." She batted at him with her fan. "This will be a long evening."

"What fun."

"Do have fun. Perhaps... one-fifth as much fun as you'd like." Taking his arm, she walked with him up the steps to the Gravenshire house, where a footman waited patiently to admit them, pretending that it wasn't odd at all for a gentleman and his lady to have a protracted conversation on the pavement. "You look regal. Just keep hold of your courage and talk. No writ claiming you are feckless can win once Britain's courtiers hear you speak."

CHAPTER 43

*J*esper knew he would be rewarded when he and his lady were alone again. He was no untried boy; he could wait that long. No matter how he wished to whisk her into some quiet corner and kiss those lips.

But it was also a reward, of a sort, when Lord Burden approached him looking like a man who'd sucked lemons.

"Sir John." He didn't bow. "I know what you're doing. Putting on a masquerade for your betters, pretending you deserve to hold the King's lands."

"Lord Burden! I know what you're doing too. How knowledgeable we are." Jesper leaned a little, emphasizing he was many inches taller. "And they're my lands."

"Ha!" Burden's fake little laugh sounded like a cough. "How dare you, sir? When we all hold our lands by grant of the King."

Jesper hadn't wasted his time with the solicitor; the man might not care about ethics, but he did know the law. "An oddly outdated view for a man of your office. Have you not read Sir William Blackstone's *Commentaries*? I thought very persuasive his description of the abolition of feudal ideas of land ownership. Haven't you read it? If you object to his common heritage, he *was* knighted by the King." Jesper gestured toward the table, as if they should both sit. "Or don't you care for that? Reading books?"

To say that Lord Burden stiffened would be an understatement. His head locked into a position over his shoulders that reminded Jesper of a toad.

Jesper merely nodded, taking his seat opposite, by his lady. The table was too wide for him to be expected to converse further with Burden; and that too was by design.

He couldn't imagine having to worry about every detail of a night like this, much less the dozen more evenings like this his wife had arranged with the help of the Duchess.

But he paid close attention and did his part; given his lady's work on behalf of him and his holdings, he could do no less.

Their holdings, he reminded himself. He wasn't alone in this.

* * *

ANOTHER MAN MIGHT BE APPALLED by Eleanor's social capabilities.

Jesper just marveled. She charmed him into saying clever things within hearing of the judges. She ruthlessly flattered the ones awestruck by the Duke's precedence and sympathized with those who felt out of place.

If she dropped little comments here and there that made no sense to *him*, but drew from some knowledge she'd gained by some connection she didn't bother to describe, he left her to it, with thanks.

It crossed his mind to ask the Duke if he'd known Eleanor was his match, back when the man had started him thinking about marrying her. But he didn't really want to know.

He bowed as His Grace approached, and both of them glanced toward his wife.

"Your father would have adored her," the Duke said suddenly, making Jesper blink.

"Yes."

"I wish you'd met sooner. I wish your happiness had convinced him to try again."

Jesper glanced over at the Duchess, regally inclining her head over the table of sherry with other ladies.

"I think that's for some men," he said quietly, for after all, it wasn't really a discussion for a public place. "Perhaps you have a bigger heart. I think my father and I were made of different cloth. Only one woman will ever do for me."

His father's lack of interest in remarrying made complete sense to Jesper now. His father had lived as he'd wished. He needn't ever have spoken of his love for it to be everything to him. Jesper knew exactly how he'd felt.

"It's different," the Duke admitted, fond gaze resting on his wife. "But it's wonderful. I hope you've reconciled yourself, boy, if you ever find yourself in a like position, that you needn't live out your days alone."

Jesper didn't have words to explain his bargain with Eleanor, or their trust in each other to keep it. If something happened to him, he trusted Eleanor to go on with her life, and he would do the same. But he, at least, would never marry again.

It was a kind of peace he couldn't explain. Not to the Duke, anyway.

"You've set a wonderful example," he diverted the question with a smile, deciding this was one of those rare moments when bluntness wasn't best.

* * *

A MUTTON NECK, boiled rabbits, and a chicken in curry sauce later, and Eleanor was already looking forward to returning to Roseford.

It appalled her to think that her husband had felt the need to hold back his wedding gift. Whatever she had said or done, she promised herself silently, she would never do or say again.

But clearly his confidence in their union was not shaken, and the heavy jewel pressing against her was proof of that.

Let them claim he was foolish. Let them mock his work in mud.

He was twice the man any of them would ever be, and more than she'd ever hoped to marry.

When he cornered her behind a massive walnut chest, her arms went gratefully around his waist.

"I can't do this for weeks," he muttered against her ear, his lips teasing the soft spot there that he had discovered made her knees weak.

"You will."

"I know." Always hungry for more of her, he bent and kissed one eyebrow, a gesture she felt was unbearably sweet. "You've saved me, you know. Without Faircombe's or your father's support, Burden doesn't seem to know how to convince anyone. And the rest of the gentlemen here can't call me an oaf." One hand slid around to the small of her back; she felt its heat even through all the layers of her clothing. "Even the Duke of Talbourne won't support Faircombe's claim; nothing to do with me, Talbourne just hates the King. Of course, the court must still rule."

"This sort of thing is decided long before it reaches the court. Many of the judges are here tonight, and when they talk of you—and they will—they will not call you a pig farmer in a borrowed coat." If she arched her back, perhaps he could reach that spot at the base of her throat.

"I despise that way of deciding matters of law."

"Sir, I'm with you." As his lips traveled upward to capture hers, she sighed. This was terribly improper, and she had to admit, she loved it.

When they emerged, prepared to survive a much duller hour than they wanted by picking up play sticks with the remainder of the Duke's guests, Lord Burden, still lurking about, took the chance to land one more blow.

"There's something unseemly about a man blatantly desiring his wife."

Jesper seemed to choke on thin air, and though Eleanor felt she needed to check and assure herself that the folds of her gown were all lying properly and the styling of her hair had not moved, Jesper just laughed and laughed and laughed until Burden simply left without bidding the Duke farewell.

* * *

SOME OF THE servants engaged in London for the duration may have been of the same feeling as Lord Burden; Eleanor had the feeling they whispered behind her back when they saw her husband's clothing scattered in her rooms.

But she didn't care. She didn't want to be without him ever again, and delighted in how often he said he felt the same.

"It's peculiar how comfortable this is," he said, one fingertip brushing at his own powdered hair. "You don't wish me to keep it, though, surely."

"Oh." She sighed as her eyes traveled his length. "Not the powdered hair, but the clothes. They do things, sir. For me and for you."

He still had no valet, preferring to let Eleanor dress his hair if she pleased, and leave it if not.

So Eleanor slid off his shoes, then his stockings, taking the chance to stroke one palm down his very masculine shin.

He went from tired to tightly focused in a moment. "Are you teasing me?"

"Did you not tease me all night?"

"No, that was touching you. And kissing you," he admitted, as Eleanor unbuckled the knees of his breeches for him before taking her favorite spot on his knee.

"It was teasing." Returning the favor, she kissed the column of his sun-browned throat.

"No, it would be teasing if I weren't willing to carry through. I would have been happy to carry through. But no, you would have complained that we were in a *public place*."

"I thought you only accosted ladies out of doors."

"You may be right." Surging up under her, he carried her over the small space to the bed and, putting her down on it, began to roll off one of her silk stockings. "Though I would take up accosting a lady indoors if you wanted to stay in London."

"Why, because I have been *allowed* to come crawling back to London society and attend a few dinners, courtesy of Her Grace's intervention?" Eleanor rolled her eyes. "Yes, what a pleasure it has been. I am transported. I may faint."

"If you ever change your mind, my lady. Only say so, and it's done."

Rebby Coombes seemed to enjoy London, and mostly because of her freedom from her husband, though Eleanor thought it helped that her services of an evening weren't really needed. For a baronet, Sir John had become quite adept at removing hatpins, panniers, and difficult shoe buckles.

When his fingers moved to the brooch on her dress, she pretended to wag her finger at him.

"Have a care with that. It's my wedding gift. It's the most valuable thing I have." Then she spread her arms. "After you."

"What a silver tongue you have." He sank down next to her, tasting her kiss as if to confirm it. "I have to say I was hoping for more of a hell-cat. No titled lady would do the things I'd like to do with you."

"I'm sorry to argue with you, sir," she whispered against his lips, "but you're mistaken. Nearly any lady would do anything for a love like yours." Then she smiled into his kiss. "Even in a public place."

EPILOGUE

Almost ten years later

There was no way to hide how the Grantley heir constantly roared through the house, running, never walking, from place to place, and almost always at the top of his voice.

So why had Lady Grantley tried to hide the rip in the back of his son's coat?

"What's wrong?" The coat had disappeared somewhere since they'd returned from the village. Jesper wasn't sure what made it so important.

She rolled her eyes at him as they sat in the parlor, very proper, but side by side. He would take any chance to be near her, and while she was always, *always* proper in public, she never put him any farther away.

And he would be grateful for that all the days of his life.

"Nothing. Michael tore his coat."

"I saw that Michael tore his coat. Also that you tried to keep me from seeing it. Why hide it?" The distant sound of their son trying to ask Mrs. Peterborough politely for bread and butter, even at the top of his voice, couldn't be hidden; nor had any of his other activities, right down to the time he'd launched himself from the top of the stairs and tried to fly.

His beautiful lady turned her face and bit her lip.

"Since most faults are mine," he said mildly, "I suppose you are just trying to spare me some obvious critique?"

Her look was severe, and she thumped his knee.

"I am embarrassed," she admitted to his buttons, unable to look him in the eye. "I have so tried to curb my temper, and yet somehow I have infected him with it."

That wasn't the whole story. Well, she'd tell him later, in their chambers. He doubted Michael had lost his temper for no reason. The boy got hot when crossed, but not over nothing.

"Ah. That doesn't bother me. Just let us make sure he makes good use of it." He managed to get an arm around her, so slender still. "You do."

"Only with effort."

"You will show him the right example."

"I love your faith."

"I know," he said, kissing her temple, knowing she wouldn't kiss him back in such a public place, but storing all the banked embers he could create for their fire tonight.

"While you are practicing faith," she said, pretending not to notice his kisses but giving away their presence with the flush on her cheek, "*you* might show him a good example."

For ten years Jesper had done exactly as he liked when he liked, working in the mud and the trees and the rain.

But he always dressed for dinner.

"My hair is combed. Every button in place. What do you want of me, my lady?" Jesper made an enormous effort and didn't begrudge it, because it had the benefits she promised: others took him seriously, and she looked at him with approval.

With longing.

"Stop making me blush in public."

About to make a flippant remark, Jesper could see her bite her lip. She meant it. "I'm sorry, my lady."

It was clear her upset exceeded her usual restraint. "Not at all, Sir John, it's just—what if I give him all my worst habits?"

Jesper could see he would have to soothe her with words. Not his first choice, but he didn't shy from a challenge.

"I don't think you *have* bad habits," he murmured. "But if you think you might give him your honesty? I hope you *do*."

She made an unhappy noise. "I've had such a bad temper before."

"To bad people. See here. Perhaps London causes short tempers. We stay out of London; no short temper. Perhaps Michael will be the same way."

"I don't want him to lose sight of what's important. How to treat people. What to value. I want him to respect himself. And ladies."

Jesper didn't point out that Michael might run like wildfire but he still washed his hands. Aside from today's torn coat, he didn't ruin his things, though he did take off his clothes at every possible chance. As for the rest, Jesper thought that rather depended on the ladies.

"Those worries are years off."

She tossed him a cutting look. "How much time do either of us have to raise him?"

His heart had given him little more trouble since his illness had been discovered. He grew tired, sometimes; more so as the years passed. Sometimes it pained him a little.

Jesper suspected it would make his life shorter than hers; then he felt guilty for hoping that was true.

"You aren't with child again?"

She had barely recovered from the last attempt. It was all they fought over, her determination that they have more children, his determination that she stop trying. They didn't fight often, and usually both felt like they won, since what they wanted was more years with each other, and with Michael.

But Jesper had learned to be wary of guessing when to avoid the danger of another child, especially since she still loved for them to sleep together.

"No," she calmed him with a word. "Please don't look like that. We still have a bargain. We care for Roseford. We've got an heir. And we survive, sir. No matter what."

As always, he felt he could do it, because *she* could. If he had to leave her alone, she would carry on, just as if he were here. And he'd do the same.

"You drive a hard bargain." He'd be restrained, if she liked. But no one was looking. He kissed her knuckles. He was really very restrained, given how constantly he wanted to touch her. "I didn't think titled ladies were like that."

"Well, I never wanted to be a titled lady." She squeezed his hand back, her eyes promising him more when they were truly in private. "I've only ever wanted to be your wife."

"And you are the only wife I ever wanted." It was hard to feel cheated by time when she'd made his life so much richer than he ever imagined. When he thought of his father, he wouldn't trade their years alone; but he hoped his father had had a time in his life like this. And that his mother would have approved his father's choices, and Jesper's biggest choice.

The one that made Roseford come truly alive.

Mrs. Peterborough stopped at the parlor door. "I'm just going up to shutter the windows, Sir John, Lady Grantley. You can go in to dinner if you like. It's going to rain."

Eleanor's happy gasp, the way she turned to Jesper with her eyes alight—Jesper congratulated himself on proposing before any of those fools in London.

"Oh, Sir John. Let's go see!"

"What about dinner?"

"Young Master Michael has already run outside to catch frogs," Mrs. Peterborough put in, looking up at the corner of the parlor as if she weren't telling on him.

Eleanor just laughed. She loved it when he was like his father, thank God. "And you gave him apples earlier, apart from the bread and butter he just had. I know his secrets. And yours."

"Let's go see the roses blooming." The rain would wash away some petals, Jesper knew, but open others. At this time of year, the harvest of roses was rich, yet still not to be wasted.

And his so-proper lady walked straight out the front door with him, her linen cap with its ruffles instantly plastered to her hair, which she'd never once powdered since they'd left London.

"What are Mrs. Peterborough's secrets?" Jesper prompted, watching to see that her footing was fair as they walked down the hill, the rain soaking them both within moments. It was a shocking thing to do, but the servants would pretend not to see.

"Sometimes when we are not there, she calls him simply Michael," Eleanor confided.

"Hm. Lady Grantley, I think your sense of propriety is askew. Now you walk down to the footbridge with me, and I'll tell you what makes a really shocking secret."

"In the rain?" She kept her hand in his, warm summer droplets running over them both. "I was hoping you'd ask."

* * *

It's hard to leave Roseford...

Get your free bonus scene between Jesper and Eleanor, and keep reading to choose whose story to read next!

AFTERWORD AND ACKNOWLEDGEMENTS

The day my husband was diagnosed with heart failure was the loneliest day of my life.

Of course the story unfolded more slowly than that. A collapse; a trip in an ambulance; a sharp-eyed doctor who (thankfully) wanted to rule out a heart attack quickly; the nurses who wheeled him here, there, and everywhere, for tubes, images, consultations.

For me it all coalesced into the night I drove home, alone, in the dark, after updating every family member, because my husband wanted me to get some sleep. I hadn't wanted to argue with him, but was more terrified than I had ever been before that I could lose what made my life most worth living.

My husband was able to reverse his heart failure, likely virally caused, entirely with *health care*: prescriptions and physical therapy. His heart might not be one hundred percent perfect, but *he* is, and still the inspiration for every one of my love stories.

I don't know what the *Lords and Undefeated Ladies* series means to you, but to me it's a big middle finger to everyone who has ever said that people in the past who had health problems, disabilities, what have you, would simply have died. Of course they didn't. They survived and had lives, just like people do today, because lives are rich and precious. They always were, and they still are.

These books believe in love, and everyone's right to both love and the freedom to pursue it. It's not up for debate, for me or for any of my characters.

In 1785 physicians were just beginning to discern that rheumatic fever, with which they'd been familiar for centuries, had developed a new trick. Millbank's 1989 article "Emergence of rheumatic fever in the nineteenth century" summarized how before then, there are no records of cardiac disease following a bout of the fever; but after that, it became increasingly clear that a certain percentage of rheumatic fever sufferers who survived the disease still died later, of what, it became increasingly apparent, was heart damage.

The 18th century was a cornucopia of scientific developments, but the scientific method was still under development. It would be years before the hugely influential anatomy textbook of Dr. Baillie, a real historical figure, was published, and circulated Dr. Pitcairn's 1788 theory about rheumatic fever's damage to the heart.

Still more years had to pass before physicians could rely on more than just the occasional self-reported patient. They needed larger populations whose health information was recorded so that scientists could discern patterns, and correlate survival rates with wealth, location, diet, activity, and ultimately genetics. The mechanisms of science, when conducted well, are slow but sure.

No one's fate is certain. But science is a sure and sound method of discovering more truth.

Jesper has a damaged heart valve, of course, not heart failure like my husband, though a great deal of my husband's recovery was based in exercise. Jesper is perfectly strong, and likely his vigorous activity has kept him that way. I suspect that he has been brought up to simply sleep if he feels fatigued, and surely his collapse at Gravenshire house taught him to be much more careful when he felt faint. We don't know what other similar episodes he had in his life; there must have been a few. I suspect knowing his condition helped him understand his body better, and make better choices. Readers of *Not Like a Lady* know that he did not live to a very old age, nor did his wife. But I like to think that between them they set Michael many good examples, even if I wish Eleanor had been a little more willing to let Michael see her emotions. And obviously, Jesper and his lady felt they had a rich, full life.

My stories are fiction, not medical advice.

Other notes:

Jonathan Swift's "A Treatise On Good Manners and Good Breeding" was widely anthologized, for Mr. Swift was and is an amusing author. I find myself agreeing with this essay, while still drastically disagreeing with his "A Letter to a Very Young Lady, On Her Marriage." Such is the quality of an interesting moralist.

It also seems natural that both the Grantleys would ultimately be interested in Blackstone's *Commentaries*. It too contains a great many things to agree with and to disagree with. I'm so grateful to all the libraries of the United States for their commitment to sharing knowledge and electronic resources, across boundaries, as freely as they can; but I must specifically point to Project Gutenberg (gutenberg.org) which has been providing electronic copies of classic works in English for over twenty years, and is a jewel of modern life.

The English muffin isn't so called in England, of course, and in this period these easy little breads were apparently common. Horse bread or bannock is heavy and chewy, and one can imagine the delight in a fresh buttered English muffin compared to the type of bread on which you survive. I thought after twenty years of baking bread I knew a lot. The research for my serial *Ladies' Own Bakery* has uncovered a whole world of people recreating our ancestors' baking practices, and I continue to be fascinated.

The complex, stiffened, lacy concoctions of Georgian fashion aren't always my cup of tea, and very different from the Regency; I must thank my friend Elizabeth, who has sewed many a Georgian gown, for all the guidance she's given on the various fashions of the day, and apologize for any mistakes I've made or liberties I've taken.

I did long for a chance to visit a ball at Ranelagh, which was closed by the time of my later novels, and wish we could have spent more time there. Many untoward things happened at the fringes of the crowd in that vast dance hall; I suspect we'll have to know more about them in time. (We will meet Lady Lawson, of the high-flying heels, again.)

Eleanor's view of London was inspired by Wenceslaus Hollar's 1647 panoramic etching of London, which I highly recommend. He took the view from the tower of what is now Southwark Cathedral. Not a cathedral in 1785, it was nonetheless a church just as Jesper saw it, with a centuries-long history and full of the spirits of kings. Quite a fine place for Jesper and Eleanor's hurried wedding.

I hope if you've read my other books you enjoyed getting to see old places in new ways (David Castle, for instance, spent much more time in Roseford's portrait gallery in *Crown of Hearts*, and of course readers of *The Caped Countess* have already visited the vast city Gravenshire house). If you are a lover of *Ladies' Own Bakery* and wish we'd visited Leicester Square, never fear, our London friends will find their way there in *The Lord Trap*.

NEXT IN LORDS AND UNDEFEATED LADIES

A sneak peek from
The Lord Trap...

"I'm in love with Lord Callendar. So I'd like to marry you."

She was surprising the way an incoming cannonball was surprising.

"Lady Viola, I don't believe we know each other well enough for this conversation." He hesitated. "I don't believe I know *anyone* well enough to have this conversation."

"I am pressed for time."

That only confused Bradley Waite more. Lady Viola was maid in waiting to the powerful Duchess of Talbourne, still young, and delicately lovely. She had no reason to feel pressed for time.

And she was Oliver Burke's sister—or as he was now styled, Lord Rawleigh. His best friend. They'd come home together from the wars.

Oliver would kill him.

He decided on a delaying tactic. "Why me?"

Lady Viola was always brutally accurate in her assessments. "You are not desirable. London society ignores you. You're free of bothersome mothers. I would not be depriving anyone by taking you."

* * *

Sign up for insider news and first looks at new books at judithlynne.com

ABOUT THE AUTHOR

Judith Lynne writes rule-breaking romances with love around every corner. Her characters tend to have deep convictions, electric pleasures, and, sometimes, weaponry.

She loves to write stories where characters are shaken by life, shaken down to their core, put out their hand...and love is there.

A history nerd with too many degrees, Judith Lynne lives in that other paradise, Ohio, with a truly adorable spouse, an apartment-sized domestic jungle, and a misgendered turtle. Also an award-winning science fiction author and screenwriter, she writes passionate Regency romances with a rich sense of place and time.

If you enjoyed No Titled Lady, help keep these books coming - share a review at Amazon, Bookbub, or Goodreads!

Sign up for the first information on new books from Judith Lynne, as well as sneak peeks and exclusive content, at judithlynne.com.

READ MORE

*After **No Titled Lady:***

Not Like a Lady (the story of Sir Michael, Eleanor and Jesper's son, and Letty, his homeless horse trainer)

The Countess Invention (the story of Cass Cullen, inventing under the name of *Mr.* Cullen, the daughter of that cabinet maker and the viscount's daughter; and Oliver, surprisingly enough one of Lord Rawleigh's sons)

What a Duchess Does (the story of that little boy with the gray eyes who was the Duke of Talbourne's son, and Cass's cousin Selene, well trained to be a duchess—plus the return of the revolting Burden family)

Crown of Hearts (the journey back to Roseford for Anthony, Letty's only friend and mysterious problem-solver of all the previous books, and David Castle, in his own way a man of the people)

He Stole the Lady (where one of Lord Faircombe's grandsons seduces the American heiress picked for his brother - look for more about the Faircombe sons in an upcoming series of their own)

And in other series,

The Caped Countess (the story of the Duke of Gravenshire's granddaughter and Lord Ashbury's third son, back from war)

There are more books on the way from Judith Lynne!

ALSO BY JUDITH LYNNE

Lords and Undefeated Ladies

Not Like a Lady

The Countess Invention

What a Duchess Does

Crown of Hearts

He Stole the Lady

No Titled Lady — Series prequel

The Lord Trap (Forthcoming)

Cloaks and Countesses

The Caped Countess

The Clandestine Countess (Forthcoming)

Ladies' Own Bakery

Ladies' Own Bakery Season One: The Collected Episodes

Made in United States
North Haven, CT
07 June 2023

37484516R00157